A DEADLY WAKE

A DEADLY WAKE

An Inspector Andy Horton crime novel

Pauline Rowson

Fathom

A Deadly Wake

First published in 2020 by Fathom

ISBN: 978-1-9160915-6-6 (paperback)
ISBN: 978-1-9160915-5-9 (ebook)

Fathom is an imprint of Rowmark, Hampshire, England PO11 0PL

Pauline Rowson
Adventure, mystery and heroes have always fascinated and thrilled Pauline. That and her love of the sea have led her to create her critically acclaimed gripping range of crime novels set against the backdrop of the sea on the south coast of England.

The Inspector Andy Horton Series
Tide of Death
Deadly Waters
The Suffocating Sea
Dead Man's Wharf
Blood on the Sand
Footsteps on the Shore
A Killing Coast
Death Lies Beneath
Undercurrent
Death Surge
Shroud of Evil
Fatal Catch
Lethal Waves
Deadly Passage
A Deadly Wake

Art Marvik Mystery/Thrillers
Silent Running
Dangerous Cargo
Lost Voyage

Inspector Ryga 1950 set mysteries
Death in the Cove
Death in the Harbour

Thrillers
In Cold Daylight
In For the Kill

For more information on Pauline Rowson and her books visit www.rowmark.co.uk

Authors Note

DI Andy Horton's investigations into the disappearance of his mother, Jennifer, over thirty years ago, has been touched upon in many of the Horton novels, in which he has unearthed some startling revelations. In this, the fifteenth in the Horton series, there are more surprises to come. In order to help the reader quickly catch up on the mystery of Jennifer's disappearance, and to accompany Horton on his final journey in his quest to get to the truth, I have included a prologue. I have also included a cast of characters who are connected, in some way, with the Jennifer Horton mystery.

Acknowledgement

My grateful thanks to John Holmes for his cartographic expertise.

Cast of characters in the Jennifer Horton Mystery

Jennifer Horton – Andy Horton's missing mother
Eileen and Bernard Lichfield – Andy Horton's foster parents
Susan Nash – Jennifer's colleague at the casino
Andrew Ducale, left a photograph on Horton's boat of six men taken during the student sit-in protest at the London School of Economics in 1967
Professor Thurstan Madeley, compiled an archive file on the 1967 student sit-in protests at the London School of Economics
Dr Quentin Amos, former lecturer at the London School of Economics in 1967
Wyndham Lomas - a beachcomber artist
Lord Richard Eames
Gordon Eames (Richard Eames' brother) – dead
Anthony Dormand aka Brother Norman – dead
Rory Mortimer – dead
James Royston – dead
Timothy Wilson – dead
Zachary Benham – dead

Prologue

A ndy Horton sipped his coffee on the deck of his small yacht in the Portsmouth Marina and stared across Milton Lake at the lights of the houses opposite. The crisp April breeze, after blowing a gale all day, had finally run out of energy and now barely lifted the limp halyards, causing only the occasional and feeble protest as they slapped against the masts. It was cold for April, but Horton didn't mind that. In fact, he hoped the bracing night air would clear his head of the grime and bustle of London where he'd been banished on a course for the last two days.

Putting down his mug, he stretched his hand in his jacket pocket and took out his wallet to retrieve a creased black and white photograph from within. It was of six men and, written on the back in black ink, was a date, 13 March 1967. He had discovered the photograph in June, tucked under a cushion on his boat, left deliberately for him to find by a man named Edward Ballard, who had already departed the marina. Horton had been unable to find any trace of Ballard, but in December he learned that Ballard's real name was Andrew Ducale, and he was the twin brother of his last and loving foster mother, Eileen. Horton also believed it was Ducale who had taken him from care and placed him with his sister, Eileen, and her police officer husband, Bernard. With them Horton had found the stability and love that had been wrested from him at the age of ten when his mother disappeared on a foggy November day. They were dead now. If only they had told him what they knew about his mother, Jennifer. But they had remained silent and let him go on believing she had taken off with another man because she hadn't wanted the burden of a kid.

His gut tightened as he thought back to the November day when his life had changed. He'd come home from school to find their council flat in a tower block in Portsmouth empty. There hadn't been anything particularly unusual in that, his mother was often out shopping or at work. She worked as a night croupier at a local casino and sometimes did overtime. He'd made himself something to eat, watched some television, then got himself to bed. When she still hadn't returned the next morning, he was perplexed but thought there must be a simple explanation. He was ten and didn't think the worse of situations. There followed what seemed like endless days alone. As they drew on, he began to get more worried. Each day he hoped she would be there after school and, in the morning when he woke. But she wasn't. A teacher, noticing his dishevelled state and disturbed manner, reported it to the head teacher who called in social services.

For years Horton despised his mother, before deliberately blocking out all thoughts of her. Then, eighteen months ago, before Ducale left the picture on his boat, an investigation into the murder of a man found on a burnt out boat in Horsea Marina had led him to a vicar in Portsmouth who had kept a record of all press cuttings mentioning Horton. The vicar had written beside them, "Jennifer Horton's boy". He had died before Horton could ask him why the interest, but it had sparked his. He'd begun to make enquiries about Jennifer's disappearance. He'd got more questions than answers.

He took a breath. The sound of laughter from a boat on another pontoon drifted across to him as a car started up in the marina car park. His eyes returned to the picture of six men. He could recite their features from memory, he'd stared at them so many times.

His first port of call after finding the photograph had been the London School of Economics' archive files; the only significant event he could find that had happened on 13 March 1967 was the student sit-in protests there, and all the men in the picture looked to be students. He had hoped to find the identities of the six men and other references to them, but there had been nothing. Only the fact that Professor Thurstan Madeley had compiled an archive file on the 1967 sit-in protest.

Horton recalled the aloof man in his late-fifties with a domed head culminating in thinning grey hair, bright, shrewd and curious hazel eyes, and a wide mouth with lips a little too thin. He'd contacted Madeley in August and had arranged to meet him in the Castle Hill

Yacht Club at Cowes on the Isle of Wight, six miles across the Solent from Portsmouth. He had shown Madeley the photograph and asked if he had recognized any of the men. Madeley had said he didn't and that the photograph must have come from a private collection, but he gave him a lead, Dr Quentin Amos, a former lecturer at the London School of Economics.

In Amos's urine smelling flat in Woking, Amos told Horton the names of five of the men in the picture, and that Jennifer had been involved with them and the Radical Student Alliance, helping to support and organize the protests. Amos had died before Horton could question him further, but Amos left a manila envelope with his solicitor to be given to Horton on his death. Disappointingly it had been empty but, written on the back, had been a set of numbers 01.07.05 and 5.11.09. Horton had interpreted these as being a grid location, which, with a bit of manipulation, could be nearby Gosport. Had Amos been trying to tell him that was where Jennifer had been heading on the day she vanished?

Gosport, just across the narrow entrance of Portsmouth Harbour, had been home to the Royal Naval Hospital Haslar where Horton's foster father, Bernard, a former Royal Air Force police officer, had been laid up after being wounded in Northern Ireland at RAF Aldergrove during the Troubles in 1978. Not far from the hospital was where MI5s communications training centre had been and was still based.

Over the last nine months Horton had discovered more about the men in the picture and some startling and disturbing facts about them and his mother, Jennifer.

Dormand, with a beard, second from the left, had his arm around the shoulders of the man on his right, Rory Mortimer, who also sported a beard. Dormand, Horton had located in October, masquerading as Brother Norman, a monk in the Benedictine Northwood Abbey on the Isle of Wight. The abbot had no idea of Brother Norman's true identity, and Horton hadn't enlightened him. Dormand was dead and had been since October when he'd taken off in the night on a small boat on a storm tossed Solent. His body hadn't been recovered and neither had the boat. Horton supposed it was possible he had put in somewhere, but he doubted it. Even if Dormand had survived, he had told Horton he was terminally ill. That could have been a lie, but the man had the gauntness of sickness and death about him.

Dormand had confessed to Horton that he had killed Mortimer under orders from British Intelligence who he had worked for. He said that Mortimer, like James Royston, next to him in the picture, and Timothy Wilson, the man on the far left, had been a traitor, selling the country's secrets to the Russians. Horton discovered that Royston had died of a heroin overdose in a sordid bedsit in 1970, and Wilson in a motorbike accident in 1969 on a deserted road on Salisbury Plain on a calm, clear April night. That left two of the six men.

Zachary Benham, on the far right of the photograph, had been killed in a fire at the Goldsmith Psychiatric Hospital in 1968, along with twenty-three other men who had been locked inside their ward.

Horton's mind ran over the conversation he'd had with Dr Gaye Clayton, the forensic pathologist, in March about that hospital fire. She knew all about it, not only from a professional view but also because her father, Dr Samuel Ryedon, an eminent Home Office Forensic Pathologist, had been fascinated by the fire. There were several factors that were suspicious to say the least. Gaye had told Horton that her father had been abroad at the time of the incident but, on his return to the UK from America in 1974, he'd asked questions about it only to be told the file was closed. Only one pathologist had been appointed, a Dr Jocelyn Jennings, who had been under extreme strain and suffering from depression following the death of his only child, a son, aged fourteen, found hanging from a tree in the garden. Jennings had been killed in a car accident in the Brecon Beacons in Wales three months after completing the examinations on the fire victims.

Horton had read the inquiry report, but Gaye had furnished him with more information, which her father had managed to ferret out before being warned off. Horton hadn't explained to Gaye the reason for his interest and she hadn't asked him for it, for which he was grateful.

The identity of the victims had been compiled from the list of patients in the ward, but they hadn't been matched with dental records. There were no personal items or ID on the bodies, or in their lockers, because they hadn't been allowed any, but cigarettes and matches had been stated as the cause of the fire. Neither were found at the scene, and the patients certainly wouldn't have been allowed them. It was considered that someone had given them to a patient, or he had stolen them from a nurse or visitor.

The patients had been locked in the ward, as was normal practice in psychiatric hospitals in the nineteen sixties. There had been no sealing off the crime scene, which again wasn't unusual in 1968, and the extent of the fire had made it difficult to amass evidence.

The scene had been contaminated from the start. Firemen, desperate to get the blaze under control, had doused the ward with water. Charred remains of some of the patients had been found against the door, frantic to escape the flames. The firemen had walked over them and some of the other remains, not realizing they were doing so, while some patients had perished in their beds. No toxicology tests had been carried out on the bones to determine if drugs had been used on the victims. Their remains were gathered and taken away by the undertakers without any note of where they'd been found. The room had been photographed after the event and after all the remains had been removed.

Had Zachary Benham really died in that fire? Dormand had said Benham had been killed, but was that the truth? Then there was the testimony from a former casino colleague of Jennifer's whom Horton had traced, Susan Nash, who told him that Jennifer had turned deathly pale, as though she'd seen a *ghost* enter the casino. Shortly after that she had disappeared.

Horton again studied the sixth man in the picture, second from the left. Amos hadn't known who he was, but Horton had recognized him when he'd met him in the Castle Hill Yacht Club in August. He'd been there with Professor Madeley. Lord Richard Eames hadn't denied it was him. In 1967, Eames had been down from Cambridge visiting his friend Timothy Wilson, but Eames had claimed to know nothing about Jennifer Horton or her disappearance. It was clearly a lie. And since January, Horton had wondered if he was mistaken. There was a chance the sixth man could have been Eames' wayward brother, Gordon; they had been very much alike, but Gordon, the black sheep of the family, had been found dead on a beach in Australia in 1973.

So where did that leave Horton? A question he'd posed so many times over the last few months. His enquiries regarding these men had got him no closer to the truth behind his mother's disappearance on that foggy November day in 1978. He firmly believed that Richard Eames, like Andrew Ducale and the late Antony Dormand, worked for the intelligence services. Dormand had also told him that Jennifer had worked for the intelligence services while in Portsmouth, providing information on the IRA. That being the case, Horton thought his chances of getting to the truth were practically nil.

He tucked the photograph back inside his wallet and withdrew a grubby business card. On it was a name only, Wyndham Lomas. He was another mystery, one Horton didn't think he was likely to solve. He didn't even know if Lomas was connected with Jennifer's disappearance, or if he was connected with Lord Eames, only that Horton had met him on Eames' private beach at his Isle of Wight property in October, the same time that he had unearthed Dormand at the monastery.

Neither Lord Eames nor any of the family or staff had been at home. The house had been shut up but with a remote security monitoring system in place. Lomas had materialized out of thin air and had vanished into it just as quickly. Horton hadn't been able to trace him since. There was no record of Lomas on any of the databases Horton had access to. Lomas had claimed to be a beachcomber artist looking for flotsam and jetsam to turn into art. Maybe he had been. But Horton had been curious about the sun-tanned man in his early sixties and had asked the fingerprint bureau to see if the prints on the card matched with anyone on criminal records. They hadn't. He'd tucked the card away along with the memory of that meeting.

Aside from learning that all those in the photograph were dead – unless the sixth man was Lord Eames – and that Jennifer had known them, been involved with the Radical Student Alliance, and that she must have taken the picture, he was no further forward. Perhaps he never would be. Perhaps it was time to forget the past and move on, to concentrate on securing greater access to his nine year old daughter, Emma, and live in the present. But fate has a funny way of working and, as he retired for the night and turned his thoughts to the crimes of Portsmouth that would be burdening his desk in CID, fate was about to throw the final pitch in the twisted tale of Jennifer's life.

One

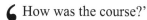How was the course?'

'Mind-numbingly boring. I'd rather have been shut up in the interview room with DCI Bliss for four days,' Horton replied, throwing himself in the seat opposite Sergeant Cantelli.

'That bad?' Cantelli's dark eyebrows shot up.

'If she had wanted to inflict torture on me for disobeying her every command, she couldn't have found a better way of doing it. Interrogating computers is not my forte, Barney, and never will be. It's about as thrilling as counting the cars on the motorway. No, correction, counting cars is far more exhilarating.'

'Walters might disagree.'

'What might I disagree about?' Walters ambled in with a bar of chocolate in one hand and a newspaper in the other.

'Computer work is boring,' Cantelli answered.

'It beats physically chasing after villains. You can get a lot of intelligence from computers.'

'So I've been told, several times over the last two days,' Horton said wearily. 'And it may be true but it's not my cup of tea.'

'Talking of which.'

'Fetch it yourself, Walters. Oh, and while you're at it, mine's coffee, black, no sugar, and a tea for Cantelli.'

Walters waddled out to the machine in the corridor.

'Where is Bliss? I didn't see her car in the car park,' Horton asked.

'Lecturing on a new recruit course for two days.'

'God help them. On what?'

'No idea. Probably on form filling. You know it's her speciality.'

There were probably several on Horton's desk waiting to be completed. Though, to be fair, the increasing amount of paperwork wasn't solely down to her. It was just the way the job was done now. It was all about keeping exact and intricate records of every scrap of conversation, and tip-toeing around suspects and villains. The instinctive coppers like him – those that had a nose and feel for crooks, and a handful of unregistered informants from the shady criminal classes to tap into – were out of favour. Too many coppers gazing at computer screens and not enough out on the streets. He asked what had come in during his absence. Aside from the usual house burglaries and drunken assaults, Cantelli told him there had been a nasty spate of highway robberies.

'Not of your Robin Hood variety,' he said. 'And I sincerely hope not the Dick Turpin kind. It's not been violent yet, but there have been threats. Motorists are being conned out of cash by a gang of three, two men and one woman, in their late twenties or early thirties, clean shaven, casually dressed, Caucasian. The woman stands by a supposedly broken-down car, looking upset, and flags down the motorist. She claims she has run out of fuel and has no cash or has lost or left her purse elsewhere. She offers gold jewellery or, in two cases, her watch in exchange for money. The gold is fake, the watch a cheap imitation. Unfortunately, some of the motorists have fallen for the scam. They've usually been conned out of cash of about ten to twenty pounds but yesterday, a woman was made to hand over cash and jewellery to the value of two hundred pounds. So the gang have really hyped up the ante.'

Horton didn't much care for the sound of this.

'They've been operating primarily along the seafront, at The Hard and Old Portsmouth. Traffic are increasing their patrols of those areas and uniform are asking around on the street, but they can't be everywhere.'

Walters, returning with the teas and coffee, caught the end of the conversation. 'There's nothing on the CCTV cameras so far.'

'And none of the motorists have dash cams,' Cantelli added. 'But we did lift some fingerprints from the vehicle targeted last night. So we might get lucky.'

'How many robberies have there been?' Horton asked, concerned.

'Three at the weekend, four on Monday and two yesterday. Most in daylight with two at dusk, Monday and yesterday. They took a gold watch, diamond ring and silver charm bracelet from the last woman targeted, so those items might show up in a pawnbrokers or jewellers, and Walters is keeping an eye on what crops up on the internet and on social media. One of the gang might be stupid enough to brag about it, or offer the items for sale. Stealing items which can be identified could be their downfall.'

'Let's hope so. Talking of jewellery thefts, any development on the Trehams robbery?' That was Detective Superintendent Uckfield's case. The Major Crime Team were investigating an aggravated burglary which had taken place two weeks ago at a substantial house to the north of Portsmouth. Victoria Treham, the owner, had been alone. Her husband at work. She'd been threatened, tied up, and the safe opened and stripped of extremely valuable and precious jewellery.

'If there is, we've not heard of it,' Cantelli answered.

Horton's office phone was ringing. He rose.

'Someone knows you're back,' Cantelli said.

'At least it won't be the wicked witch in the wardrobe,' Walters called after him.

Horton placed his motorbike helmet on the floor behind his desk and lifted the receiver. It was DC Mark Leonard of the Arson Task Force with the news that there had been a fire at the sailing club at Tipner.

'Not the building, but three boats have been destroyed in the yard,' Leonard announced.

Horton knew the club well. They'd had a murder investigation close by it last June, when a woman's body had been found on a sunken barge off the old quayside. The club and its quay were on the western shores of Portsmouth, just north of the international port and naval base. Gaye Clayton, the forensic pathologist, kept her sailing dinghy there. Horton hoped hers wasn't one of the three boats that had been torched. He asked if Leonard knew whose boats had been destroyed.

'That's the reason I'm calling you. The club secretary, Richard Bolton's here, and has just broken the bad news to me,' Leonard replied. 'One of the boats belongs to a retired dentist by the name of Venda Atkinson, the second to Councillor Dominic Levy.'

'Head of the police committee.'

'The same.'

'Not good. Levy's opinion of us isn't high at the best of times. He's bound to start jumping up and down, bellowing for results.'

'Then he'll have company because the third dinghy belongs to the Chief Constable.'

Horton emitted a groan.

'Yes, a double whammy.'

'Does Meredew know?'

'He will any moment now. The club secretary is on the phone to him. The fire could have been worse but for the fact that shortly after it was started, it was reported by a passing yachtsman heading into Horsea Marina.'

'What time was this?'

'One thirty-four, a.m.'

Late to be sailing, but not completely unusual. Horton had done a lot of night sailing himself and last night had been clear and still, which had probably helped prevent the fire from spreading too rapidly. That and the early call from the passing sailor.

'Watch Manager, Greg Hammond, is with me, and Elkins and Ripley of the marine unit are assisting. There's no sign of any forced entry into the boatyard from either the road or seaward side. Hammond's found fragments of glass and burnt rags, so it looks like a Molotov cocktail job and, judging by how the glass has shattered over a wide area, I'd say it was thrown into the yard. It could have been thrown from the road, but whoever did it would have needed to stand on a car bonnet or roof, or be an ace javelin thrower or shot putter.'

'Or a cricketer with a good overarm delivery.'

'A Donkey Drop.'

'Eh?'

'A ball with a high trajectory before bouncing, only this one didn't bounce and wasn't made of leather. Not that we've tested the theory of it being lobbed from the road, but we have from the seaward side. Elkins has done a mock up with a partially filled plastic bottle not glass, you'll be pleased to hear, Inspector, and even though you don't quite get the same impact or trajectory, both he and I think that was how it was done; the fence is lower on the harbour side.'

'Could this passing yachtsman be the arsonist?'

'He doesn't fit the usual profile. He's sixty six and a retired civil servant.'

'There's always the exception.'

'We'll keep an open mind.'

'Were those dinghies targeted specifically or the club in general?' Horton mused.

'Don't know yet. Might be someone with a grudge against the club, I'll follow that through.'

'Or a grudge against Levy or Meredew.' Horton could think of a few in the city who had been vociferous about the pompous, egotistic Councillor Levy and his lack of ability. But would they stoop to arson? Slagging him off in the press and at meetings, and plotting behind his back to find something with which to disgrace him, yes, but setting fire to his dinghy and risking the fire spreading? Horton doubted it but when roused, even sane, decent and generally law-abiding people could commit all kinds of crimes.

He wasn't sure about those who might have a grudge against the Chief Constable. Paul Meredew had taken up the post just over a year ago, following Superintendent Uckfield's father-in-law's retirement. Horton had only met Meredew once, when he was on his newly appointed Calvinistic tour of the station, trying to appear fair, full of bonhomie, tough on crime and criminals and supportive of the troops. No one believed him. They'd heard it all before, several times. Horton had sensed a restless impatient man, driven and ambitious.

Leonard said, 'It could be that the arsonist has a thing against the retired dentist, Ms Atkinson. Maybe she pulled the wrong tooth.'

Horton smiled. 'Could the arsonist be someone who was turned down for membership and thought he'd get even?'

'Bolton, the secretary, insists that no one has been rejected membership, but he said that new members have to be proposed by an existing member. Councillor Levy proposed our chief.'

'Who proposed Levy?'

'A fellow councillor on the leisure committee. Levy became a member two years ago, and the chief last May. I don't know who proposed Venda Atkinson and neither does Bolton, she's been a member for years.'

'Maybe someone got black-balled, despite being proposed, and didn't take too kindly to it.'

'Bolton was at pains to tell me that, at the last committee meeting, they had agreed to do away with the proposal system from 1 July and let anyone apply. I gather they're desperate to get new members.'

'Financial problems?'

'There's a lot of competition in their field nowadays and not as many young people taking up dinghy sailing. But if the arson was an insurance job, or a rival club trying to cut out the competition, then the clubhouse would have been targeted.'

'Perhaps the arsonist was unlucky in that there just happened to be an eagle-eyed night sailor heading into the marina further up the harbour. Or maybe this arson has more intimate implications.'

'You mean an affair. A jealous lover and love triangle?'

Perhaps the chief was putting it about as much as Uckfield. Although that would take some doing. Sometimes Horton thought Uckfield was trying for the Guinness Book of Records. He seemed to change his lovers almost as often as he changed his socks, despite being married with two daughters. So far Uckfield hadn't been found out but give it time.

Leonard continued, 'As we both know, the usual arsonist gets his jollies from seeing the fire take hold and watching the big red fire engines arrive. He also likes an excited audience to witness his destruction. He didn't get that here, not at that time of night. Even if it had been daytime there are no houses here and only a handful of businesses, so it's not your usual location for an arsonist. The club has its own CCTV cameras. We might get something from them.'

'You'd better keep me updated when you can. The chief is bound to start breathing down my neck.'

His prediction was fulfilled. Two minutes after he had replaced his phone, it rang again. Meredew curtly announced himself and angrily demanded to know if Horton had been informed of the crime.

'I have, sir.'

'And what do you intend to do about it, Inspector?'

'DC Leonard and Watch Manager Hammond are highly experienced in these matters, sir. They have considerable expertise in detection and arson.'

'I want more than a detective constable and fire officer overseeing this. Send Sergeant... whatshisname?'

'Cantelli, sir.'

'Yes. Tell Sergeant Cantelli to get down there immediately. I'd go myself if I wasn't on my way to London for a meeting.'

Thank God for that. 'I'm sorry, sir, but Sergeant Cantelli is due in court this morning. I can send DC Walters and while he is there, he can examine the CCTV footage. He's expert at that.'

'Then I suppose that will have to do,' Meredew grudgingly accepted. 'I expect to be kept fully informed, Inspector.'

'Of course, sir.' Horton rang through to Leonard and relayed the news. Then to Walters in CID, he said, 'You're off to the sailing club to assist Leonard. Chief's orders, so watch your manners.' Addressing Cantelli, Horton said, 'I told the chief you were due in court.'

'I'm sure I must be at some stage. There's your phone again. Hope it's not the chief with new instructions already.'

'Why do I get the feeling it's going to be one of those days?'

'Isn't every day one of those days?' Cantelli called out as Horton headed back into his office.

Horton was pleased to see it wasn't the chief but Jane Ashley from the fingerprint bureau.

'I've got a match on fingerprints from that card you gave me last October,' she announced.

Horton scrambled to recall what she was referring to before he realized it was the grubby business card the beachcomber, Lomas, had given him on Lord Eames' private beach.

'They match with a man in the mortuary on the Isle of Wight,' she said.

'Lomas?'

'That's just it, no one knows. It's why the prints were sent over to us. There was no ID on the body.'

'Do you have a description?' Horton remembered the easy-going man in his early sixties, sturdy, about six feet, with a close-cropped greying beard and short grey hair.

'No, just the prints.'

'But you're sure they're his.'

'Positive. Do you wish me to inform Sergeant Norris on the island?'

'No. Leave it with me.'

Eagerly, Horton rang through to the mortuary. It was a pity that, having found Lomas, it was too late to ask him why he'd been trespassing on Lord Eames' private beach. Perhaps his belongings might tell Horton more.

After a slight delay, the mortician confirmed that the unidentified male was in his early to mid-sixties, and had been brought in five days ago, on Friday. The post-mortem had taken place on Monday, and the death was due to natural causes.

'Cardiomyopathy,' the mortician proclaimed. 'Dilated cardiomyopathy to be precise. The heart's ability to pump blood was weakened because of an enlarged left ventricle.'

'So no suspicious circumstances surrounding his death?'

'Not according to the pathologist's report, unless you tell us otherwise.'

Horton had no reason to. He replaced the receiver and called Sergeant Norris of the island's CID. He'd worked with Norris a few times, a rotund, solid, plodding man who had always viewed him with suspicion. That was because Norris's former boss, Detective Inspector Birch, a dry insect of a man, had despised Horton. The feeling was entirely mutual. But Birch had retired, and his replacement had yet to be appointed.

'The man found dead on Friday, without an ID,' Horton said peremptorily, when Norris came on the line, 'what can you tell me about him?'

'You mean the man in a log cabin in Luccombe Bay? Died of heart failure. No suspicious circumstances,' Norris cautiously replied, echoing the mortician's remarks.

Horton knew the bay. It was on the east coast of the island, secluded and small with no properties. Just rocks, shingle, sand and a cliff prone to landslips. He'd sailed past it but never into it. He didn't recall seeing a log cabin, but then he hadn't really been looking for one and, out at sea, he probably wouldn't have seen it anyway.

'Who discovered him?'

'A woman. She'd motored into the bay on a small boat. It's inaccessible by any other means.'

'What took her there?'

'She's a geologist. She was fossil hunting.'

That coastline was renowned for fossils.

'She'd met the man once before and spoken to him,' Norris continued. 'He told her his name was Ben and that he lived alone.'

'Ben?'

'Yes, why?

14

Not Wyndham then. 'Go on.'

'The cabin door was open when she arrived, and there was no sign of Ben. She called out to him, entered and found him dead on the floor. There was nothing on the body or in the cabin to give us an identification. If she hadn't arrived when she did the poor man would still be lying there now. The officers who attended said there was no evidence of foul play,' Norris re-iterated, slightly defensively.

'How did they get to the bay, it being inaccessible?'

'I called up the marine unit.'

Good, that meant Sergeant Elkins would have been on the scene. Horton could get the full picture from him.

'Why the interest, Inspector? Do you have new information?'

'Fingerprints have come up with a match, to a man called Wyndham Lomas.'

'A wanted criminal?'

'Not as far as I'm aware, just someone we were eager to trace,' Horton hedged, thinking he should cross his fingers when he lied, but it wasn't a lie. *He* had been keen to find Lomas because anyone on Lord Eames' land, and anyone connected with Eames, was of interest to him. 'I met him once, in October, on the island during an investigation. He told me he was a beachcomber artist.'

'Well there are wood sculptures at his cabin.'

That seemed to confirm it. 'I'll be over shortly to ID the body. I'll update you after that.'

Horton rang through to the marine unit. 'Are you still at the sailing club, Dai?'

'Yes, but there's not much more we can do here. We were just on our way to Horsea Marina to ask if anyone came through or went out of the lock in the early hours of the morning, save for the man who reported the fire.'

'Postpone that for now.' The chief wouldn't be pleased, but Horton would get round that if he ever found out. 'I need you to take me across to the island on the RIB.' The RIB would be much quicker than the ferry and could moor up on the River Medina at Newport, the island's capital where the hospital was based. It was also flat bottomed, which meant it would be able to get into Luccombe Bay. He told Elkins about the match of fingerprints with the body found in the cabin, and how he had met the man in October. He requested that

15

Elkins pick him up from the secure berth at the international port in fifteen minutes.

Horton grabbed his sailing jacket and stopped long enough to brief Cantelli, giving him the same information he had Elkins. Then he made his way through the subway that ran under the motorway and across the busy port car parks to the secure berth where the RIB was waiting for him.

Two

'It's pretty basic,' Elkins said in answer to Horton's question about the log cabin as Ripley swung out into the harbour. Horton had given Ripley instructions to head there first. 'Clean though. No sign of a struggle or any damage. No paperwork, mobile phone, computer or anything that could tell us who he was. Looked like a heart attack to me but I'm no medic.'

'Well you're more or less right. Did you take the doctor to the bay to certify death?'

'No. We picked up two officers from Shanklin, and we agreed that it looked pretty straightforward. Ripley left us in the bay while he returned to Shanklin to fetch the undertakers. We then transported them, the body and the two officers back to Shanklin. The body was taken straight to the mortuary at Newport in the undertaker's private ambulance.'

'Did you talk to the woman who found him?'

'No. She'd already left the bay after discovering the body. I assume she's been into the police station to make a statement.'

'I assume so too,' although Norris hadn't said.

Horton postponed further questions. Firstly, because they weren't necessary when he would see Lomas' cabin for himself shortly, and secondly because, as they picked up speed in the Solent, the noise of the RIB's engine prohibited it.

The grime and fuel-filled air of the last two days in London slipped away from him as they crossed the busy Solent. There were several yachts and a few motorboats enjoying the spring weather. A cruise ship was heading towards the port, and a large container ship loomed on the horizon. Within minutes the RIB was rounding the chalk cliffs of Culver, on the island, heading past the coastal town of Sandown and beyond that Shanklin with its short promenade, nestling beneath the town perched high on the cliffs. After rounding the headland, Ripley slowed the RIB and the sheltered bay of Luccombe came into view. Lying under the cliffs was a wooden hut which looked little more than a large shed.

'I'm surprised it hasn't been buried by a landslip,' Horton said, eyeing the trees and shrubs above it, some of which had already slipped and fallen on to the beach, both to the left and right of the cabin.

'Give it time, and it will,' Elkins replied as Ripley drew closer to the shore.

'I see what you mean about it being basic. ' As they drew closer Horton could see a small window to the right of the door and a rickety veranda.

'Wait until you see inside.'

Ripley nudged the boat on to the sandy shore and silenced the engine. Horton jumped off for'ard and, with Elkins, they pulled the police RIB higher on to the shore out of reach of the incoming tide and about ten yards away from the cabin. The upper line of seaweed told Horton that high water never reached the cabin. Unless there was a fierce easterly wind and exceptional high tides, then it might just grace the veranda. Heading for the cabin, Horton nodded at a well-maintained and immaculately varnished wooden boat on a raised shingle bank. 'Does that belong to the dead man?'

Elkins answered, 'No idea. Probably.'

'And those, I take it, are Ben's handiwork?' Horton drew up in front of the cabin where there was a sturdy hand-carved wooden bench and two wood sculptures. One was of a seagull about to take flight, the other a watchful owl, both beautifully executed. To the right of the door was a pile of driftwood. Lomas had indeed turned *his flotsam and jetsam* into art. Who had he sold to? How did he sell them? Horton guessed he must have used the boat to transport them to his customers because there was no other way he could have done so unless there was a path up to the top of the cliff. Norris had said the bay was inaccessible. Yes, by road but perhaps not on foot. Even if there were a footpath, Lomas couldn't have hauled his masterpieces up there.

'He was obviously a talented artist.'

'If you like that sort of thing.'

'And you don't? You're a philistine, Dai.'

Elkins shrugged his big shoulders with a smile.

The exterior of the cabin had been repaired in places and quite expertly. Perhaps Lomas aka Ben had done that, being handy with his tools and wood. The door was unlocked, as Elkins had said. Horton stepped inside.

'This certainly is pared down living,' he announced, eyeing the faded blue, soiled, sagging two-seater sofa and paraffin heater. There was a green canvas camp bed resting against the far wall, clearly old, as was the navy-blue sleeping bag on it. Over that was an orange blanket. The pillow was covered with a faded and slightly stained striped cotton pillowcase. The dusty wooden floor was devoid of any carpets or rugs. Yet, despite its humble bleakness, the cabin had a comfortable lived-in feel, and the smell of wood reminded Horton of traditional wooden boats, the kind he loved but had little spare time to care for. There was an attraction about this kind of living, he thought, cut off from the world and all its sordid problems, but to be without contact with Emma, his nine year old daughter, would be too hard for him to bear. As it was, Catherine, his estranged wife, was determined to keep him away from her as much as possible.

On a wooden table underneath the window was a large white mug, a glass, and a half empty whisky bottle. Had alcohol been found in Lomas' blood stream? Possibly.

'Anything changed since you were last here on Friday, Dai?'

'No.'

Ripley also shook his head.

'Tell me what you found.'

Elkins answered, 'The deceased was lying face down on the floor beside his bed. His arms were outstretched, slightly at an angle, not crumpled up. I'd say he got up, collapsed and died.'

'What was he wearing?'

'Shorts, a T-shirt and sandals. We didn't find any pyjamas, only those clothes over there.' Elkins nodded to a wicker chair on which Horton could see a pair of worn and faded khaki shorts, two T-shirts, a couple of darned woollen jumpers and a few pairs of socks and pants. Lomas had been wearing shorts, a T-shirt and sandals when Horton had met him.

He said, 'He couldn't have slept in his sandals, so he either fell ill after putting them on when he woke up, or he died before he got into bed. Anything found in his pockets?'

'A penknife, harmonica and steel comb.'

Horton crossed to the table by the window and regarded the mug. He felt a reluctance to pick it up, even though he wouldn't be spoiling a crime scene. Perhaps it was ingrained training. The brown sludge in the bottom of the mug indicated that it had at one time contained coffee or possibly a strong brew of tea. The whisky glass looked clean. On the table was an oil lamp and four unusual looking knives.

'The tools of his trade,' Ripley said, peering at them. 'Not that I know anything about wood carving, but that's what they look like to me.'

Horton agreed. They all had matching light-wood shaped handles and the name Flexcut on them. They appeared well used. The blades looked sharp, although he didn't test them, and they were of varying widths and lengths, obviously used for different purposes in the woodcarving business. Beside them was a curved shaped implement with a hook. There was no evidence of Lomas aka Ben having conducted his wood carving inside the log cabin. Perhaps he tidied up after he'd been working or carved his sculptures outside.

In an alcove to the left of the heater was a tiny kitchenette. There was no fridge or sink. A Calor gas stove, the type used in camping, was perched on a small table on top of which was a well-used kettle while beside it was a medium sized saucepan and frying pan. Next to the table was a rickety cupboard with faded checked curtains instead of doors. Horton pushed them aside to find two shelves. The top one held two clean blue and white willow-patterned plates, two blue mugs and some cutlery, along with a couple of tins of food, two jars, one jam, one marmalade both, by the labels, made locally. The lower shelf contained Ben's shaving and washing gear; flannel, soap, razor blades, shaving brush and shaving foam, the cheap variety.

Elkins said, 'The toilet's a portable sea one at the rear of the cabin. God knows how he disposed of its contents. He could have ditched it in the sea, illegal of course, but who's around to check? No idea how long he'd been living here, but the local police might have more information on him by now. Perhaps one of his customers has come forward.'

'Sergeant Norris didn't mention anything when I spoke to him earlier.' Horton gazed around. 'He wouldn't have needed to make much money living this way. Let's take a look at the boat, obviously his mode of transport.'

Had Lomas used this boat to motor around to that inlet adjoining Eames' property in October? Horton hadn't seen or heard a boat, but then it could have been hidden on the shore in amongst the trees and bushes. And Lomas could have used oars; there were two inside the boat. It was well cared for, but two things in particular interested him.

'Notice anything unusual about it?' he asked.

It was Ripley who answered, 'The keel's been planed, either to make it easier to get into this bay or to make the boat go faster. And it's got a powerful outboard engine. With that it could get up to a good speed. Fifteen horse power I'd say. And, up on the plane, it could do about twenty knots.'

'So why the need for such speed when everything about Ben indicates a leisurely, slow paced lifestyle?'

'Maybe he delivered to customers on the other side of the island, or even over on the mainland,' Ripley ventured.

Maybe. Horton had seen all he needed to here. He instructed Ripley to make for Newport and moor up in the River Medina. From there Horton walked the short distance to the hospital, while Elkins and Ripley remained with the RIB. After showing his ID, Horton followed the mortician through to the chilly mortuary with its familiar nauseating smell which he tried to block out. He prepared himself to meet the mask of death of a man he had briefly met but, as the large refrigerated drawer slid open, Horton stared down at the dead man with grey stubble and collar-length grey hair, puzzled.

'Are you sure this is the man found dead in his cabin in Luccombe Bay?' he asked.

'Positive, Inspector. It's not who you were expecting?'

It certainly wasn't. This was not Wyndham Lomas, the beachcomber.

Three

'I'd like to see his clothes and belongings.'

'Of course.'

The mortuary attendant slid the body back into the deep freeze and Horton followed him to a bench on which were two plastic bags. In one were the dead man's clothes as Elkins had described – khaki shorts, a navy-blue short-sleeved T-shirt, underpants, and a pair of brown leather sandals. The latter were the same style and type Horton had seen on the suntanned feet of Lomas. He extracted them.

'They're quality leather. Handmade, I'd say,' the mortuary attendant said.

Horton agreed. They had also seen considerable wear. The leather was pitted and cracked, but clean. The rubber sole had been repaired, probably many times. The inside was so worn as to leave indentations of the toes, and the maker's name and size had rubbed away. Fastened at the side with an old fashioned buckle, they sported wide criss-cross leather straps across the front of the foot, were open-toed with a closed heel.

'Jesus Sandals we used to call them back in the nineteen sixties and seventies when they were fashionable,' the mortuary attendant added as Horton replaced them in the bag. 'Which is when I'd hazard a guess those were made.'

'He's hung on to them for a long time.'

'Quality like that lasts.'

Horton turned his attention to the items in the small bag, which were the contents of Ben's pockets, as Elkins had described. Here was the penknife, but it wasn't the usual kind. Firstly, it was incredibly old, with the bone handle worn and the name on it faded, but he could make out what looked like 'Oar Carver'. Secondly, when he flicked it open it revealed two blades on either side of the handle. Both looked to be exceedingly sharp. It could well be an offensive weapon used to wound and kill but given the faded name on it and what he had seen in the cabin, he judged this to be one of Ben's woodcarving implements.

He turned his attention to the harmonica. Again, he thought it was antique, although he was no expert. There was a name on it, more legible, 'Marine Band.' The comb was an ordinary steel one.

'What was the time of death?'

The mortuary attendant picked up the file on the table and flicked through some papers. 'Sometime on Thursday 28 March. Difficult to say when exactly. His body was discovered the following day. He was brought here at two thirty-two p.m. on 29 March. He'd been dead for at least twenty-four hours.'

'Were you the person who took his prints?'

'Yes. I sent them over to the police station as requested.'

'And this was when?'

'Friday about four p.m. It was one of the first things I did, after undressing him. In fact, I took two sets, one before I washed him and another afterwards, before the post-mortem. I put the prints in a sealed envelope and despatched them by our internal post to the police station. I also scanned his prints into the computer and emailed them to the fingerprint bureau with a copy sent to Sergeant Norris's email address.'

'Any distinguishing marks on the body?'

'There was some scarring on his back, possibly the result of an accident, which had stripped away the skin, or it could have been caused by scalding, but that was all.'

Horton asked for a copy of the autopsy report and waited while the mortician printed it off. Outside the mortuary, he read through it. It was fairly basic, which was to be expected because there hadn't been any need for a full forensic post-mortem, there not being any indication of foul play. The pathologist estimated that Ben had been in his early sixties. There were several moles on his body and some damage to the epidermis on his arms, legs, neck and face, some giving indications of melanoma; arthritis in his joints and some mild lung damage. The scarring on his back was old and the report confirmed what the mortician had just told him.

Horton tucked the report into the pocket of his sailing jacket and headed for the police station, trying to fathom out how Ben's fingerprints could have got on the business card that Lomas had given him. The internal post could have been tampered with, he supposed. The fingerprint file which had been sent to the police station could have been replaced with one containing the prints of the man he had met, Wyndham Lomas, but they would also have to match with the prints the mortuary attendant had emailed over to the bureau and to Norris. And why would anyone tamper with the files? They wouldn't of course. Could Ben be an identical twin of Wyndham Lomas? There were similarities in looks, age and build. Did identical twins have the same fingerprints? He was sure they didn't, but he rang through to Jane to check. It was as he thought, the prints of identical twins were similar but there were distinct differences, so that quashed that idea. He told Jane that after viewing the body, it wasn't the man he had been expecting.

'It's a perfect match on the prints we received, both the physical copies and those emailed,' she confirmed.

'Then there must have been two sets of prints on that card or make that three; mine, Wyndham Lomas's and Ben's. Lomas's got rubbed off in the process of me giving you the card to lift off the prints but the other man's remained.'

Jane agreed that must be the explanation. And if that was so, then where was Wyndham Lomas? Why hadn't he come forward to identify his friend? *If* Ben had been his friend. Horton had no evidence of that. Lomas had said *he* was an artist, but from what Horton had seen in that cabin, it was Ben who had been the artist. Perhaps they had both been artists and friends and, after October, Lomas had moved on to pastures new and had not kept in touch with Ben. Indeed, Ben would have been a difficult man to contact, not having a phone or a valid address.

Norris rose as Horton entered the untidy CID office with almost as many empty desks as Horton's own CID office in Portsmouth. Horton knew that wasn't on account of officers being out on enquiries. Desks were aplenty, people to sit behind them was an entirely different matter. Norris had put on a few pounds since Horton had last seen him in October. He confirmed that he had received an email containing the prints, and a hardcopy of the prints had been couriered to the bureau's offices at Netley on the mainland.

Horton then relayed the fact that the body in the mortuary was not the man he had been expecting to see, the one he had met in October,

Lomas. The name meant nothing to Norris. Horton asked if an appeal for anyone who had known Ben to come forward had been made.

'Of course,' Norris said, slightly stiffly, taking the question as a slur on his ability. 'We were too late to get it into the County Press, it being a weekly newspaper. There'll be full details in this week's, which will be out tomorrow. Aside from that we sent details to the local radio stations who have broadcast it; we've circulated it on social media and to all the doctor's surgeries, citizens' advice bureaus and community centres this side of the island. No one's come forward so far. Officers are also asking around the shops and clubs in Shanklin and Sandown. Ben must have shopped somewhere, although that doesn't mean he talked to anyone let alone gave them chapter and verse of his life history.'

'Have you circulated it to the boatyards and marinas?'

Norris looked surprised for a moment, then uncomfortable.

Horton continued, 'Ben had a boat, he might have put in somewhere. You say that the bay is inaccessible?'

'Yes. There's a narrow lane which branches off from the main Shanklin to Ventnor road, just before the Devils Chimney, an old smugglers haunt.'

Horton knew it. He'd taken Emma there once. A narrow stone opening in the cliff with ancient stone steps and a decidedly creepy atmosphere.

'There are no properties down that lane, and the only house it leads to is Beachwood House. The lane stops at the footpath that stretches north to south from Luccombe Down to Ventnor. Directly opposite the lane is the entrance to Beachwood House, a large manor house and grounds that belonged to Cedric Halliwell. There was a footpath once, not far from the property, which led down to the bay just south of Beachwood House, but I'm going back five years, could be more. The cliffs there are notorious for landslips, so parts of the path kept disappearing. The council patched up the footpath for years with wooden steps and the like, but it got to the stage where it no longer made any sense to keep renewing it, so they closed it down. It's completely overgrown now. No one would know it had once existed.'

'Is the house empty? You said 'belonged.'

'Yes. Halliwell died in February. He was a recluse by all accounts.'

Another one, thought Horton, like Ben. He asked to be kept

informed and hurried back to the RIB where he updated Elkins and Ripley.

'I'd like to see if there's a footpath from Ben's cabin up to Beachwood House, and as I haven't got any transport, aside from your boat, you can take me back to the bay and we can climb up from there.'

'*We*,' Elkins said, clearly aghast at the prospect.

'The exercise will do you good, Dai. *If* we find a path.'

'Then let's hope we don't.'

But Elkins was to be disappointed. The path, which was little more than a track, was behind the cabin. Elkins eyed the steep climb with horror and despair. 'Can't Ripley go? He's much younger and fitter than I am.'

'Which is why he's not going.'

'If I keel over with a heart attack, on your conscience be it.'

'I'll give you mouth to mouth.'

'I bet you say that to all the girls.'

Horton smiled and struck out ahead of Elkins, up the steep and twisting path through the sprouting ferns, bushes and brambles. The land to his right, seaward, had slipped in three places. One was a major landslide where trees and shrubs had been upended and had slid down the cliff exposing fresh light brown soil.

'For God's sake, Andy, be careful. We don't want to end up down there,' Elkins implored as the earth slipped beneath Horton's feet and scree slid down on to the shore.

'OK, I'll save you from a fate worse than death. I'll go on ahead and see where this ends up. Probably in nothing but a tangle of bushes and trees. If the cliff gives way you can come and dig me out.'

Elkins looked relieved, and then guilt ridden.

Horton said, 'Go back to the RIB. I'll join you shortly, and if I don't you can call the rescue team.'

After a moment's brief hesitation, Elkins turned back while Horton carefully continued upwards. The ground was sticky with mud from the heavy rain a week ago and his shoes were soon covered in it. Where a landslip had occurred it had cleared a view to the sea until the path twisted onwards and upwards. It had been used, that much was clear. There was still evidence of footprints, and the ends of the shrubs were broken back. The prints were difficult to make out, could be Ben's sandals, could be a boot or shoe, but it had to be Ben, because if not, who else?

The birds were chirping away and the trees and bushes a mass of buds and blossom. After a considerably steep climb, he came out on to a wide expanse of cultivated, untamed grass. Dotted around it were clumps of Rhododendron and other shrubs in what had once been a landscaped garden, but it was the house beyond it that drew Horton's attention and interest. Norris had been wrong, there was access to Ben's cabin from the landward side, albeit dangerous. This had to be Beachwood House, the late Cedric Halliwell's residence. It was a substantial, sprawling mock Tudor edifice built possibly around the nineteen thirties or perhaps much later. It was a large dwelling for one man because, according to Norris, Halliwell had been something of a recluse, so Horton assumed he had lived alone. Did Halliwell have any relatives? If so, they looked to be in line for a tidy inheritance. Maybe one of them had taken the path down to the bay.

As he made his way towards the house, he saw there were shutters on the top windows and most of the ground floor windows, except those of an orangery that abutted part of the rear and gave on to a stone terrace. Perhaps once there had been a family living here and laughter and shouts had rung out around the rooms or through the gardens, or perhaps he was just being fanciful, imagining a childhood he'd never been privileged to experience. Yes, he'd shared a large house with other children from the age of ten to fourteen, but they had been a succession of bleak, characterless, sterile children's homes.

He pushed away the memories and stood back to study the house. The exterior was badly in need of re-decorating and repair. Perhaps Halliwell had grown old here and hadn't had the energy or the inclination to get workmen in, or perhaps his resources had dried up. Or perhaps he just didn't care how he had lived and had been content for it to fall down around him as some people were. Had Cedric Halliwell known Ben? Norris said Halliwell had died in February. Horton wondered when Ben had taken up residence in that cabin.

There would be a magnificent view from the upper floor, across the Solent to the coastline of Hayling Island and Selsey, he thought. It was a view he wouldn't mind waking up to every morning. Instead, he had second best, waking up on board the small yacht he lived on in the marina. It had taken some adjusting to living in the confined space and alone after his marriage had broken up, but that was nothing compared with the desolation he had felt at the fact that Catherine had chosen to believe he could be capable of forcing himself on a woman he'd had under surveillance. An accusation for which he'd been suspended. He'd been exonerated but too late to save their marriage. Their divorce had come through last June.

He walked to the front of the property. The gravel driveway and surrounding gardens were in the same state of disrepair as the rear. Ahead was a gatehouse, also in a dilapidated state with shuttered windows and a rusting iron gate pushed back into overgrown shrubs. A pockmarked sign declared this was "Private Land" and that "Trespassers would be prosecuted". The footpath from Luccombe to Ventnor, which Norris had told him about, did indeed pass in front of the property and opposite, was the narrow lane which led to the main road. There was no one about.

Horton tried his mobile phone to tell Elkins he was all right, although he'd probably know that given that the sergeant was keeping his eyes skinned on the cliffside for any movement of earth. But he couldn't get a signal.

Time to return to the RIB. He'd like to know the extent of Cedric Halliwell's land. Did it incorporate the bay and Ben's cabin? Who was the executor of Halliwell's estate? Maybe he or she would know. It might give them a clue as to Ben's true identity. Not that it was Horton's problem. It wasn't his case, and Ben's death wasn't suspicious. He was just curious to know what the link with Wyndham Lomas had been because of the prints on that card, but he resigned himself to the fact that he'd probably never find out.

He followed the steep path downwards, taking care where he trod, but he'd only gone a short distance when the earth slipped beneath him. Instinctively he reached out. His fingers connected with the trunk of a young tree, but the lifeline came away in his hand and, crying out, he slithered and slid several paces down the side of the cliff. Cursing, he frantically grabbed at another young tree and just in time as the ground was violently swept from under him and he was suddenly face down eating earth, choking and spluttering, with vegetation and dirt showering down on him. Would the tree hold? Would his strength? Elkins might need that rescue party after all. The roaring earth filled his ears. He kept his eyes and mouth tightly shut. His arm was stretched to breaking point. He braced for the fall, knowing he would need to relax and go with the movement of the earth to avoid any broken bones. That might be the best that could happen. The branch gave way slightly. He slipped another foot. This was it.

Then, as suddenly as the landslip started, it ran out of energy and stopped. He could hardly believe it. Anxiously he waited, his breath coming in gasps, his heart thumping. Yes, all was still. It was safe to open his eyes. He breathed a huge sigh of relief and began to move gently and slowly for fear of kicking off another landslide. Still clinging to the young tree – he wasn't confident enough to let go yet – he twisted his body round prior to standing. Then involuntarily cried out for staring up at him was the hollowed sockets of a human skull.

Four

'I hope you haven't got me all the way over here for some silly sod of a walker who got too near the cliff edge and fell,' Detective Superintendent Uckfield grunted uncharitably as he clumsily clambered off the police RIB. Ripley had taken it back to Portsmouth while Elkins, looking mightily relieved that he hadn't made the trek to Beachwood House, had waited on the shore with Horton. During that time Horton had called Sergeant Norris, told him what he'd discovered and that the head of the Major Crime Team was on his way over. He asked Norris to find out who Cedric Halliwell's executor was. Uckfield had brought with him DC Jake Marsden from his team, and three scene-of-crime officers, including the photographer, Jim Clarke.

'Not unless he managed to bury himself,' Horton replied, because after recovering from his initial shock, he had seen clear signs that the corpse hadn't been the victim of a landslip but a murder. 'If he'd fallen, he'd have been at the bottom of the cliff not half way down it. And, judging by what I saw of the skull, he didn't get his injuries from hitting his head on a rock.'

'You could be wrong.'

'I could be, but a man found dead in this cabin five days ago, the owner of the house at the top of the cliff dead since February, and now a third –'

'A hat trick you'd say.'

'Suspicious is the word I'd use. It certainly needs looking into.'

'You're expecting me to climb up there?' Uckfield said horrified, squinting up at the cliffs.

'Why not? I did.'

'But you're not a detective superintendent.'

And never likely to be, thought Horton. He didn't want promotion, not anymore, maybe not even before. But Catherine had been keen to see him get on, so he'd obliged. Now it didn't matter what Catherine wanted. And neither am I overweight, Horton thought, eyeing Uckfield's corpulent figure which made even DC Walters and the sturdy Sergeant Elkins look slender. Horton said, 'From what I could see the body looks intact, but I didn't hang around to clear all the earth away for fear there might be another landslip.'

'Now you tell me.'

'Inspector Horton is right,' DC Marsden piped up. 'This whole area is unstable.'

'That's a great comfort,' Uckfield said sarcastically, setting out for the cabin, while Ripley swung the RIB back out into the bay. He was to collect the firefighters from nearby Shanklin. They, with their rescue equipment, would transport the body down the cliff.

'I'm a keen amateur geologist and fossil hunter,' Marsden brightly continued.

'Plenty of old fossils in the station,' muttered Uckfield.

Marsden made no comment. He valued his career too much for that. 'This cliff is mainly comprised of Lower Greensand. It's a loose, unconsolidated sandstone, like the rubble used in construction,' he explained to Uckfield's baffled glared. Horton hadn't known what it meant either, although he'd felt it on his face and had brushed it off his clothes. 'It contains sands of varying grain size with some amounts of siltstones, mudstones, containing smectites and limestones.'

'If you say so,' sniffed Uckfield.

Horton indicated the path and asked Elkins to remain behind for which the sergeant smiled his thanks. They'd only gone a few steps when Uckfield began to pant, while Clarke, the photographer, the slender Beth Tremaine and stooping Phil Taylor seemed to find the trek easy, although Taylor was muttering something about the trees and burgeoning bushes playing havoc with his hay fever. He sneezed to prove it. Uckfield tossed him an angry glare, fearful Taylor might bring down the earth in an avalanche on top of them.

Marsden, clearly just getting into his stride, both physically and verbally, continued to give them a geology lecture, 'The Lower Greensand Group was deposited during the Early Cretaceous Period, which lasted for approximately forty million years from 140 to 100 million years.'

'I think our remains are more recent than that,' said Horton, but how recent he couldn't say. There was hair left on the scalp and some traces of flesh. It would need the expertise of Dr Clayton to give them an indication of time of death.

'Lower Greensand is one of the most landslide-susceptible formations in the UK, so this could give at any moment.'

Uckfield looked nervous. 'Is it much further?'

'No,' Horton replied.

Marsden continued enthusiastically, 'When fresh and unexposed to air, the greensand is soft which makes it much easier to collect fossils. You can simply use a knife or trowel, and any fossils you do find will be in excellent condition.'

'Yeah, well the only fossil I'm interested in collecting now is the one Inspector Horton has dug up,' snapped Uckfield. He stumbled, and a slither of earth fell beneath his feet, causing him to mutter an oath. Horton reached out and steadied him.

'It's just down there,' he said, gesturing to where he'd left the corpse, hoping it was still there and exposed.

'And I'll be down there in a minute,' Uckfield growled. 'Let's get this over with. You lot stay here,' he commanded the crime scene team in a voice barely above a whisper, as though speaking loudly would cause an avalanche. Horton thought it good advice; the fewer of them trampling around here the better. He wondered if it would have been wiser to wait until the firefighters had arrived and applied safety harnesses to the crime scene officers. Too late now. He led the way around a virulent shrub and through some ferns until they came to a small clearing of earth. He could hear the sea below them, washing on to the shore, and where the shrubs had been upended and the cliff had given way in places, he could also see it through the gaps. The tide was going out.

The remains were exactly as Horton had left them an hour ago. If he hadn't come here the body could have lain buried for years, maybe forever. The same could have been said about Ben in his cabin, if the geologist on a fossil hunt hadn't arrived when she did.

Horton stepped cautiously aside to allow Uckfield and Marsden a view of the remains. The corpse gave off no stench, but it wasn't the prettiest of sights, although Horton had seen worse. The jaw gaped wide, displaying yellowing teeth which seemed to look huge in the cavernous spectre. The soft flesh of the eyes, ears and nose had decomposed and been eaten by insects and animal life.

Horton said, 'You can see what I mean about the skull. It's battered and there's a small hole on the right temple that looks as though it could be a bullet wound.'

'How did the other two men you mentioned die?'

'Ben of cardiomyopathy, heart disease,' Horton summarized. 'Cedric Halliwell from Beachwood House above us, I don't know, but it was deemed to be of natural causes.'

'Then maybe one of them shot this poor bugger before keeling over.'

That would be convenient, thought Horton. Even so, enquiries would have to be made.

Uckfield turned away and Marsden followed suit. Horton joined them on what he hoped was more solid ground, but he wasn't banking on it.

Uckfield instructed the crime scene officers to do only the basics. 'We don't want any more bodies to retrieve.'

The three of them, already wearing scene suits, placed their masks over their mouths and, while Clarke manipulated his tall, lean body into a position where he could take photographs without falling down the cliff, Beth Tremaine and Taylor began to carefully clear the earth around the remains. Horton found himself holding his breath. He suspected Marsden and Uckfield were doing the same.

It didn't take much to expose the rest of the body, which was intact. What remained of the clothes – fragments of trousers, a suit jacket, shirt and a pair of rotting slip on shoes – indicated it was probably male. Horton said, 'He doesn't look like a hiker, not in those clothes, and neither is he dressed as though he's come off a boat and climbed up here.'

Uckfield addressed Marsden, 'Is it possible he might have fallen from a footpath and ended up lying on his back?'

'Landslips are pretty unpredictable, sir. The soil could have gradually given way around and under him, without disturbing the position, but you need to ask a forensic geophysicist that.'

Uckfield said he had seen enough, and he told the crime scene officers not to hang around or disturb the corpse further than was necessary. 'Any sign of a landslip, leave the body. We can retrieve it later if necessary.'

Back on firm ground, the RIB was just pulling into the bay with the firefighters on board. Uckfield ordered Marsden to escort them to the body. To Horton, he said, 'No point in calling the doctor out to certify death, we know the poor bugger's dead. And we don't want any more people trampling about up there.'

Horton agreed and said, 'It's unlikely we'll be able to search the area for any personal belongings or forensic evidence, it being so unstable, but we might be able to search the base of the cliff in case anything of the victim's has fallen down here.'

'Never mind that for now,' Uckfield dismissed impatiently. 'I think it's about time you told me what you were doing here, and how you managed to stumble over matey up there.'

Horton had been expecting this and, as he had waited for Uckfield to arrive, had been considering how much to impart. His relationship with Uckfield went back to their first day in the force when they had forged a friendship which had seen them being best man at each other's weddings. Horton's suspension just over two years ago had tested that relationship and, since Uckfield's promotion to Superintendent, Uckfield had put some distance between them. Horton knew full well where Uckfield's loyalties lay, and if it came down to an official reprimand or enquiry, Uckfield would sacrifice their friendship on the altar of his career. Horton decided the bones of the truth would be sufficient. Besides, he didn't have many facts, and there was still so much he didn't understand, especially given the revelation of this corpse.

He told Uckfield how he had met Lomas on the private beach of Lord Eames' property in October, before the investigation into the disappearance and subsequent death of a private investigator whose body had been found there. Lomas had given him a business card and, because Horton had been curious about him, he had asked Jane to check it for fingerprints.

'You mean that, during the investigation, you didn't reveal a possible suspect?' Uckfield declared disapprovingly and incredulously.

'I felt sure he wasn't one, which was confirmed.'

'What you *feel* has nothing to do with policing.'

'You sound like DCI Bliss now.'

'Well she's right and you're wrong,' Uckfield snapped. 'You can't keep going against the rules, Andy. You've already sailed too damn close to the wind. One more time and you'll be out. I can't –' but he didn't get any further. He cried out and clutched his side, doubled up in pain.

Startled and concerned Horton said, 'What's wrong? Are you OK, Steve?'

'Just a stitch from climbing up that damn cliff,' Uckfield panted.

But it looked more than that to Horton. He caught Elkins' eye who, witnessing the scene, made to hurry forward, but Uckfield, despite his pain, managed to wave a podgy arm for Elkins to stay back. Through gritted teeth, he said, 'Go on.'

'I forgot about him,' Horton lied, 'and that we still held his prints. But when the prints matched that of the unidentified male in the mortuary, I came over to identify him. But it's not the man I met, so there must have been another set of prints on that card that at some time got wiped off.'

Horton saw Elkins' worried expression and shook his head slightly. Uckfield took a few breaths, then his expression of pain lifted and, cautiously, he began to straighten up. 'Who is this Lomas?' he asked tentatively, as though waiting for the spasm to return.

'He said he was an artist. He was on Lord Eames' beach looking for driftwood to turn into art.'

'And what were *you* doing on that private beach?' Uckfield asked, now seemingly recovered.

'I was due to appear in court here on the island, but the two men who had stolen sculptures from the abbey, one of which had been donated by Lord Eames, changed their plea to guilty, so I broke the good news to the abbot and then thought, as I was along that part of the coast, I'd call in and tell his Lordship.' Uckfield eyed him dubiously. Horton knew it was a bit nebulous. It had been an excuse, a failsafe device in case Eames was at home in October, which was highly unlikely given that he usually only occupied the property during the major international sailing regatta of Cowes Week in August. Horton hadn't really known what he had hoped to achieve by seeing the house, or what he had hoped to accomplish by walking through the private wood to Eames' beach. All that happened was he'd met Wyndham Lomas.

'Eames wasn't in, the house was closed up, as you know from the ensuing investigation. And nothing was picked up on the security monitors.' A fact that still niggled away at Horton. Why hadn't an alert sounded when he and Lomas were trespassing? Or if it had, why had no one questioned him. He didn't know about Lomas. The security system was monitored by Mike Danby's company and Danby, being ex-job and a friend of Horton's, would have told him if Lomas had been located and questioned. Horton had encountered Danby many times since last October, but he'd given no indication that any of his operatives or monitors had registered his or Lomas's presence.

Uckfield said, 'This landslip corpse could be Lomas then?'

'I guess he could be, but the clothes seem wrong. When I met him, he was dressed very casually in shorts and a T-shirt.'

'He must have changed since then!' Uckfield seemed to be back to his usual self.

Horton admitted that was the case. He added, 'While Taylor and Tremaine are here, they can take prints and DNA samples from Ben's cabin, and from Cedric Halliwell's house. If Dr Clayton can lift fingerprints from the dead man, we might find a match in one or both of those places, which will give us a connection.'

'We'll need a warrant for the house,' Uckfield declared.

'Sergeant Norris is finding out who the executor is. He or she could give us permission, which would save time.' Horton's phone rang. 'It's Norris.' He listened for a while, said, 'No I'll speak to him. Give me his address. Can you arrange for the body to be taken to the mortuary? We'll bring it into Shanklin, there's a slipway at the end of the promenade.' Norris confirmed he'd arrange it. Horton said he would update him later and rang off. To Uckfield he said, 'The executor is a local solicitor by the name of Peter Chilcott, based in Shanklin. I'll call on him.'

'*After* Ripley's taken me back to Portsmouth. I'll leave Marsden with you.'

'Do you want me to ring Dr Clayton?'

Uckfield said he did. He gave instructions for the scene-of-crime team to examine the cabin as there was no one to apply for permission. Before climbing into the police RIB, Uckfield turned back to Horton. 'You're not to mention what happened. It was just a stitch in the stomach, caused by too much exercise. OK?'

'If you say so, Steve.'

'And tell Sergeant Elkins that.'

Horton did, but he could see that Elkins didn't believe him.

He called Dr Clayton who said she was in Exeter but would be back in Portsmouth tomorrow. She confirmed she would examine the corpse and conduct the post-mortem on the Isle of Wight. Horton asked if she had heard about the fire at the sailing club.

'No. Is there much damage?' was her shocked answer.

Horton told her.

'Well that's a relief, although not for those whose boats have been destroyed. Random destruction or targeted?' she asked.

'The jury's still out on that. Can you think of any reason why someone should have a grudge against the three victims, or the club?'

'Not against Venda Atkinson. She's loved by everyone.'

'Not so Councillor Levy? He seems to have plenty of enemies.'

'Yes, he's brash and full of himself.'

'And the Chief Constable?'

'Love's himself too, and thinks he knows it all when it comes to sailing, which I can assure you, Andy, he doesn't. If I hear anything on the grapevine about the fire, I'll let you know. Ask Clarke to email me the photographs of your body. I'll look at them on the ferry on the way over tomorrow.'

Horton then called Cantelli and relayed what had happened while he watched the crime scene officers and DC Marsden descend the cliff. He asked if there had been any progress on the highway robberies.

'A woman called in to say that she thinks she might have witnessed the latest robbery while she was walking her dogs. Walters has gone to interview her. He got back from the sailing club an hour ago. He says the CCTV images show no sign of life, either front or rear. He's left Leonard to break the news to the chief.'

'Lucky old Leonard.' Horton rang off and addressed Taylor as the firefighters came into view carrying the corpse in a body bag on a stretcher, 'Anything?'

'We've taken soil samples and we've bagged up twigs, stones and insect carcases. There's no sign of any personal belongings, but they could be scattered around the cliff or ditched elsewhere.'

As Horton had already conjectured and expressed to Uckfield. He told them to examine the cabin and the boat, and to bag up the woodcarving tools, mug and bottle on the table. There might be some prints and DNA to be extracted from them. Possibly those of the corpse, who could have descended to the cabin and been killed on his way back up to Beachwood House. Had the landslip corpse been a visitor to Beachwood House. Perhaps a friend of Halliwell's? Or possibly the reverse, an enemy, and he could have been killed on his way down to the cabin. By Halliwell? Or by someone else who had been staying at the house? Horton only had Norris's word that Halliwell was something of a recluse. For all he knew, he could have thrown riotous parties or had a stream of guests or family visiting. But Horton recalled the semi-derelict state of the house. Halliwell could have been frail and elderly and completely unconnected with the landslip corpse, which was much more probable. Perhaps he'd had someone caring for him. Horton told Marsden he was to accompany him to the solicitors.

Ripley wasn't long returning with the RIB – the powerful boat could make the round trip across the Solent comfortably within an hour. Within minutes Horton was climbing on board with Marsden, the two firefighters, Elkins and the corpse. Another ten minutes saw the stretcher being placed into the private ambulance with blackened windows at the seaside town of Shanklin. The incident drew some attention from a few passers-by and promenade strollers, some of whom took pictures on their mobile phones. Those would no doubt appear on the internet shortly, along with a great deal of speculation.

Elkins bought some sandwiches and drinks from the nearby café for himself, Ripley and the crime scene team, while Horton and Marsden, also equipped with refreshments, set off on the steep climb to the town centre. Horton hadn't eaten since breakfast and that was over eight hours ago. The day was racing away. It was just after four thirty.

Weaving their way past the day trippers, Horton, ignoring Uckfield's threats about not mentioning his episode, asked Marsden if he had noticed anything wrong with Uckfield, medically.

'He seems his usual self to me, sir,' Marsden replied.

Then perhaps that incident had been the first, and maybe the climb up the cliff *had* been too much for Uckfield. If so, he should look at dieting and getting fit, but Horton wasn't going to volunteer telling him.

He asked Marsden about his possible promotion to sergeant. Marsden smiled. 'In May. I take up my new rank and position on Operation Pelican.'

That was a major Hampshire police drug-busting operation. Horton warmly congratulated him and wondered who Marsden's replacement would be in Uckfield's team.

They turned left towards the railway station and, halfway down the road, drew up outside a large double-fronted, turn of the century house, which had been converted into offices. It boasted the name of Peter Chilcott Solicitors. Horton hoped the solicitor hadn't already left for home, because he was curious to learn more about the late Cedric Halliwell and his close neighbour, Ben, which could possibly tell them more about the landslip corpse.

Five

'This is the first I've heard about a cabin in the bay and about a man found dead in it,' Chilcott declared with some hostility as though Horton had deliberately placed both there to annoy him. Behind square-framed glasses, his hazel eyes blinked hard. His podgy fingers, sporting a couple of gold rings, one with what looked like a diamond in it, fiddled with his pink tie.

Horton didn't take to the rotund solicitor, but then maybe he was biased towards them because of Catherine's who seemed determined to make his life as difficult as possible by blocking his request for greater access to his daughter. Though, to be fair, they were only working under her instructions. His own solicitor, Frances Greywell, was a million miles away from this pompous individual with a round pink face and a thin film of sweat on his forehead and upper lip. Ms Greywell was efficient and professional and doing the best she could but for all that, she seemed to be up against a brick wall.

They had been shown into the boardroom at the rear of the building. Marsden had retrieved his notebook and pen from the inside of his jacket pocket and looked expectantly at Chilcott. Horton thought Chilcott's surprise genuine. He obviously hadn't heard the news on the local radio or seen it on the internet.

'We thought the cabin might be part of the late Mr Halliwell's estate,' Horton said.

'Not according to the Land Registry,' Chilcott crisply replied. 'The boundary of the deceased estate goes to the top of the cliff which leads down into the bay.' Chilcott pulled at his right ear which Horton noticed was larger than his left.

'How long had Mr Halliwell lived there?'

'He purchased the property fifteen months ago, January.'

So bang went Horton's earlier idea of the property having been in the family for years and neglected as the owner grew sick or old. Horton was almost certain the cabin was older than that. 'Would the cabin have required planning permission?'

'Probably.' Chilcott ran a chubby forefinger down the side of his right cheek and again blinked hard. 'And it wouldn't have been granted given that there are no utilities laid on in the bay, no water, sewage, gas etc. and no access to it either. It's also a highly volatile area. Landslips.'

Horton nodded and Marsden scribbled. Chilcott shifted and was about to speak, but Horton said, 'How did Mr Halliwell die?'

'I really don't see that this has anything to do with that vagrant.'

'Probably hasn't, but humour us, Mr Chilcott.'

The solicitor looked taken aback for a moment. 'If you must know, it was a heart attack on board his boat, a motor cruiser.'

'Where?'

'In the Solent. Ryde Inshore Rescue found him. They'd received a call from the Captain of the Wightlink Catamaran about a drifting boat. They went on board and found Mr Halliwell dead.'

'Where did he keep his boat?' Halliwell couldn't have kept it permanently moored in the bay, and a motor cruiser was definitely not the wooden boat he'd seen in front of Ben's cabin.

'Bembridge Marina.'

Horton had put in there many times. It was on the north of the island. By the sounds of it, Cedric Halliwell wasn't as much of a recluse as Sergeant Norris had said. 'Was he under the doctor for any underlying medical condition?'

'No. In fact, he wasn't registered with a doctor. I really don't see the reason for all these questions, Inspector.'

'Is Beachwood House the only property he owned?'

'Yes.' Chilcott looked at his watch.

Horton ignored the hint. 'Did Mr Halliwell own a car?'

'No. He didn't own any form of transport, except the boat.'

Maybe he didn't have a driver's licence, thought Horton, or had surrendered it, being elderly. But then Horton didn't know exactly how old Halliwell had been when he died. He asked.

'His passport states he was sixty-four.'

Horton had envisaged someone in their eighties, so he'd been wrong on that count too.

Chilcott was saying, 'I'd have put him a few years older than sixty-four, but we can't all look younger than our years.' He smirked as though expecting some comment or compliment. Neither Horton nor Marsden responded. Horton would have said Chilcott was mid-forties but maybe he was being kind.

'Who is the next of kin?' he asked.

'There isn't one. Mr Halliwell named me as his executor and told me that he was single and had no children or living relatives.'

So that ruled out Ben being a relation. Perhaps there wasn't a connection between the two men. Yet someone had used that footpath, and someone had killed the landslip corpse. He was curious to know who Halliwell's benefactors were but first, he asked, 'How substantial is the estate?'

Chilcott blinked twice, as though he didn't understand the question. He bristled and fingered the knot of his tie. 'I can't see that it is any business of yours.'

Calmly Horton said, 'It is when we are trying to establish the identity of a man who lived and died in the bay beneath Mr Halliwell's estate and that of a body found on the cliff just below his grounds.'

'Body? What body? You mean there have been two deaths?' Chilcott was genuinely shocked and puzzled.

'Yes. We're treating the second death, the one found on the cliff, as suspicious.'

'I don't understand.'

'Neither do we at the moment, Mr Chilcott, which is why we are here and why we'd appreciate your co-operation. As both deaths occurred so close to the late Mr Halliwell's estate, we have to ask these questions.'

'You should have explained all this to begin with,' Chilcott snapped. 'I still don't see how it can be relevant to my late client, but Mr Halliwell's estate is worth approximately six million pounds, maybe more.'

'That much!' Marsden declared, stunned.

Chilcott's eyes swivelled to the young detective. 'The house, contents and grounds amount to approximately two million, and Mr Halliwell had bank accounts in Guernsey and Zurich and an offshore account in the Cayman Islands, so you can see that handling his estate is not a straightforward matter.'

Horton was growing ever more curious about the late Cedric Halliwell.

'How long had he been a client?'

Chilcott shifted, clearly uneasy. 'Since January.'

'Last January?' A year after he'd purchased Beachwood House?

'Yes. He asked me to draw up his will.'

Even more curious. Why would someone that wealthy entrust a substantial estate on his death to be dealt with by a small local solicitor? Horton would have thought an international law firm with expertise in handling the dismantling of complex financial accounts would have been more suited. OK, so Halliwell was dead, and perhaps he hadn't cared what would happen to his estate on his death. Maybe he had walked into the offices of the first legal firm he had come across on the island to make his will. Perhaps he had been in a hurry and he had intended to change solicitors when he had more time. But that didn't wash because he'd had a year since purchasing Beachwood House to make a will, so coming here on the spur of the moment seemed to be out of it, unless he had been told in January that his days were numbered. A month later he was dead.

'Do you know how he amassed his wealth?' asked Horton, also wondering why Halliwell hadn't spent some of that wealth on renovating Beachwood House, which was falling down around him. Maybe he hadn't had the time or had been miserly. Rich people often were.

'Of course not. And it wasn't my place to ask him.'

No, thought Horton, Chilcott wouldn't have wanted to probe and risk losing a valuable client. 'There was nothing in his paperwork to indicate his past occupation?'

'No.'

Truth or lie? Horton wasn't quite sure, but he knew the solicitor was uneasy about something.

'Did he employ any staff? I understand there is a gatehouse to the property.'

'There is, but that has been empty for years.'

'You entered it?'

'Well, no.' Chilcott looked uncomfortable. 'It's shuttered, and Mr

Halliwell told me it was empty.'

Horton thought it strange that the solicitor had taken his dead client at his word and hadn't been curious to see inside the gatehouse.

'As far as I am aware, there were no staff at any time, or if there were then Mr Halliwell didn't keep employment records. There was no contract labour to settle, no gardener, window cleaner, domestic cleaners. At least no one has come forward saying they are owed money, and there were no outstanding bills to be paid. There were no invoices either, the latter of which he must have destroyed.'

'He might have scanned the paperwork to his computer,' Marsden said. 'And paid his bills online.'

'Was there a computer?' asked Horton.

'Not in the house or on the boat, and neither was there a mobile telephone, laptop or any kind of device.'

'Don't you think that unusual?' Horton said.

Chilcott shrugged. 'Not everyone embraces technology. He might have been a technophobe.'

'So how did you liaise with him?' Marsden asked.

'He came into the office in person on 19 January and asked if I could have a will ready for him to sign by the 23rd. It was a bit of a rush, but it was fairly straightforward, so I agreed.'

And the fee Chilcott would have charged Halliwell would have reflected that. Halliwell must have indicated he was a wealthy man, or perhaps the fact that he owned Beachwood House had been enough for Chilcott to weigh up his client's worth and agree to the quick turnaround.

'The will was witnessed by myself and my secretary. Mr Halliwell gave me a set of keys to the house and the safe and told me I would find his papers there in the event of his death, those papers being fairly limited, as I've indicated. There was his passport and details of various bank accounts, and that's it. I didn't expect his death to occur quite so soon after making his will. Nine days in fact after he'd signed it. He was found dead on his boat on 1 February. Perhaps he knew he had a heart condition and had been told he hadn't long to live.' The small eyes blinked again three times, and the podgy finger again stroked the chubby cheek.

This was sounding decidedly strange to Horton. All right, so there were some eccentric people and maybe Halliwell was one of them, but the absence of employees, contract workers, and paperwork gave him the impression that Halliwell was keen to keep a low profile. Now why was that? His suspicious mind automatically leapt to the thought that Halliwell might have been in hiding because he was a crook, or because he was on the run from someone or something. He was probably wrong but the discovery of two bodies close to Halliwell's house set his police antennae vibrating like a pneumatic drill.

He said, 'There must be financial accounts. After all, Mr Halliwell would have been a taxpayer.'

'He wasn't. He hadn't been in the country long enough. He wasn't classed as a UK resident. His main residency was the Cayman Islands. He came back to the UK on 18 December and died on the 1 February, on his forty-fifth day here. He would have paid tax on his assets if he had been in the country for forty six days. But there you go. He has no residencies abroad, so I'm assuming he must have sold the place he owned in the Cayman Islands before deciding to return to the UK, perhaps because of that heart condition, and the proceeds of that are in his offshore account there. He was a British citizen, and the money from the sale of any of his overseas property and other assets will be released to me when probate is granted, but being subject to overseas laws, it will take time.'

And expense, thought Horton, knowing that Chilcott was the type who would spin it out and inflate his fee accordingly.

'He won't pay death duties either,' Chilcott continued. 'Because he was not 'domiciled' here. There is no Inheritance Tax on 'excluded assets' such as foreign currency accounts, overseas pensions and other investments.'

Horton took it that Chilcott was right about these tax technicalities. Even if he wasn't that would be down to him and the Inland Revenue.

'Do you have a photograph of Mr Halliwell?'

'Only his passport one, and you know how awful they are.'

'Describe him.'

'A pleasant man, well spoken, intelligent, about six feet tall, grey haired going thin at the temples, a heavily lined face, grey eyes, tanned, slender, well dressed. No jewellery,' Chilcott said the latter as though it was minus point. 'Now, if that's all, I have an evening meeting to attend.'

Horton rose, and Marsden quickly replaced his notebook and

scrambled up. Horton noted the relief on the solicitor's face.

'Thank you for your help, Mr Chilcott. We may have to return if our enquiries make it necessary.' That drew a frown and a couple blinks. 'Oh, and we will need access to Beachwood House.'

Chilcott started with surprise, and his face flushed. 'But why?'

'We could execute a search warrant, but it would be much quicker if you, as executor, would let us have the keys.'

'I really can't see how it will help you. The man found dead on the cliffside has nothing to do with Mr Halliwell.'

'I didn't say it was a man.'

Chilcott's flush deepened.

'But it probably is,' Horton added. 'And Ben is most certainly male. Perhaps we could request permission from the benefactors, although that might be lengthy and time consuming. How many are there?'

'I don't know exactly.'

Horton looked puzzled. 'But surely you –'

'There is only one benefactor but several members so to speak. Mr Halliwell left his estate to a monastery, here on the north of the island. The Benedictine Monks at Northwood Abbey are the sole beneficiaries.'

That surprised and intrigued Horton. He thought it an unusual legacy. 'Did he say why he was leaving his estate to the monastery?'

'No, and it wasn't my business to ask,' came Chilcott's frosty reply.

Pity. 'Was he Catholic?'

'Not that I'm aware of.'

'Did Dom Daniel Briar know of this bequest before Mr Halliwell's death?'

'You know the abbot?' Chilcott asked.

'I've had dealings with the abbey.'

Chilcott sniffed as though he disapproved. 'The abbot was totally shocked by it.'

'Then Mr Halliwell wasn't a regular visitor to the abbey?'

'I really have no idea.'

Horton would ask Dom Daniel Briar, but it was getting late, just after five, and from his previous contact with the abbey, Horton knew that after five thirty, from Vespers onwards, the monks would be in prayer and discussion. He'd talk to the abbot tomorrow if Uckfield permitted it. This wasn't Horton's investigation. But the fact that he knew the abbot, that he could also liaise with Dr Clayton here on the island before and possibly after she conducted the post-mortem on the landslip course, and that DI Dennings was otherwise fully engaged on the Trehams robbery, meant he had a fair chance of being involved for another day at least.

Six

Uckfield gave his permission after Horton had reported back to him two hours later. The scene of crime team had lifted prints and hairs from Ben's cabin, but there had been no sign of flesh or blood. Horton had also brought Sergeant Norris up to speed before leaving the island, and requested he contact the planning department to see if anyone had ever applied for permission for the cabin to be erected in the bay.

Trueman had set up a crime board and Clarke's photographs were already on it. There was another crime board close to DI Dennings' office detailing the Trehams robbery but, judging by the lack of activity in the incident suite, that investigation looked to be at stalemate, which Sergeant Trueman confirmed. He also said there had been no reports of missing persons that could fit the landslip corpse, but once they had a more detailed description from Dr Clayton and possibly fingerprints and DNA, they could run a match.

Horton handed over the passport photograph of Halliwell. 'It's not brilliant. The passport expires this year, so it's ten years out of date.' He gave a résumé of what Chilcott had told him.

'I'll make some enquiries with Her Majesty's Revenue and Customs and the Border Agency and see what I can find.'

That done, Horton returned to CID for an update from Cantelli on the sailing club arson, the highway robberies and anything else that the villains and lowlifes of Portsmouth had cared to throw their way during the day.

Cantelli looked frazzled. Horton took the seat next to the sergeant in the empty CID office. 'Don't tell me, the chief's been on the phone.'

'Several times,' Cantelli answered somewhat wearily. 'He's seconded Walters to the Arson Task Force to make, as he calls it, a quick arrest. It would be nice to know *who* to arrest. Leonard was brave enough to suggest to the chief that it could be a member of the club with a grudge against him, Councillor Levy or Ms Atkinson, but he stoutly rebuffed that as "ridiculous". He's more inclined to go for a staff member or ex-employee with a chip on his shoulder and has ordered that they all be interviewed, hence Walters continued input.'

'He could be right. And the witness who claims she saw the highway robbers, what did Walters get from her?'

Cantelli's dark-featured face lit up. 'A good description of the vehicle but not the registration, the thieves had deliberately obscured that, but we've got the make and the colour of the car, and a description of the woman who held up the witnesses' car. I've circulated details across Hampshire, and to bordering counties, Dorset, West Sussex, Surrey in case they've moved on. How about you? You've had a fun day.'

'Which is more than the poor bugger I fell over had when he was last alive.' Horton told him what he had unearthed.

'Any ideas?'

'No, just lots of questions. Are the three dead men, Halliwell, Ben and the landslip corpse connected? Or is it just a fluke that all have a link with that area? Two have died of natural causes and the third murdered, although Gaye hasn't confirmed that yet. But it looked remarkably like a bullet in the head to me.'

'He could have committed suicide and the gun fell down with all the earth and debris in a landslide.'

'And the damage to the skull?'

'Caused when he fell.'

'It's possible but the skull damage looked too violent for that.' He told Cantelli that Halliwell had left his entire estate – some six million pounds – to the Benedictine monks at the abbey.

'Blimey, they must have been praying hard,' was Cantelli's response. 'It's a powerful motive for murder, but I can't see a monk committing it.'

Cantelli's remark pulled Horton up sharply and made his mind race. Dormand, one of the men in that photograph from 1967, posing as Brother Norman at the abbey, had admitted to being a killer. But Dormand was dead and had been since October, and the landslip corpse looked to be more recent than that, although Dr Clayton would confirm whether that was the case. And besides, why would Dormand want to kill the landslip corpse? Dormand had said he had killed in the name of British Intelligence, and Horton couldn't see what a body under Beachwood House had to do with the intelligence services.

'You being a good Catholic boy, Barney, do you have any ideas as to why Halliwell should leave his fortune to the abbey, aside from the fact he might have been Catholic or a lapsed Catholic?'

'Maybe it was to atone for a sin.'

'It would have to be a pretty big one to warrant that amount.' Horton had briefly wondered if Halliwell might be a criminal or on the run.

'Perhaps he had been raised as a Catholic but had led a wicked life. His wealth could have been made on the back of fraud, embezzlement, murder.'

'Or robbery,' Horton added thoughtfully. If that were the case, then when and who had he robbed? Someone who had sought revenge? 'From what Chilcott told us about Halliwell, all of those sound feasible.' He relayed the gist of it, adding, 'He could have been involved in a crime years ago and, with the proceeds, took off to the Cayman Islands. That was where he ended up before the Isle of Wight, at least.'

'Wonder what made him go to the Isle of Wight. It's not a tax haven like the Channel Islands or the Cayman Islands.'

'He might have some past connection with the abbey.'

'Maybe he hoped to cleanse his money, or his soul, by leaving a massive legacy to the monks. Although you'd think if he had wanted forgiveness, he'd have given the money away before his death.'

'He only returned to the UK in December, according to Chilcott, after having liquidated his overseas assets, so perhaps he intended to but never had the time. Maybe he confessed to those sins.'

'It wouldn't have been to the abbot, because he wouldn't touch the money if it had been illegally acquired.'

'Perhaps he could have been persuaded. Six million pounds can do a lot of good for a lot of people. Perhaps Dom Daniel Briar has been instructed to give it away to the poor and needy, although Chilcott made no mention of it. The abbot could have a letter to that effect which Halliwell gave or posted to him. I'll check that out tomorrow.'

'Just as long as you don't ask me to accompany you.'

Horton smiled. Cantelli got seasick looking at a wave. 'Wouldn't dream of it. Not unless Uckfield orders it.'

'Then I'll volunteer to question every citizen of Portsmouth in connection with the chief's arson.'

'Be careful, he might take you up on that.'

Horton told Cantelli to go home. Walters had already sloped off, but then it was almost eight o'clock. Horton made for his office where he wrote up his report on the discovery of the body. Marsden was writing up the interview with Chilcott. He answered some emails then headed home. It was nine thirty when he reached the marina and, after eating in the Indian restaurant, he boarded his yacht and made a coffee.

The day's surprising events ran through his mind. If it hadn't been for those fingerprints being identified as those on the card which Lomas had given him in October, he'd never have discovered the body, and the enquiry into Ben's identity would have rested with Sergeant Norris. If he hadn't kept the card in the first place... if he hadn't asked Jane to check the fingerprints... if he had told her to destroy them... but then life was full of ifs. It was just one of those quirks of nature, or rather coincidence. It seemed bizarre, but then coincidences happened more often than many thought. This one had thrown up three men – Ben, Halliwell and the landslip corpse – all surrounded in mystery. All connected? Possibly and possibly to some distant crime. And what of Lomas? Was he also a criminal? Had *he* killed the landslip corpse? He must have known Ben to have had a card with Ben's prints on it. Unless he had randomly picked it up from somewhere.

He tried to clear his mind of thoughts of the case, but it refused to co-operate. It was too late to go for a run. Besides, running on top of a curry was not the best thing to do. And neither did it seem the best thing to have eaten before retiring. His sleep was fitful and filled with dreams of a skull staring at him, and when it began to laugh, he jolted awake with a shout. He was relieved to see it was close on six thirty. Time for a run along the promenade to blast away those dreams. Two hours later, refreshed, showered, shaved and dressed, he headed for the ferry on his Harley, wondering if Gaye would be on the same sailing. Disappointingly, she wasn't.

On board, he had breakfast, a bacon roll and coffee, and called

Cantelli to check if there had been any developments overnight on the sailing club arson and the highway robberies. There hadn't been and, miraculously, it had been a quiet night for crime. It was just after ten when he pulled into the hospital car park. Five minutes later, he was in the mortuary where he found Gaye already suited up, examining the naked remains of the corpse. Maybe he shouldn't have had that bacon roll either.

'Not much of the male anatomy left but enough for even DI Dennings to tell our corpse's gender,' she said by way of greeting.

Gaye, like him, was not a fan of the muscle bound, fifteen stone, plodding detective who she had nicknamed Neanderthal Man.

He smiled as he got his churning stomach under control, and his curiosity began to overcome the nauseating smell that neither Gaye nor the mortuary attendant seemed to notice. But then it went with the job, just as he rarely noticed the stench in the cells.

'And, as you can see, there's hardly any flesh left on his legs, upper arms, around the shoulders, or on his face, but there is some on the lower abdomen and chest,' she pointed out. 'The process of human decomposition is still relatively unknown, despite considerable research and in this case, because of where he was found, there are some additional factors to consider. I've looked at Clarke's photographs of the body in situ, and spoken to Jamie Spring, a forensic geophysicist. The cliffside where the body was found comprises of Greensand.'

'So DC Jake Marsden told us, deposited during the Early Cretaceous Period, which lasted for approximately forty million years.'

'You obviously paid attention,' she said smiling. 'Yes, and Greensand is not the world's best preservative. The sandy composition means the soil and rock will be dry and will oxidize material such as the human body, resulting in fairly rapid decomposition and skeletonization.'

'Which means his death could be quite recent.'

'Yes, but you're looking at weeks not days, and don't ask me how many weeks, not until I've done a little more delving.'

'Can't you give me a guesstimate?' he asked, thinking he could rule out Dormand aka Brother Norman having disposed of the victim. But then he already had.

'Possibly two months. Could be earlier, could be a lot later given what Jamie has told me. Why? Have you some idea of who might have killed him?'

'If it's later than 1 February it rules out Cedric Halliwell, the owner of Beachwood House above the cliff where the body was found. He died of natural causes on 1 February. But the man found dead in the cabin in the bay's a possibility. He died last Thursday, again of natural causes.'

'You have suspicions about that?'

'No. Not really.'

'But I can see you're wavering. I can hear it in your voice.'

'Only because three deaths all so close together in time and location makes me wonder. Although it's not unheard of for two men to die naturally and a third accidentally in close proximity. But I don't think this one,' he nodded at the corpse, 'was accidental.'

'On the face of it, I'm inclined to agree with you. There is considerable trauma to the skull.'

'Could that have been caused in a fall?'

'From the landslip? I doubt it. And no kind of landslip could have caused that neat round hole. I'll tell you more once I've conducted the autopsy.'

'Any idea of his age?'

'Mid-fifties to late sixties. I'll extract DNA and try to get fingerprints but there's not much skin left,' she said, peering at the hands. 'I'll scrape off what skin I can and put it over my own fingers to see if we can get an imprint.'

Horton had seen both Gaye and Jane Ashley, the fingerprint bureau supervisor, do that a few times. It didn't sound pleasant, but it often worked.

'Anything about the clothes or shoes that strike you as unusual or significant?' he asked. They were in large plastic evidence bags on a nearby bench table ready to be despatched to the lab.

'The fabrics are man-made which is why they're still evident. Natural fibres such as silk, cotton and wool rot a lot quicker, and are biodegradable. The shoes were probably leather slip-ons because their remains show no trace of eyelets or laces, although the shoelaces could have been made of cotton and the ends of the laces, usually of plastic or metal, could be buried in the soil, but I'd still expect to see eyelets in the leather. There was nothing on him to give any identification. I'll have more answers for you later. You'll just have to be patient and wait.'

'For you, Gaye, forever.'

She laughed. Horton smiled and left for the abbey.

Seven

'You have news about Brother Norman?' the abbot, a small, wiry man in his late fifties, greeted Horton half an hour later with an anxious expression.

It was a natural assumption for the abbot to make regarding his visit. 'No, sorry, Father.'

A mix of relief and disappointment crossed Dom Daniel Briar's narrow, lined face. Horton knew that he still clung to the hope that Dormand, aka Brother Norman, as he had known him, was alive. They turned towards the piggery.

'I'm here because I understand that the monastery has recently come into a substantial legacy.'

The abbot looked at Horton with surprise, and then a shadow crossed his clear blue eyes. 'You're referring to Mr Cedric Halliwell's bequest.'

'Yes. How well did you know him?'

'I didn't. I never met him. None of us did. You're wondering why he left everything to the abbey,' Dom Daniel Briar said, quickly interpreting Horton's puzzled expression. 'I have no idea, Inspector. I am grateful, although I understand that the property might take some time to sell. It is, I have been told, unique, large and in a landslip area. But time is of no consequence to us.'

'There will be money in his bank accounts which can be released to you before the estate is sold, and there is also his motorboat, which will be sold unless you decide to keep it.'

The abbot smiled. 'Our small dinghy is enough for us.'

A group of noisy school children came rushing up to the piggery. The abbot turned right on to the public footpath that led to Fishbourne and the car ferry which Horton had arrived on that morning.

'Could you, or one of the Brothers, have known Mr Halliwell under another name?'

'You mean he could have been a monk here at one time?'

'Or perhaps he stayed in your guest house.'

'I suppose it's possible. We haven't seen a picture of him or had him described to us.'

Horton showed him the copy he'd taken of the passport photograph and relayed the description Chilcott had given him, but the abbot looked blank and shook his head. 'He's not known to me, but I will ask my Brothers.'

'Could he have confessed to you or any of your Brothers?'

'Not to me, but again I will ask the others.'

'I'll email you the photograph.'

Horton didn't think he'd get a positive result. A rough-hewn wooden bench caught his eye, reminding him of the one outside Ben's cabin. He noted that this was dedicated to one of the monks who had died two years ago. He said, 'There was a man living in a cabin in the bay beneath Mr Halliwell's land. He died last week, and we're anxious to identify him. He was mid to late sixties, sturdily built, tanned, with grey cropped hair. From what I've seen in his cabin he was an incredibly talented wood carver.'

The abbot's head whipped round, and his blue eyes widened. 'You don't mean Ben?'

It was Horton's turn to look surprised. 'I do. You knew him?' he asked keenly.

'I'm sorry to hear he's died. Yes, I knew him. Well, Brother Norman did.'

Horton's mind grappled to pull together the implications of this while his rational side fought hard to say there was nothing unusual or suspicious about it. But there was, especially given that Brother Norman was a phoney.

'Ben carved that seat for us,' Dom Daniel Briar said, pausing before it.

Horton's pulse raced, but he disguised his keenness and asked when Ben had carved it.

'Last August and September. It was Brother Norman who recommended Ben.'

Was it indeed? This got even more interesting. 'Tell me about

Ben?' Horton asked as they sat on the bench he had carved.

'He first came to us last May with some of his small wood carvings asking if we would care to sell them in the shop. Brother Norman showed them to us, and we all agreed it would be a good idea. They were very popular. He also carved the squirrel and the owl in front of the abbey, a great hit with young people.'

'Do you know why he came here specifically? Did Ben know Brother Norman previously?'

'If he did, neither man said. I only met Ben a few times and then not for long. Brother Norman dealt with him. I know nothing of Ben's background; he didn't volunteer it and I didn't ask. Brother Norman might have known more, but it's not our habit to pry.'

Pity. 'Could you ask your Brothers if they know more about Ben?'

'Of course, Inspector, if it will help.'

'Did Ben work on this seat here at the abbey?'

'Yes.'

Which meant he'd have had plenty of time to have conversations with Dormand aka Brother Norman. Had the two men known one another before meeting up here? Had Ben been a monk at the Italian abbey where Dormand had been before coming here, as the abbot had previously told him? A fact that Horton had checked and had confirmed. But that didn't mean Dormand had genuinely been a monk there; that too could have been a cover. Was he being over suspicious? Was he seeing conspiracies everywhere? Possibly. Maybe he was losing his sense of reasoning and reality.

The image of those sandals found on Ben's feet flashed before Horton's mind. Jesus Sandals. They were similar to the ones he had seen on Dormand's and Lomas's feet. The abbot sported the same style. Had Ben and Lomas been real monks while Dormand a phoney one? And how did this fit with the landslip corpse and Cedric Halliwell and his bequest to the abbey? Maybe it didn't because in May, when Ben had first come here with his wood carvings, and in August and September when he had carved this seat, Halliwell, although the owner of Beachwood House, hadn't been living there. He'd only arrived in December, according to Chilcott. So perhaps Halliwell had been totally unaware that a cabin was in the bay beneath his house and that someone was living in it.

Horton pushed the myriad of questions buzzing around his head aside. 'What was Ben like?' he asked.

'Content, pleasant, amiable. He said he'd been practising woodcraft for about twenty years and had made a good living from it, enough for his needs he said, which were small.'

'Did he have an accent?'

'No.'

'Was he religious?'

'Not in the sense that he joined us in prayer or spoke of God. He might have been religious in his own way, of course.'

'Did he ever talk about or mention the name Cedric Halliwell?'

'Not to me and, judging by the surprise of my Brothers, not to them either. He might have done so to Brother Norman, but sadly we can't ask him.'

No, thought Horton. 'Have you ever heard the name Wyndham Lomas?'

'No.'

'Maybe your Brothers have?'

'I'll ask them for you, Inspector. Is he a friend of Ben's?'

'Possibly. I'm keen to trace him. He claimed to be an artist.'

'I will enquire.'

Horton thought it time to tell the abbot about the landslip corpse. Dom Daniel Briar expressed surprise and concern at the news.

'We're not yet sure how the man died,' Horton added, 'but his death is being treated as suspicious. And because his body was discovered just below Mr Halliwell's property, I would like your permission to enter Beachwood House. There might be something inside that can help us with our investigation and with discovering Ben's identity, *if* Mr Halliwell knew Ben. I'd also like to look over Mr Halliwell's boat.'

'Of course you have my permission. I will give instructions to Mr Chilcott to release the keys to you.'

'Thank you. Have you been inside the house?'

'No. I've left all that to Mr Chilcott. I will telephone him immediately and authorize it. You will keep me fully informed, Inspector?' The abbey bell sounded. 'I'm sorry, but I have to go. That's the bell for Sexts.'

'Of course. I'm sorry to have taken up so much of your time and without bringing you any good news.'

'You'll let me know if you hear anything about Brother Norman?'

'I will.' But Horton thought the abbot would wait a while for that. Forever, in fact.

Returning to his Harley, Horton called Uckfield, relayed what Gaye had said and the news he'd discovered from the abbot about Ben. 'If Ben knew Cedric Halliwell then perhaps that was why Halliwell decided to bequeath his estate to the abbey, knowing that Ben wouldn't want it, and Halliwell felt grateful to the abbey for selling Ben's work and commissioning him. Not that it gets us any further with the landslip victim. I'll stay on the island until Dr Clayton has finished the post-mortem, and while I'm waiting, I'll get the keys from Chilcott, and take a look round Beachwood House and Halliwell's boat.'

Uckfield grumpily agreed. Horton wanted to give the abbot time to call Chilcott, so he made for Bembridge Marina where Chilcott had said Halliwell had kept his boat. The Solent glimmered in a clear turquoise sky. There was barely a ripple on the water, and he could see several yachts making the most of the weather. The buildings of Portsmouth were so sharply in focus that he could almost make out every detail. Not a good sign weather-wise, so local folklore had it. Rising amongst them was the tower block where he had lived with his mother until he was ten. He'd sit and gaze out of the window, counting the boats in the Solent and wishing he could be on them having an adventure. Well, he got there in the end. Now he wished he could give Emma that adventure. Instead, she spent time on Catherine's rich boyfriend's luxury motor cruiser that was almost as big as the Isle of Wight ferry he could see streaming through the calm waters towards Portsmouth. Or she'd be on her grandfather's larger yacht.

He wound his way along the road that led to the National Trust land which had once been a golf course with public access through it, recalling how the January before last he had met Thea Carlsson, crouching over the body of her brother with a gun in her hand. During that full-scale murder investigation he had got close to Thea. He hadn't believed from the start that she had committed the murder. She had claimed to be psychic. He was sceptical about that, but she seemed to sense his difficult childhood and the presence of his mother.

There had been his own flash of memory of being here as a child, long before the marina had existed. His mother had been ahead of him, with a man. She'd turned and called his name. He'd run to her, laughing. He could remember nothing of the man. Why couldn't he? Perhaps because he had been too young, only five or six, or perhaps because the man hadn't made any impact on him, which meant he couldn't have seen him regularly, and he hadn't conjured up any strong feeling about him. He couldn't remember how they had got to the Isle of Wight. Had it been by private boat or the ferry? All Horton knew was that he had been happy. His mother had been too.

He parked just outside the marina office and was surprised to see the police RIB on the pontoon. He bumped into Elkins coming out of the office.

'What are you doing here?' Horton asked.

'Booking my summer holiday,' came Elkins' sarcastic but good-natured reply, before he added, 'There have been some thefts from the harbour, a couple of outboard engines and a motorboat. The latter probably used to transport the outboard engines away.'

'I'd have thought you'd be occupied following up the Chief Constable's sailing club arson.' Walters had told Horton earlier that morning on the phone that he was interviewing the staff and the club's suppliers. Meanwhile, DC Leonard was reviewing previously unsolved arson cases, looking for similarities and checking if any known arsonists had recently been released from prison and were knocking around the city.

Elkins said, 'We've already spoken to the lock master at Horsea Marina who says that no boats entered or left the lock at the critical time, save for our lone night sailor who reported the arson. But what are you doing here?'

'Looking at the late Cedric Halliwell's boat. Care to join me?'

'Might as well.'

They entered the marina office where Horton introduced himself and explained why he was there.

'Poor man,' said the woman behind the desk. 'He should never have gone out on the boat. Not that it was the cause of his death, but he might have been found sooner if it had been a clear day. There was a terrible mist in the Solent,' she explained to Horton's baffled look.

'Was it misty when he left here?'

'Yes, all day, it never lifted.'

And Horton knew that fog or sea mist was the sailor's worst nightmare, so why chance it? 'What was Mr Halliwell like?'

'I only saw him twice, once when he looked over the boat with a view to purchasing it, and the second time when it was his. He was a quiet man, nicely spoken, polite, in his sixties. We didn't know the boat had gone with him on board until Ryde Inshore Rescue brought it back and gave us the sad news.'

'When did he purchase it?'

'Mid-January. He bought the boat and the berth together. Mr and Mrs Wakelin were the previous owners. They had it for sale privately. They'd put a card in the chandlers on Embankment Road which said interested parties should enquire at the marina. I handed him the keys, as we were instructed to do if anyone asked about it. He looked over the boat alone, came back and said he'd have it. Four days later it was ·his. He didn't bother with a survey.'

A rush job then. Halliwell must have owned a telephone at some stage to have phoned the Wakelins and his bank to arrange payment.

'Do you have the Wakelins' address?' Horton asked.

'They're living in Portugal now. I don't know where. It was why they were selling the boat, to move abroad. I have their mobile number, would you like that?'

Horton said they would. She relayed it to Elkins.

Horton wondered if he would find a logbook on board, or had Chilcott taken that? In fact, Horton hadn't asked Chilcott if he had been on board Halliwell's boat and taken any paperwork from it, but he would when he collected the keys. He asked for the boat's name and where it was moored, then, with Elkins, set out the short distance along the single pontoon which stretched out from the shore. It branched left, leading into the small harbour. The wind was strengthening, causing ripples across the water like corrugated iron, and the cloud was building from the south. Opposite came the pulsating beat of machinery from the gravel pit on the northern shores of Bembridge. There were a couple of dog walkers on the sandy beach and a handful of people sitting on benches outside the café next to the sailing club. A number of small craft bobbed gently in the harbour and, to his right along the Embankment Road, were the row of houseboats which had been there as long as he could remember.

Halliwell's boat, *Tradewinds,* was sandwiched between a sailing yacht and another motorboat. It was a much more modest craft than Horton had anticipated, especially for a multi-millionaire who could have bought such a vessel as a tender for a mega yacht. But then, judging by the state of Halliwell's house, he had been a man who hadn't liked to parade his wealth or spend his money. The four berth boat was clean and well cared for with a green rear canopy stretching over the cockpit.

'Talk to Ryde Inshore Rescue, Dai, see what you can find out about the rescue.'

'I'll also see if I can get hold of the Wakelins.'

They returned to the shore where Horton bought sandwiches from the café for them all and, after eating them on board the RIB, he returned to his Harley and made for the solicitor's office. Chilcott grumbled about releasing the keys to the boat and the house but did as had been requested by the abbot. He confirmed that he had been on board the boat, but had found no paperwork nor a logbook. Horton thought that slightly unusual but made no comment.

He set out for Beachwood House, not expecting to find much save some old sticks of furniture, dust and cobwebs. What greeted him though was something startlingly different and totally unexpected.

Eight

Maybe he was hallucinating. No, this ultra-modern and exquisitely decorated hall was real and so completely different from the exterior that it was like entering a parallel universe. He'd liked to have seen Barney's reaction to this. Elkins would have been as equally flummoxed. Why hadn't Chilcott told him what to expect? Surely he must have thought this contrast with the dilapidated exterior completely unusual? Did the solicitor have no imagination at all? Was the rest of the house like this, he wondered, eyeing the white painted walls hung with large, vividly coloured abstract paintings. Around the hall were dotted blue-grey contemporary armchairs and a sofa and, in the middle of it, a full sized snooker table.

His feet echoed on the light grey ceramic tiles as he moved towards the snooker table and played with the brightly coloured balls as he gazed around. All the doors that gave off the hall were open, save for one farther down on his right. There was a lingering odour of paint. It was as though no one had lived here. He wondered if the snooker table had ever been used. The cues hung tidily on the wall.

Why had Halliwell chosen to keep the exterior so dated and shabby? To deter would be thieves? No one would think there would be anything of value to steal here, judging by the exterior, and the thought of the Trehams robbery flitted across his mind. He had seen a photograph on the crime board of their expensive prestigious property behind gates equipped with security cameras. It was like saying to any would-be burglar casing the area, herein lie rich pickings.

He hadn't yet seen the rest of this house, but he expected it to be similar to the hall. Clearly Halliwell must have spent a fortune on this, because Horton didn't think this had been executed by a previous owner; it looked and smelt too new for that. If Halliwell had commissioned this refurbishment when he had purchased the property fifteen months ago, then Horton would have thought he'd have kept receipts and records of it. Maybe Marsden had been correct when he'd said that Halliwell might have kept invoices on a computer. But where was that?

He crossed to the room on his left and found an expansive drawing room which mirrored the hall both in contemporary design and opulence. The shutters were drawn but even through the dim light he could see that the flooring, fittings and furniture were of the highest quality and all new. He looked for a light switch but couldn't find one. Perhaps the lights were controlled wirelessly, possibly by voice command. There were more pictures on the walls, but unlike those in the hall they were traditional scenes of life. The room looked like something out of an interior design magazine of the type Catherine loved. Maybe she would get the chance to live in a house like this if she stayed with Jarvis. Horton was certain she would. Emma would get the kind of bedroom he could never provide, even if he decided to move from his boat to a flat or a house so that he could have her to stay overnight. One of Catherine's objections to granting him overnight stays was that his boat was totally unsuitable for a young girl to reside on board. It was too small and too cold. He'd told his solicitor, Ms Greywell that it did have two cabins, an efficient heating system, an inboard shower and toilet and, in the summer, it wasn't at all cold. But he could never compete with Peter Jarvis when it came to wealth and luxury, a thought that disturbed him. He was afraid Emma would prefer her wealthier potential stepfather to her real father.

He pushed the thought aside as he stepped into a smaller sitting room that fed off the drawing room. It was equally beautifully refurbished with more scenes-of-life paintings on the walls. The sitting room in turn gave on to the kitchen, which occupied the complete rear of the house. It was like something out of Cape Canaveral with a pared-back grey stone floor, chrome fittings, white cabinets and a grey slate worktop. A walk-in pantry was the size of most people's kitchens. This was in sharp contrast to the orangery which contained old wicker furniture, dust and decaying plants.

He returned to the hall, and crossed to the room opposite the drawing room. Inside was a grand piano, a stool and nothing else. Did that mean Halliwell had been an accomplished pianist? He couldn't have been famous otherwise there would have been obituaries in the newspapers about him and people at his funeral. But maybe there had been. Horton hadn't asked Chilcott about the funeral. It hadn't seemed relevant. He recalled though that Chilcott said he didn't know what Halliwell had done for a living.

He thought about Ben's old harmonica as he climbed the sweeping staircase covered with a brightly striped carpet of green, grey and blue with brass stair rods. Dust covered the brass stair rail. Ben's lifestyle, had been so totally different from this – a little camping stove for cooking and a plastic bowl for washing up and ablutions.

Here in the upper hall were more brightly coloured abstracts. He peered at the artist's name: Jethro Dinx. It wasn't one he recognized but then he wasn't an art expert, although he had spent some time working on the arts and antiques squad. He guessed that these paintings, like the others in the house, were valuable. Another thing that Chilcott hadn't told him.

There were six rooms upstairs. One was a large and elaborately decorated marble bathroom with a freestanding bath, walk in shower and double basins set in a marble unit, which revealed no items. There was a bedroom decorated in pale blue and cream, and off it, a spacious shower room, again exquisitely outfitted. He found no toiletries, clothes or shoes in any of the wardrobes. Chilcott must have cleared them out. Had he done that himself or engaged someone to do it?

He entered what was clearly Halliwell's study at the rear. The safe was in an alcove in the wall, and open. Again, as in keeping with the rest of the house, here was the same clean lines, quality furniture and tasteful decoration. There was a modern desk with nothing on it, a large executive leather chair, a contemporary sofa and, to the right of the shuttered French windows, a small table on which was a pair of binoculars. Horton opened one of the shuttered windows and, taking the binoculars, focused them in.

There were a few yachts and a ferry far out in the English Channel, but it wasn't those which caught Horton's attention. Through a clearing of the trees and low shrubs to his right, he could see Ben's cabin. So why hadn't Chilcott looked through these and seen the cabin? Horton could also see the landslip area.

Replacing them, he returned to the hall. There had to be a basement and right enough, opening the door beyond the staircase, he found stairs and, this time, a light switch. He expected to find nothing but dust and spiders. Once again, he was taken by surprise. The light oak stairs descended into an awe-inspiring cellar that was beyond anything he had ever seen.

Curved wooden shelving ran around the walls on both his right and left forming a U, with a ladder against one of them of the kind that you pushed around to reach books on the higher shelves. Here though, instead of books, were wine bottles lying on their side. A single elaborate bronze star-shaped light hung from a central pendant, and the room was also floodlit with uplighters. Beneath the two curved wine racks, almost opposite him, was a back-lit shelf that sloped downwards with slats, against which a few bottles lay. Below this were more partitioned sections containing wine bottles, interspersed with shelves, some of which held wooden cases. In the centre of the cellar was a two shelved unit displaying wine glasses and, beneath them, a closed in cupboard. Above it was a grill that discreetly contained an air conditioning unit which quietly hummed. Halliwell had obviously been something of a wine connoisseur. And this was also something that Chilcott hadn't mentioned. He must have called in a wine specialist to value all this because Horton, although no wine expert, knew that no one went to this much trouble or expense for a few bottles of plonk. The monks would have a merry time with this lot, he thought. Or perhaps they'd sell it off and add to their inheritance. When had this cellar been fitted out? It, like the rest of the house, looked and smelt new, and whoever designed and built it had been a specialist.

Horton locked up, his mind mulling over what he had seen, wondering if in the short time Halliwell had resided at the property, forty-five days, he had engaged a cleaner or a domestic agency to clean for him. Chilcott had said not, or more exactly that he hadn't found any paperwork to indicate otherwise. There was dust on the surfaces, but then Halliwell had been dead for almost nine weeks, so there was bound to be.

He wondered if the pattern would be repeated in the gatehouse. It wasn't. A drab, empty hall greeted him which mirrored the rest of the building. It was dated and dirty, hadn't been used for years, and was empty.

He made for Chilcott's offices which were closed when he arrived.

He hadn't realized how late it was – just after five. He'd also missed a call from Gaye, which he quickly returned. She had finished the autopsy and was about to make for the ferry. Horton said he would meet her on board. He found her at the bow on the upper deck.

'I got you a coffee,' she said.

'Thanks.' He sat opposite her as the ferry began to slide out of its berth and the small cluster of houses around the tiny Fishbourne green and shore slipped past them on their left.

'Have you found out anything more about your mystery man?' she asked.

'Which one? There are three. Cedric Halliwell, Ben and the landslip corpse. I've discovered more on the first two.' He gave a quick résumé of what he had learned from the abbot and seen at Beachwood House.

'Perhaps Halliwell was just eccentric,' she said with a look of surprise.

'Ben, too, I would say. Living as he did in that cabin.'

'It's certainly an interesting case.'

Made more so, Horton thought, with that connection with the abbey. He'd made no mention of Brother Norman being Antony Dormand, or where Lomas fitted into this, if he did.

'Your turn,' he said.

'Your landslip corpse had broken his leg in two places twenty years ago at least. He's also had knee replacement surgery about fifteen years ago. I hope to be more precise after I've heard from the manufacturers. I've emailed them.'

'Don't tell me that a new knee comes with a number stamped on it?' Horton said half-jokingly.

'Yes, and the make,' came the surprising reply. 'I found evidence of metal in the remains and a product number etched on it. There is an x-ray identification service whereby orthopaedic surgeons can submit digital copies of x-rays of implants to help identify the products used in the absence of access to the patient's, or in our case the deceased's, medical records. If I can pinpoint the product, I might be able to track back and find the orthopaedic surgeon who carried out the operation, and where it was conducted.'

'That sounds like it could take forever.'

'Possibly, but there's always dental records, if you can find a dentist to identify them, and that might be just as time consuming, given he used a dentist in this country. But I managed to lift some fingerprints and have sent them over to the bureau, and I've extracted DNA so you can try for a match on the DNA database. *If* he's on it.'

'We got some hairs from Ben's cabin which could be his, so I'll request samples be taken from Ben's body in the mortuary to check his DNA, but they could possibly be the landslip corpse's, if he was ever there. What else did you get?' Horton asked eagerly, sipping his coffee.

'He was five feet eleven inches tall, a lean man and, as I said earlier, about mid-sixties. There are no marks on what was left of the skin, which in fact was fairly comprehensive on his back, thighs and calves. That indicates he was buried and wasn't disturbed until you came along. As to how he died, I can confirm he wasn't shot. But you're certainly looking at homicide. He was stabbed in the head.'

Horton gaped at her.

'Unusual yes,' she said, taking a sip of her tea. 'Many people think the skull is too tough to be penetrated by an instrument, but it's not. In this case your victim was stabbed in the left temporal region, as you saw, just above the ear. It's an area of the skull that is more susceptible to stab wounds.'

'Would the killer know that?'

'He or she might have been lucky, or perhaps it was the only area of the skull that immediately presented itself to the killer. The instrument used was small and round, about one inch where it impacted and tapering down as it penetrated further, about six inches in length. It could have caused an intracranial haemorrhage and death but, in this case, might not necessarily have killed him outright, because I also found perimortem cranial fractures, those caused around the time of death by a heavy blunt instrument, something smallish and round.'

'So someone stabbed him in the head, the victim fell –'

'Or was pushed to the ground.'

'And then he was battered with a round heavy instrument and buried.'

'Correct.'

'Not nice.'

'No.'

Horton left a brief silence as he considered this and drank his coffee. There had been no heavy instrument like that in Ben's cabin or in Beachwood House, but then if either Halliwell or Ben had killed the landslip corpse they'd have disposed of the murder weapon, or weapons in this case. And there was nothing to say that either man had been the killer.

'Anything more on time of death?'

'As I said before, it's difficult to be precise. You're looking at anything up to two months. There's not much more I can tell you, Andy, except he was fairly healthy for his age, no lung or kidney damage, no sign he was poisoned or drugged and no heart disease, unlike your other death, the man in the cabin.'

'And the owner of Beachwood House.'

'Want me to review the autopsy reports on both men?'

Horton said he did, although he didn't think they would spark anything new. They talked more about work. Gaye said she was off to the States in a month's time for a three month Home Office exchange working in Seattle.

Horton felt disappointed. 'I'll miss you. And I mean both professionally and personally.'

'Then come over and we'll do some sailing.'

He smiled. 'I might take you up on that.'

'I hope you do, Andy,' she said, eyeing him steadily. He felt a little uncomfortable under her gaze. 'You look as though you could do with a change of air and a rest.'

'Do I look that bad?' he joked.

'Just a little tired and worn down.' Then she smiled. 'Trust me, I'm a doctor.'

He returned the smile, though he felt uneasy. 'Well, I sincerely hope I don't become one of your patients.'

'Me too.'

'There's a month before you go, plenty of time for us to have dinner together and go sailing here if you fancy it.'

'I do very much. Just give the command.'

He said he would after he knew which way the case was going to progress. He might not even be involved with it any further, in which case, if she was free at the weekend, they could sail over to the island then. But Gaye had another engagement. The weekend after that was a possibility. That tentatively agreed, they parted company as the ferry came into Portsmouth and the tannoy announced that passengers were to return to their vehicles. As he made for the station, he wondered if Gaye had wanted to ask him about his research into the fire at the Goldsmith Psychiatric Hospital which they'd discussed in January, and in which Zachary Benham had perished along with twenty-three other men. He felt he was holding out on her, and he didn't want to but years of hiding his feelings and keeping silent about his personal life and problems was a hard habit to break.

He reported back to Uckfield and requested that he continue to follow up Cedric Halliwell. 'I'd like to see if there are any prints we can lift from Beachwood House and the boat, and re-interview Chilcott, the solicitor. There are a pair of powerful binoculars in the house and you can see Ben's cabin from what was Halliwell's study. If Ben was living there before 1 February, when Halliwell died, then he must have known about him, and I can't believe that Chilcott didn't look through them when he was retrieving the paperwork from the safe, which according to him was scarce.'

Uckfield gave his permission, adding that he couldn't spare anyone to assist him. 'I've got my hands full with the Trehams robbery.'

'Any progress?'

'Nothing. There are no fingerprints, no footprints and no hairs in that study, except those of the dogs who didn't bark because they'd been drugged.'

'How?'

'In their meat or drink probably. Victoria Treham wouldn't let us open up her darling Huskies – Botus and Kobi – to analyse their stomach contents. We did examine their shit though. I left that pleasure to the lab. Nothing. It was probably in a drink. There's nothing on the Treham's CCTV over the gates and grounds, not even a shadowy figure, so God alone knows how they got in. Probably materialized out of the mist like *Brigadoon*, only they weren't wearing kilts, which is about all Mrs Treham *can* tell us. The description she gave us is worse than useless – two men, tall, well built, Caucasian, she thinks. Not that she saw any flesh so they could have been all colours of the rainbow, and neither did she see their hair, *if* they had any. She saw only the slits of their eyes through their balaclavas. They spoke gruffly, no accent. And none of the stolen jewellery has surfaced on the internet or with any jewellers. Probably already got the stuff out of the country.'

'Could it have been an inside job?' posed Horton, sure this must have crossed Uckfield's mind. 'After all, the dogs didn't alert her before they were drugged, and we all know our Sherlock Holmes.'

'Eh?'

'The dog that didn't bark in the night.'

'Oh that.' Uckfield waved it aside. 'No, Mrs Treham was genuinely distressed. I don't think she's faking it. Trueman's checked the Trehams' credit rating and financial situation, and they're loaded. Maurice Treham is a big shot investment banker in the City.'

As if that made him above suspicion, thought Horton.

'The hired help's alibi checks out, and she claims never to have seen the safe, which could be a lie. She could have passed the information on to someone, but she seems genuine enough. We're checking out contractors and visitors.' Uckfield shifted a buttock and winced. Retrieving a handkerchief from the pocket of his trousers, he wiped his brow.

Horton made no comment, but he could see that Uckfield was in pain and trying desperately not to show it. Uckfield gruffly dismissed him, and Horton returned to his office after a quick word with Trueman who told him that Halliwell had never paid UK tax or national insurance because he hadn't lived in the country. He'd also discovered there was no driver's licence in his name, or car registered to him. Horton asked him to check with the Land Registry for the extent of Halliwell's property.

The CID office was deserted. Both Cantelli and Walters had left for home. Horton rang Cantelli and broke the bad news that he was to accompany him to the island tomorrow and follow up the leads on Halliwell. Horton could have detailed Sergeant Norris on the island to assist him, but he'd much preferred to have Cantelli.

'I'd better stock up on the seasickness pills then,' Cantelli said resigned.

'The weather forecast is for a bright calm day.'

'Huh!'

Horton smiled. He had no idea of the weather, but he hoped for Cantelli's sake his prophecy would be fulfilled.

Nine

❛ You told me it was going to be calm,' Cantelli said when they were on board and easing out of Portsmouth Harbour. 'This is calm.'

'It's blowing a gale.'

'Only a force five.'

'That's a hurricane.'

'No, Barney, it isn't. You'll be fine. Drink your tea. Want any breakfast?'

'And bring it up? No thank you.'

'Then read through my reports. It'll help take your mind off things while I answer this call. It's Bliss, unless you want to...' he held out his phone.

'It's you she wants. Not me.'

Horton answered it. Four minutes later he came off the phone with a sad shake of his head. 'Absence certainly doesn't make the heart grow fonder in her case. She wasn't pleased to learn that two members of her CID team are on a Major Crime Team investigation, but I told her to take that up with Superintendent Uckfield.'

'I bet she didn't much like that either.'

'No, and despite us being otherwise engaged, she wants regular updates and results on both the highway robberies and the arson. I told her DC Leonard was following up convicted arsonists recently released, and that Walters had drawn a blank interviewing staff and suppliers unless we check all their alibis which would take a huge amount of time. Thank God there were no highway robberies yesterday. Anything new occur to you on the landslip murder?'

'Haven't got through all the information yet.'

'Then I'll leave you in peace.' Horton stepped out on to the deck and found a fairly sheltered spot where he returned some calls from the previous day's messages and watched the promenade slip slowly past them. After he'd finished his calls, he bought himself some breakfast and a coffee, along with a tea for Cantelli, and returned to the sergeant. While he ate, they discussed the case. Cantelli couldn't throw any more light on it than Horton could, save that he thought the house of contrasts interesting and that Chilcott had been economical with the truth.

Horton's phone rang. He was pleased to see it was Sergeant Elkins.

'I've spoken to the volunteer, Jason Arlett, at Ryde Inshore Rescue, who boarded Halliwell's boat. Arlett works for Grinstead Marine Engineering in Ryde. He said the call came through at about two p.m. on 1 February. There was a sea mist all day. It was bitterly cold. When they saw the craft, they noted that there was no one at the helm and the engine wasn't running. He thought the owner might have fallen overboard or been taken ill. They hailed the vessel, but there was no answer. They fixed a line to the stern and Jason and a colleague boarded her. They found Halliwell lying face down in the main cabin as though he'd got up from the helm, felt ill and collapsed. They took the boat back to Bembridge. It was low tide so they couldn't get into Ryde marina. A uniformed officer was waiting for them, PC Wetherton, and a paramedic, who wasn't needed, but she confirmed death and the body was taken to the mortuary at St Mary's Hospital Newport.'

'Anything strike Arlett as unusual?' Horton knew Elkins would have asked that question.

'No. He said there was a mug on the table, but he can't remember if there were dregs in it. Everything was clean and tidy. No bedding in the for'ard cabin but a sailing jacket on the bunk.'

'Did Halliwell have a course plotted on the radar?'

'No.'

'Any paperwork on board?'

'Arlett didn't see any, and neither was there a logbook or if there was then it had been put away in one of the lockers. Neither he nor any of his colleagues searched the boat.'

'What did Halliwell look like?' Horton asked, then quickly added, 'apart from being dead?' before Elkins could make some witty reply.

'Thinning grey hair, receding at the temples, medium build, mid-sixties, about six foot, lean face, heavily lined. He was wearing deck shoes, casual brown trousers and a navy-blue jumper. Oh, and a good wrist watch, a Tag Heuer. Arlett is observant and he knows his watches, as do I. Tag Heuers don't come cheap. Arlett couldn't see a computer and there wasn't a mobile phone. PC Wetherton went through the pockets but there was nothing remarkable in them, just a wallet. No credit or debit cards, no driver's licence, just two twenty pound notes and a ten pound note. No coins in his pockets either.'

'House keys?'

'Only one on the key ring that was in the helm.'

A list of the contents would have been passed to Chilcott, along with the actual items, all of which would eventually belong to the abbey.

'I wonder where he was going on a bitterly cold, misty day.'

'*If* he was going anywhere, save up or down, depending on how good a boy he'd been in life,' Elkins elaborated.

'Suicide?'

'It's a possibility, but not sure how he did it unless he threw the empty bottle of tablets he'd taken over board before passing out? Maybe they brought on a coronary.'

'The post-mortem didn't find any evidence of drugs in his system.'

'Then I'm wrong. I usually am. The canopy over the cockpit had been unzipped at the aft but not pulled back. But then it was bitterly cold and misty. I've also spoken to Mr Wakelin who said that Halliwell paid for the boat by a transfer of funds from a bank in Guernsey. He gave me a contact number he had for Halliwell but it's a dead line, as you'd expect.'

Horton asked Elkins to relay it to Trueman and ask him to check out the number and provider, but Horton suspected it might have been a pay-as-you-go phone as Halliwell hadn't wanted Chilcott the solicitor to have the number. He wondered why.

He relayed the information to Cantelli.

'These Tag Heuer watches, how much are they worth?' Cantelli asked.

'About six thousand pounds.'

'You're kidding!'

Horton shook his head. 'Halliwell *was* a millionaire.'

'Wonder what happened to it.'

'We'll ask Chilcott.'

The solicitor wasn't best pleased to see them some fifty minutes later.

'I can only spare you half an hour. I have a client appointment at ten,' he said tersely the moment his secretary closed the boardroom door behind them. Cantelli took the seat beside Horton, his pencil poised over his notebook, chewing his gum with a slight frown of concentration. He'd survived the sea crossing without the slightest hint of queasiness. Horton had told him his seasickness was all in the mind. Cantelli had said, 'I'll remind you of that when I'm throwing up on the way back.'

'Were you surprised at the contrast between the interior and exterior of Beachwood House?' Horton launched without any preliminary exchange.

Chilcott blinked hard, as though he didn't understand the question. After a moment he shifted and said, 'Well, yes, I was a little.'

'Would the interior have been like that when Mr Halliwell bought the house?'

'Definitely not. Jacob Sundridge was ninety-three when he died in 1997, and the property had been neglected for some years before that. In fact, Sundridge didn't live there but in London. It was bought as a holiday retreat, but he hardly ever used it. He had a successful publishing business which his nephew now runs. His estate was left to that nephew, Orion Sundridge, who immediately put Beachwood House up for sale. It took years to offload, not only because of its decaying state, but also because of its position in a landslip area. Insurance is almost impossible to get and extremely expensive if you can get it. I wasn't involved in the sale of the property. But being local, with contacts in the property business, I knew all about it. Orion Sundridge instructed a London agent and his own lawyer in the city.'

'And Mr Halliwell? Who did he instruct? You have the deeds I take it?'

'Not yet. They're with a legal firm in Guernsey, Selwyns. I've spoken to them on the phone. They handled the purchase for Mr Halliwell.'

Then they could be worth talking to, thought Horton. He'd call his old friend, Inspector John Guilbert of the States of Guernsey Police, and ask him to make enquiries about Halliwell. The fact that Halliwell had instructed a Guernsey lawyer could mean he had split his time living between there and the Cayman Islands.

Chilcott said, 'The current Beachwood House was built in 1937 on the site of the old manor house, which Jacob Sundridge had demolished.'

'So Halliwell had it completely re-modelled inside to his own design. Who did the work for him?'

'I have no idea,' Chilcott archly replied. 'I mentioned to you before that I couldn't find any invoices or receipts for anything in the house.'

'Not even for the paintings and the wine?' Horton asked slightly sceptically.

'No.'

'You've seen that cellar?'

'Of course.' Chilcott shifted, and his eyes darted to Cantelli and back to Horton.

'Then you must know that some of the wine must be very valuable.'

'Of course. I've had them valued.' Chilcott bristled.

'By whom?'

'Wight Barn Wines. They're a reputable Island company with an international reputation,' he added, as though Horton was about to criticize his choice of valuer.

'I'd like a copy of their report.'

Chilcott made as if to protest, then changed his mind. After all, he had been instructed by the abbot to give them every assistance. With slightly ill grace he said, 'I'll get my secretary to copy it.' He reached for his phone, but Horton forestalled him.

'I'd also like an inventory of all the items you found in the house and on the boat. Was there a logbook?'

'No.'

The previous owner would have kept hold of his, and Halliwell, not owning the boat for long, might not have got around to supplying his own. Maybe Elkins was correct about the suicide theory, because Halliwell wouldn't need a logbook if his intention was to kill himself on board the first time out.

'I'd also like copies of the provenance for the paintings,' Horton said.

'There weren't any.'

'Don't you think that strange?'

'Why should I? It's not my job to comment on my late client's peculiarities.'

No, thought Horton, all Chilcott wanted was to get his hands on a substantial fee for handling the estate. He left a short pause. The solicitor sniffed and looked down at the boardroom table. Outside, a car started up and a seagull screeched. Just when Chilcott looked set to break the uneasy silence, Horton said, 'What did you do with Mr Halliwell's clothes?'

'Gave them to a charity shop.'

'The abbot requested you do so?'

'Yes.'

'All of them?'

'Yes.'

Horton thought if the solicitor had been the same size as Halliwell he might have kept them. But Chilcott was short and round whereas Halliwell, by all accounts, had been tall and slim. Besides, Chilcott was younger, in his mid-forties, Horton had estimated, and his taste in clothes was a little on the flamboyant side. Today, his suit was a loud black pinstriped one accompanied by a lemon coloured tie that contained small white motifs which looked like tiny smiling faces.

'What about Halliwell's personal belongings, jewellery for example?'

'There wasn't any.'

That was a lie. Horton sensed Cantelli's interest, but he didn't show it. 'I understand he was wearing a watch when his body was found.'

Chilcott flushed and pulled his ear – the larger of the two. 'I'd forgotten, yes, he was. It was only a cheap one.'

That wasn't what Arlett had said. Maybe he had been mistaken or the Tag Heuer had been a fake. Horton let it go for now.

'The watch also went to the charity shop,' Chilcott said.

'Which one?' asked Cantelli.

Chilcott looked startled, as though he hadn't expected Cantelli to be capable of speech. 'The Red Cross in Shanklin High Street.'

Cantelli took some time writing this down.

Irritably, Chilcott said, 'Is that it because I really am extremely busy?'

'We're sorry to keep you but appreciate your help,' Horton said smoothly. It didn't mollify the solicitor. 'There are a just a few more questions, Mr Chilcott. There were some binoculars in Mr Halliwell's study, did you see them?'

'Of course.'

'Did you look through them?'

'Why should I want to do that? I see the view of the English Channel every day. My apartment overlooks it.'

Horton nodded as though to say, of course, but he doubted anyone could have resisted using them. Perhaps Chilcott was the exception.

'Then you didn't see the cabin in the bay.'

'I've already told you I know nothing about it.'

'It's quite clearly visible from Mr Halliwell's study, especially through the binoculars and in winter when the trees are bare. He must have known it was there.'

'Well I didn't see it, and Mr Halliwell made no mention of it or anyone living in it.'

Horton held Chilcott's gaze, but his eye contact remained steady. 'Did Mr Halliwell mention the piano? He must have been an accomplished pianist to own such a magnificent instrument.'

'If he was, he never said. I didn't find any sheet music in the house.'

Cantelli looked up. 'Perhaps he was too good to need music to read from.'

Chilcott shrugged.

'Did you make enquiries about his background or if he was known in musical circles?' Cantelli asked.

'No, why should I?'

'In case anyone wanted to attend his funeral.'

'I put an announcement in the *Daily Telegraph, The Times* and the local press, but no one showed up.'

'That's sad. Was he buried or cremated?'

'I can't see —'

'Just humour us, Mr Chilcott,' Horton interjected. 'We'll be out of your hair a lot quicker if you do.'

He pursed his lips and scowled. 'Cremated. Eventually,' he added.

So that blew an exhumation. Not that Horton had any reason to ask for one.

'Why do you say "eventually"?' Cantelli asked.

'He left his body to medical science and, as the Isle of Wight doesn't have a body donation process, it has to go to the nearest medical school which accepts them, and that's the University of Southampton. Mr Halliwell had made all the arrangements with the funeral director before his death.'

Then he knew he was going to die and sooner rather than later, thought Horton, which indicated he had been aware that his health problem could carry him off at any time. Or had he been afraid of someone tracking him down and killing him? The landslip corpse perhaps? Or had Halliwell died first? Gaye couldn't be certain. It was a close call, anyway. If Halliwell had killed the landslip corpse then perhaps, suffering from delayed shock or anguish at what he'd done, combined with the cold, he'd had a heart attack on board his boat and died. Horton put his concentration back on what Chilcott was relaying.

'Because of the manner of Mr Halliwell's death, alone, on his boat in the Solent, the coroner ordered an autopsy and that meant a delay in getting the body to Southampton. It has to be at the medical school within five days, but that wasn't the only stumbling block. I discovered that the medical school doesn't take bodies which have undergone an autopsy. I had no specific instructions as to what Mr Halliwell would have wanted, burial or cremation. He wasn't Catholic, even a lapsed one. At least, I don't think he was.'

Cantelli again spoke, 'Did you find a rosary, crucifix or bible in Beachwood House?'

'No, but as he had left his estate to the Benedictine Abbey, I asked Dom Daniel Briar what I should do. The abbot would have preferred a burial, which is traditional in the Catholic faith.'

Cantelli nodded.

'But there was no designated plot for a burial and the abbot wasn't certain Halliwell would have wanted that anyway, given that his original request was not to be either buried or cremated. I persuaded the abbot that it might be better for everyone if a simple cremation took place. The abbot capitulated on the grounds that a service be held for Halliwell first. Dom Daniel Briar spoke to the priest at the Catholic Church in Ryde, and it was arranged that Mr Halliwell's body be taken there for the Funeral Mass. The cremation took place straight afterwards with only myself, the priest from the church in Ryde and Dom Daniel Briar present.'

Not Ben then, Horton thought, unless he had remained out of sight or had taken up residence in the cabin after Halliwell's death, but the latter seemed unlikely given what the abbot had told him about Ben's work at the abbey. Horton was certain Ben had been living in that cabin at least from May, when he had first approached the abbey asking them to sell his woodcarvings.

Chilcott said, 'In accordance with the Catholic Church the remains were buried, not scattered, in the abbey grounds.'

The phone rang and Chilcott swiftly answered it. Replacing the receiver, he said, 'My ten o'clock appointment has arrived. Now, if there's nothing else?'

'Just copies of all the documentation you have,' answered Horton.

Chilcott picked up the telephone and gave instructions to his secretary.

'She'll be a while. If you wait in reception, she'll bring them to you.'

They obliged. An elderly man was shown into the boardroom by Chilcott himself, who was all smiles and oily pleasantries. Five minutes later, Chilcott's secretary, a woman in her early fifties, handed them a buff coloured folder.

Outside, Cantelli said, 'He's a bit on the defensive side.'

'Perhaps that's just his manner.'

'Maybe,' Cantelli dubiously replied, zapping open the car and climbing in.

'You think he's bent?'

'My nose does.'

'Your nose could be right. His description of the watch doesn't match that of Jason Arlett from the inshore rescue team. Let's see what it's listed as in the documentation.' He flipped through the paperwork. 'A Timex valued at fifty pounds. Either Jason Arlett was wrong or Chilcott's manipulated the inventory.'

'I'd go for the latter.'

'The watch must have been removed from the body in the mortuary. I wonder what they listed it as. I don't think we'll find that watch in the charity shop, but I'll get Sergeant Norris to follow it up. I'd like to talk to the wine valuers.' Horton flicked through the documentation. 'Wight Barn Wines, Niton.' He relayed the post code and, Cantelli, after punching it into the Sat Nav., pulled away and headed south.

Horton scanned the valuation report. 'There are some very expensive wines in that cellar.'

'You mean worth more than a few pounds?'

'More than a few *thousand* pounds.'

'For one bottle of wine?' Cantelli cried incredulously.

'According to this. There are two bottles *each* valued at approximately ten thousand pounds.'

'To drink?' Cantelli exclaimed. 'Seems a waste to me, in one end and out the other with nothing to show for it except a headache.'

'Not with this wine, Barney. It's not plonk.'

'I don't believe any wine can be worth that amount of money.'

'Well, the expert, Mr Charles Nansen, thinks they are. The art expert, Felicity Ellwood, is also based here on the island. But there's no valuation report for those paintings.'

'Perhaps she hasn't finished valuing them. She could be trying to discover more about them.'

'Probably. We'll talk to her later. The snooker table is listed here. Value provided by a reputable company. Six thousand pounds,' Horton added, consulting the notes. 'And the piano. Now that is interesting. It's been valued at twenty five thousand pounds.'

'For a piano!' Cantelli almost veered off the narrow road in his surprise.

'It's a Yamaha C3X Grand Piano, Polished Ebony.'

'Oh, well that makes all the difference,' Cantelli said airily.

Horton smiled. 'No one buys a piano like that for decoration. Halliwell must have been an accomplished pianist. So why didn't Chilcott advertize his client's demise in the appropriate musical periodicals?'

'Too lazy or too incompetent,' Cantelli summarized.

'Or didn't want anyone to come forward in case they obtained permission from the abbot to enter the house and could see what was missing.'

'A piano and snooker table are on the large side to tuck under your jacket,' Cantelli said smiling.

Horton returned it. 'That watch might not be the only item Peter

Chilcott has helped himself to. There might have been other more portable items he could have removed from the property.'

'Such as the wine.'

'Sounds more likely than smuggling out a painting, unless it was a small one, although I didn't note any tell-tale gaps. That piano might tell us more about Halliwell. The company who sold it to him must know more about him. It's not the sort of thing you buy online without trying it out. Likewise, the wine cellar. No one goes to that much expense and trouble without knowing his stuff, and that could mean Halliwell was well known in wine circles.'

'Doesn't get us much further with the landslip corpse.'

'He could have been a fellow musician or wine lover.'

'Or artist.'

'Wrong clothes,' Horton said, thinking of Lomas.

'Not all artists go around dressed in ripped jeans and tatty T-shirts,' Cantelli said. 'Our landslip corpse could have put on his best suit because he was calling on a wealthy patron.'

'And ended up dead.'

'Professional jealousy?'

'I doubt it, Barney, but you never know. Turn left here.'

Cantelli did as instructed and, after half a mile, pulled up in front of an impressive manor house constructed in Isle of Wight grey stone, a barn complex and some large signs that informed them they had reached the premises of Wight Barn Wines.

Ten

'I was sorry to hear about Mr Halliwell's death,' Charles Nansen said, gesturing them into comfortable leather and chrome seats around a table in the large barn which had been converted into offices. Through the tall windows overlooking the garden and fields, Horton caught a glimpse of the sea in the distance. The other walls of the barn were taken up with large well-executed photographs of wines and of the man seated in front of them, well built, dark-haired, with a beard, deep brown eyes, about mid forty. In most of the photographs he was accompanied by two other men, one of a similar age, the other about ten years older, and a dark-haired woman in her early forties. Nansen's dog, a brown Labrador, took up position by his master's side.

'You knew Mr Halliwell?' Horton asked hopefully. At last someone who could tell them what the living man was like.

'Not exactly,' came the disappointing reply. 'He purchased some wines from us. Not rare and vintage wines, like some of those in his excellent cellar, but nevertheless some of superb quality.'

'Then I take it the two bottles you valued at ten thousand pounds each is not a misprint?'

Nansen smiled. 'No. They're probably worth even more than that.'

Cantelli shook his head in bewilderment.

'The Domaine de la Romanée-Conti, or DRC as collectors like to call it, with the vintage of 1978, is one of the most coveted and expensive French pinot noirs there is. In 2015, one bottle alone was sold at auction by Sothebys for twenty thousand dollars.'

Cantelli spluttered and turned it into a cough.

Horton said, 'Do know how he acquired them?'

Nansen picked at his beard. 'No, and that's the sad and puzzling thing, because Mr Chilcott couldn't find any provenance for any of the wines.'

'And without this provenance the wine is worth less money?'

'It will put off the serious investors, but there will still be plenty of buyers who will purchase them, as well as other vintage and excellent wines in his cellar for laying down, or for the pleasure of drinking.'

'How did Mr Halliwell order his wines from you?' According to Chilcott, Halliwell hadn't a computer or a phone, although he had liaised with the seller of the boat by phone.

'He turned up here. He only came once, in January. We talked about wines, and I showed him around, then he placed an order, which we delivered.'

'To Beachwood House?'

'Yes.'

'Did he take delivery himself?'

'I believe so. Tim Jennings, who delivered the wine, will know more about that.' Charles Nansen looked a little perplexed.

Horton would speak to Jennings. 'What made Mr Halliwell come to you?'

'He'd heard of our reputation and said that, as he had only recently taken up residence on the island, he thought he'd check us out.'

That sounded reasonable. 'How did he get here?' Horton asked. This place was hardly on a regular bus route. The narrow road leading down to it was off the beaten track, surrounded by fields and rolling hills. And Halliwell didn't have a car or a licence to drive a hired one.

'He came by taxi and asked the driver to wait.'

It would probably be easy to track down the taxi company and its driver on the island, but Horton suspected that Halliwell would have confided nothing.

Nansen continued, 'Mr Halliwell told me that he'd been working abroad most of his life and wanted to settle down here. He had an aversion to crowds and wanted peace and quiet.'

'Did he say what he used to do for a living?'

'No. I assumed some kind of financier or stockbroker, not that I had any reason to make that kind of assumption but, judging by the wines he purchased from us and those I found in his cellar, he must have had considerable wealth.'

'Do you know who fitted out the cellar for him?'

'Yes. There was no mistaking it when I saw it and, even if I hadn't recognized the design and build, the name is engraved on some of the wooden shelving.'

Horton hadn't looked. He should have done.

'Simply Cellars. They're based in London.'

Horton didn't think there was anything simple about the cellar he'd seen.

Nansen said, 'They're a reputable and experienced company with an impressive clientele. The owner, Dudley Coppens, is a Master of Wine, as am I.'

'Have you spoken to them about Mr Halliwell?'

'Only briefly. I told Dudley that Mr Halliwell had been found dead on his boat. Is there something suspicious about it? Only I thought he died of natural causes,' he finally asked, looking worried.

'As far as we are aware, he did. There are just some questions we need to ask about the cellar. Do you know when it was built?'

'Just over a year ago. Dudley said they didn't deal with Mr Halliwell directly; the house was empty. They liaised through the architect, Gary Redcar.'

In that case there was probably little, if anything, Dudley Coppens could tell them about Halliwell, but the architect would be a different matter. Horton asked Nansen if he knew Redcar's contact details. He didn't, but Horton could easily get them from the Royal Institute of British Architects.

Nansen said, 'I must admit I was taken aback when I saw Beachwood House. The inside is totally different from the outside, but it does bear out the fact that Mr Halliwell was keen not to attract too much attention to himself. And that marvellous piano, a Yamaha Grand. Well, he never said anything about being a pianist, or a music lover, but then we only talked about wine. I couldn't resist playing it.' Nansen looked wistful.

Nansen's prints would be on the keyboard as well as in the cellar, but they could easily get a copy of them to eliminate him from the investigation. Horton doubted if Halliwell's fingerprints had been taken or recorded for the autopsy, it not being a forensic one, but that didn't matter too much. It was the prints of the landslip corpse and if they showed up in the house or in Ben's cabin that interested Horton. The fingerprint bureau was probably checking out the latter now, having received the victim's prints from Gaye.

Nansen was saying, 'At one time I harboured the dream of

becoming a concert pianist, but I lacked the spark and perhaps the dedication and commitment to become one. It played like a dream.'

'How did Mr Halliwell pay you?' Cantelli asked.

'By bank transfer. An account in Guernsey. Morgans Bank.'

'And he spent how much?'

'Just over three thousand pounds.'

'For one order?' Cantelli's jaw dropped.

'Yes.'

There was a small silence. The dog looked up and whined.

Horton said, 'Can you describe Mr Halliwell to us?'

Nansen looked bewildered by the question but answered, 'About six foot, medium build, grey thinning hair, receding at the temples, grey eyes, tanned as though he spent a lot of time outdoors. Mid-sixties. He looked fit and well, so it was something of a shock when I learned from Peter Chilcott that he'd died.'

'Why did Chilcott call you? I know you must have an excellent reputation on the island,' Horton added, 'but there must be other wine merchants.'

'There are, but we're the only one that handles the high end of the market, and Peter, seeing the quality of the cellar and therefore the wines, naturally thought of us. He'd also have seen our label on a couple of the crates in the cellar.'

'Of course.' Horton paused. Nansen smiled uneasily. After a moment, Horton said, 'Can you describe Mr Halliwell's personality?'

Nansen considered this for a moment as he ruffled the dog's ear. 'He struck me as a man at ease with his own company.'

'Reserved?'

'No. Confident. Someone who knew himself and was comfortable with that.'

Not many like that, thought Horton. But then perhaps Halliwell had come to terms with himself if he'd been told that a heart attack could see him off at any time. Horton asked if Halliwell had seemed well in himself. The answer was he had.

'Did he talk about his boat?'

'No. As I said, our conversation was solely about wines. That's all I can tell you about him, Inspector. I'm sorry I can't be of more help.'

But Horton could sense there was something more and that Nansen was reluctant to confide it. He thought he'd probe a little. 'You seem uncertain about that, Mr Nansen.'

Nansen's deep brown eyes shifted from Horton to Cantelli, and then back to Horton. He picked at his beard seeming to consider his next words. After a moment he said uneasily, 'When I discovered there was no paperwork for the extremely rare wines, such as the Domaine de la Romanée-Conti, I wondered how he had acquired them. And now, with your visit here asking about him, I'm considering something that struck me when I was valuing the wines which I thought couldn't be possible.'

Horton quickly caught on, and he knew Cantelli would too. 'You think they might have been stolen.'

Nansen shifted. 'I wondered if he had bought them from a dubious source.'

Horton digested this. It was possible. 'Would we be able to trace the ownership of such valuable wines?'

'You could liaise with the major auctioneers, find out which wines had gone under the hammer and when. They would keep records, but these wines might not have gone to auction. They could have been sold privately.'

Horton's picture of the late Cedric Halliwell as a possible criminal was reinforced by Nansen's information.

'Did anyone else in your company deal with Mr Halliwell?' Horton asked, eyeing the photographs. 'Except for Mr Jennings who delivered the order there.'

Following his gaze, Nansen said, 'Tim Jennings is the older man in the picture. My twin brother, Alec, is our mainland rep., so he combines sales visits with deliveries on the mainland. He's not here very often and didn't meet Mr Halliwell. Neither did Shirley, my wife. She manages the website, marketing and accounts.'

'We'd like to talk to Mr Jennings, if he's here?'

'He is. I'll find him, and he can also show you around.' Nansen rose, the dog with him.

'And if you could let us have details of when Mr Halliwell visited you, and a record of the wines he purchased, that would be most helpful.'

'Of course. I'll print them off for you while you talk to Tim.'

Nansen disappeared with the dog in tow.

Cantelli said, 'Nansen's probably gone to prime Jennings on what to say.'

'You think he's holding something back?'

'Don't you?'

Horton did, but he was puzzled over what it could be and said as much.

Cantelli said, 'Perhaps Halliwell confided something to Nansen that he feels he can't divulge. Such as where that expensive and rare wine really came from.'

'Or perhaps Nansen helped himself to some of it while doing the cataloguing. How do we know what was there? You remove a bottle and there's no trace of it, especially if you dust under and round it, unlike a picture which will leave a slightly faded and marked spot on the wall.'

'He doesn't strike me as being dishonest.'

Horton agreed but as Cantelli said there was something. Perhaps Tim Jennings might shed some light on what that might be.

Eleven

'Would you like a tasting?' Jennings asked as he showed them into the large airy vaulted warehouse to the right of the U-shaped building. It was stacked with racks of wine, cardboard boxes with the company name imprinted on them, and two long, large bench tables in the middle of the room, with a few stools beside them. Jennings was a slender man in his mid-fifties with a round open face that suited his baldness.

'On duty,' answered Horton. He didn't drink and, although he suspected Cantelli would have loved an Italian Roca, he would have declined on account of driving and the seasickness pills.

'You have good security,' Cantelli said, nodding at the steel shutters above the long wide windows that faced on to the car park. Horton had also noted the infra-red security devices in the corridor.

'Some of these wines are extremely valuable. We've never had a burglary but there's always a first time.'

'We haven't had wine thefts in Portsmouth. At least not on this scale,' Cantelli quickly amended. 'Only the occasional bottle of plonk and spirits taken from the off licence or supermarket. Perhaps that's because there aren't expensive wines on any Portsmouth premises to steal.'

'Or the villains don't know about them. It takes a discerning burglar to know which vintage to steal. Unless he or she is just lucky, which would be a shame because they wouldn't realize the value and would flog it from a car park at the back of the pub, or guzzle it without appreciating it.' He winced as if the thought pained him.

'They'd probably turn their nose up at it, preferring some cheap plonk,' Cantelli said, not entirely joking. Knowing some of their clientele, Horton thought that likely.

He said, 'Do you keep all your stock here?'

'No. Different wines need different conditions, some much cooler than we can provide. Charles and Shirley have a cellar in their house which is the one you can see behind the barns. They've also got a state-of-the-art security system. As I said, we hope it's never put to the test but with wine being an investment you can never be certain.'

'How does the investment part work?' asked Horton. Halliwell's interests were certainly throwing up some curious questions, and Horton's mind was working to put some meat on the bones of what he was learning, which made him think of the corpse. How did the landslip corpse fit into all this? Perhaps Halliwell *had* acquired the wine crookedly and the landslip corpse knew this and had threatened to expose Halliwell. Or perhaps he'd been a partner in crime. Alternatively, he could have been investigating Halliwell. He could even have come from abroad where Halliwell had lived and had traced him to the Isle of Wight.

'Investing in wines is not new,' Jennings said, pleased to display his knowledge. 'The serious wine buyers have always bought more than they needed, laying them down to drink at a later date and, if they didn't drink them, they'd sell them off. But wine investment became global in the mid-1990s, when buyers from the Far East came into the market. Up until then the best wines from Bordeaux were destined for Europe and North America.'

'We've seen Mr Nansen's valuation of Mr Halliwell's cellar, it seems a highly lucrative investment.'

'It can be. Like any other investment though it can fluctuate. Generally speaking the wine market has done fairly well. It's resilient. Fine wine is a tangible asset, and for some investors it's more accessible and enjoyable than gold and art. It's also much more transferable than shares. It's a long-term investment. You're buying for ten to twenty years, possibly more. Storing the wine correctly is also important. Sorry, you've got me on my hobby horse.' He smiled.

'No, do go on. It's all valuable information,' Horton said. This meant Halliwell must have been known in wine circles and therefore they'd get more information about him.

'Well, firstly it should be under bond to avoid paying taxes, and secondly, provenance is key to a wine's future value.'

Which Halliwell hadn't had. So perhaps he didn't care about the value, thought Horton. Or hadn't viewed it as an investment but as something he took pleasure in owning and drinking. Or, as Nansen had intimated, acquired it in a dubious way.

'Bordeaux will always be the backbone of a good investment,' Jennings was saying, 'but there are other wines that come up to the mark; Super Tuscans, Champagne and Burgundy for example. And, in Mr Halliwell's collection, as you've seen from the inventory, there are two bottles of one of the most coveted and expensive French pinot noirs that exist, the Domaine de la Romanée-Conti.'

'Mr Nansen told us about it, but he didn't say why it was so special.'

'How long have you got?' Jennings joked. 'I'll put it simply,' he continued with a smile. 'Firstly, the 1978 is incredibly hard to find. Let me explain,' he added, possibly to their baffled expressions, or possibly because he was on his pet subject. It was clear to Horton that Jennings was far more passionate about his wine than Nansen.

'Bordeaux's great châteaux make several thousand bottles of wine a year. Château Pétrus, one of the smallest and most prized, produces thirty thousand bottles a year, while Lafite Rothschild produces about twenty thousand cases. Compare that to four hundred and fifty cases for DRC's Romanée-Conti from the tiny single vineyard of just over four acres, and that makes them scarce, a big factor in their price. Put that with the fact that Asian collectors have an insatiable appetite for Burgundy, and the price goes up. Then there is the unrivalled quality. It's praised for its silkiness and balance and, because of the region's unique soil and geology, each vineyard produces a wholly unique taste and style. As the wines age, burgundies develop a special "earthiness".'

'Have you ever tasted it?' asked Cantelli.

'Once. Sublime. Only the wealthiest collectors in the world can afford Domaine de la Romanée-Conti, which makes it even more curious that Charles discovered two bottles of it in Mr Halliwell's cellar. Of course, I don't know how wealthy he was. Those two bottles might have formed part of a much larger investment, which he brought with him when he moved to the island. Or he might have been given them by an exceedingly generous person as there was no paperwork.'

And by Jennings' tone and look, Horton could see he had formed his own ideas about how it might have been acquired. He put to him

91

the same question he'd asked Nansen.

'Could the bottles have been stolen?'

Jennings frowned and sniffed as he considered his response. 'It's possible, but he didn't strike me as the type to have bought stolen goods. I could be wrong. I only met him twice. Once when he came here, and once when he opened the door of Beachwood House and took delivery of his order. He was friendly and knowledgeable. There was nothing stuck up about him.'

'Did you go inside the house?'

'Only stepped inside the hall. Impressive snooker table. I wouldn't have minded a game on that. Mr Halliwell asked me to leave the wine just inside the door. I did, and then left.'

'So you didn't see anyone else there?'

'No.'

'Or get an impression of someone else in the house?'

Jennings shook his head.

'Did the interior surprise you?'

'No, the exterior did. From my initial meeting with Mr Halliwell, I could tell he had good taste and wealth but when I drove up to the house, I wondered if I'd gone to the wrong address, or if Mr Halliwell was a phoney. Seeing that hall, I realized he didn't like to parade his wealth to the outside world. Not that anyone could see the house, tucked away as it is, and I can't imagine any burglars would bother to scout that area, but then you never know.'

Horton was interested in Jennings' perspective.

Cantelli said, 'How do you get new customers?'

'Mainly through word of mouth recommendations. The website brings in a few. Charles and Alex attend various trade shows and events.'

'And your background?'

Jennings smiled. 'Raised in a pub, here on the island. Worked in a few on the mainland, then in a succession of restaurants and hotels in London, the Cotswolds and Edinburgh, learning my trade as I went and then putting myself through various courses. Not like Charles who has a BA Hons Wine Business Degree and is a Member of the Institute Masters of Wine, as is Alec. We've all had extensive wine training both in the UK, Italy and France.'

Jennings' phone pinged. Checking it he said, 'I'm sorry, I've got to call someone.'

'That's OK, we've finished anyway.'

'I'll take you back to Charles.' As they set off down the corridor, Jennings said, 'There is one thing that I thought a little unusual. Of course, it probably doesn't mean anything but someone asked if we had or could get hold of any Domaine de la Romanée-Conti, and that's the first time, as far as we are all aware, it's ever happened.'

Horton's interest heightened. 'Who was it?'

'A man called George Caws. He left a mobile number, but when Charles called him after he'd valued Mr Halliwell's wine cellar to say that we had come across a couple of bottles that would go to auction, the number was dead.'

'When was this?' Horton asked, disguising his keen interest. Coincidence? Somehow, he felt not.

'January. He said he had been recommended by someone on the island, but he didn't say who, leastways not to me.'

But perhaps he had to Charles Nansen. And Nansen hadn't mentioned this to them. Why hadn't he? 'Can you describe him?'

'I only saw him leaving, and that's when Charles told me he'd asked about the Domaine de la Romanée-Conti. He was about five eleven, early sixties, maybe younger. It's hard to put an age on some people. He was thin. He got into a dark blue Ford.'

Horton thanked him and as Jennings departed, Nansen was waiting for them with the date of Halliwell's purchases and the list of wines. It had been 10 January, nine days before he had asked Chilcott to draw up his will. As Nansen had said the wine purchases were substantial and expensive, but nothing in the league of the Domaine de la Romanée-Conti.

Handing the list to Cantelli, Horton addressed Nansen at the door, 'Mr Jennings told us you had a visit from a man called George Caws in January asking about Domaine de la Romanée-Conti.'

'Well, yes.' Nansen scratched his beard and shifted.

'When was this?'

'I don't remember exactly.'

'Would it be in your diary?' Cantelli prompted.

Nansen consulted his phone, although he did so reluctantly. 'It was the 14 January.'

'I believe you tried to contact him after you valued Mr Halliwell's cellar to say a couple of bottles might be coming up for auction.'

Nansen flushed to the roots of his beard. 'I thought he might be interested, but the number he gave me was dead.'

'Why did he come here to enquire about such a rare wine?'

Nansen's flush deepened. 'Why shouldn't he? We do have a reputation, Inspector.'

'Of course,' Horton mollified. 'Did he say where he had come from? Or where he lived?'

'No. I only took his telephone number. He was a knowledgeable and pleasant man.'

'I'm sure he was, sir. Can you describe him?'

Nansen gave the same description as Jennings adding that Caws had been dressed in trousers, an open neck shirt and suit jacket. And no, he didn't notice his shoes.

'Any accent?' asked Cantelli.

'Not that I could hear. We talked about wine and wine connoisseurs.' Nansen stalled. Horton knew why. He helped him out.

'And you reassured Mr Caws that you dealt with a number of well to do and wealthy clients on the island, including Cedric Halliwell, and he was deeply interested in him.'

Nansen looked downcast. 'It was foolish of me, I know, but Mr Caws was highly...' he struggled to find the word.

'Plausible,' furnished Cantelli.

Nansen nodded.

'What other names did you give him?' Horton asked.

Nansen was beginning to look wretched. He did a lot of beard plucking before speaking reluctantly, 'Only one other name, and only because we spoke specifically about the Domaine de la Romanée-Conti. There's only one other customer of ours on the island who has that wine in his cellar.'

'And he is?'

'I wouldn't want him to think we tell all and sundry what he has in his cellar.'

No, thought Horton, it wouldn't do much for the company's reputation. 'The name please, Mr Nansen.'

Nansen sighed heavily; the dog whimpered. 'Viscount Lord Richard Eames.'

Horton should have guessed. Eames could afford such an exclusive wine. 'Did you talk about anything else?' he asked Nansen.

'No, just wines, our favourites, and those that were a worthwhile investment.'

'How long was Mr Caws here for?'

'About forty minutes, maybe a little more.'

'If you still have that telephone number?'

Nansen scrolled through his mobile until he found the number and relayed it to them. Cantelli wrote it down.

'You won't have to speak to Lord Eames, will you?' Nansen asked worried.

'Not if it's not relevant,' Horton said, but maybe he would enquire, just to see Eames again, although he doubted he would be at his island home at the moment, it not being August. And he had no evidence to confront him with regarding Jennifer.

Departing Wight Barn Wines they left an anxious Charles Nansen behind them. Heading back towards the main road, Cantelli said, 'This George Caws is interesting. Could he be the landslip corpse? He tracked Halliwell down and threatened to expose him as a crook unless he paid up. Halliwell kills and buries him and then takes off on his boat and dies in the cold sea mist.'

Those had been Horton's thoughts, and he said as much.

Cantelli added, 'Caws and Halliwell could have been up to the same game as Nigel Tamar. You remember him?'

'How can I forget? Convicted of wine fraud, out on bail, and absconded before sentencing. He was selling fake vintage wine, slapping labels of expensive wines on bottles which contained good old Pompey plonk.'

'Maybe Caws was in league with Nansen. We've only got Jennings' and Nansen's word that the mobile number this George Caws gave them was dead. Nansen told Jennings that. Maybe it wasn't a dead line.'

'Pull over when you can and try it.'

Cantelli did with the same result. He indicated out into the road again and resumed his theories. 'What if there were more than two bottles of this expensive wine in Halliwell's cellar which were never going to see their way onto the valuation list? There could have been three, four or more. Nansen contacted Caws to sell to him privately, which was why he looked so uncomfortable when we questioned him about Caws. Maybe he did get hold of Caws who has taken off after buying the wine. Or perhaps Chilcott did a deal with Nansen, helping himself to a bottle or two while Nansen took another few before drawing up the list.'

'It's possible,' Horton mused. 'Those bottles of wine in that amazing cellar, which you will see shortly, came from somewhere. Someone transported them there, and that someone could be the company who built the cellar. They will have a list of what they shipped.'

'But even if that list doesn't tally with Nansen's that doesn't mean either he or Chilcott helped themselves. Halliwell could have drunk a few bottles in between times.'

Cantelli was right. 'We need to find this George Caws. Turn off for Bonchurch, Barney. While we're on this side of the island I'd like to see if we can have a word with the woman who discovered Ben's body, Carina Musgrove.'

Horton had got her name from Sergeant Norris and had read the statement she had made which confirmed what both Norris and Elkins had told him. There was probably little she could add to her statement; she had only visited that bay twice and long after both Halliwell and the landslip corpse had died. But he thought it worth talking to her.

There was no answer though when Horton knocked on the door of the end house in a small row of stone terraced cottages, which faced the isolated part of a promenade, culminating in a stony shore. There was no one around to ask either. To the side of the cottage, resting on the shingle, was a boat trailer but no sign of any boat. Horton had Carina Musgrove's mobile number and, although he could call her to arrange a meeting, he decided to postpone it for the time being.

As Cantelli made for Beachwood House, Horton called Uckfield and gave him a succinct account of what they had learned. Uckfield said they'd see what, if anything, they could find on George Caws. Horton didn't think it would be much because he suspected Caws was an alias. Uckfield also said Trueman would call him back when he had details of the architect, Gary Redcar, who had remodelled Beachwood House. Horton wondered if he might be based locally on the island. If so, there was a chance he and Cantelli would be able to talk to him that day. Next, he rang Bliss and was glad when he got her voicemail as it saved him having to answer her questions. Leaving a brief update, he ended by saying that he had reported back to Uckfield.

'She's probably trying to find the chief's arsonist herself, so she can get extra brownie points,' Cantelli said.

'Knowing her as we do, she's probably giving Mark Leonard a hard time. I bet this is one occasion when Walters is glad he's in court and hopes the case will go on all day, several days.' He tried Walters' mobile number but got his voice mail. That didn't mean he was still in court. Knowing Walters he could be in the local pub or café pursuing one of his hobbies – eating. 'I'd better see that Leonard hasn't done anything stupid like pushing Bliss in the harbour.'

'I think she'd be the one to do the pushing. She came top in her class at self-defence. She's a judo and karate expert as well as being a top marksman, sorry markswoman.'

'You're making this up.'

'I'm not. Sergeant Warren told me, and he heard it from –'

'I believe you. There's no denying she's heading for the top,' Horton said as he rang Leonard. 'And she'll get there. Not like us, Barney, we'll remain lowly detectives.'

'You speak for yourself. I might make Super yet.'

Horton smiled. He was certain *he* wouldn't, and he knew Cantelli didn't want it. Leonard answered swiftly and with a note of relief in his voice. Horton knew the reason for that. Bliss.

'I've checked with the Queens Harbour Master and there are no reports of irregular boat movements in the harbour around that area two hours before or after the fire,' Leonard said. 'But it could have been a small boat that wasn't picked up on the radar. I've ruled out the arsonists who have been released from prison as possible suspects. They both have cast iron alibis. One of them had been picked up by Havant police and had spent the night in the cells, and the other is in hospital having stolen a car and crashed it into a lamppost. I'm re-interviewing the club secretary, seeing what gossip I can pick up, and I'm visiting the businesses and other clubs in the area. There's an army cadet school close by, although, as you know, Andy, the area's pretty isolated, but someone might have seen a suspicious looking vehicle or person casing the joint before the fire, travelling up and down that road or parked close by for some period of time. Watch Manager Greg Hammond is liaising with the lab over the fragments of glass and rags we found, and he's taking another look around in case we missed anything, which, as DCI Bliss has reminded me at least four times this morning, we must have done.'

Horton could well imagine. He rang off and managed to speak to Sergeant Norris before the signal gave out as Cantelli swung into the lane that led to Beachwood House. Horton asked Norris to instigate enquiries with the taxi companies on the island to find out who had taken Halliwell to Wight Barn Wines on 10 January, and if any of them had taken George Caws there on 14 January in a dark blue Ford.

'I see what you and Tim Jennings mean about the place being dilapidated,' Cantelli said, drawing to a halt outside the scuffed, scratched and battered front door of Beachwood House. 'Are you sure you didn't imagine the posh interior?'

'Quite sure. See for yourself.'

Twelve

Cantelli duly expressed amazement in every room as Horton lifted some prints from around the house, but it was when they reached the cellar that his dark eyes nearly popped out of his head.

'Blimey! You weren't kidding. My old dad would have liked this. Any Italian wines here?' he asked, resuming chewing his gum and craning his neck to read the labels on some bottles as he walked around the cellar.

'I expect so,' Horton answered, while trying to get some prints from a shelf. 'Take a look at the catalogue.' He handed him the valuation report.

'Dad was partial to a nice Chianti. Must say I am too. Ah, here's one, a 1952 Riserva Ducale Chianti Serie Ora Stravecchio Ruffino, bit of a mouthful and not sure I got the pronunciation right. Isabella is better at Italian than me.'

Isabella was Cantelli's sister and Horton often heard her speaking Italian in the café she ran on the seafront.

'Toni, my elder brother, was born in 1952. How much? Oh, a snip at three hundred pounds,' Cantelli said brightly and sarcastically. 'I think Toni will have to do with a Chianti from the supermarket for his birthday.'

'They sell some good wines.'

'Under a tenner yes. I'd even stretch to twenty five, maybe thirty pounds but no more.'

'Where's your Italian spirit?'

'Evaporated. My mother's practical English side has asserted itself.'

Horton smiled.

Cantelli continued, 'Here's the name, telephone number and web address of Simply Cellars.' He indicated a small brass plaque on the centre piece shelf. Withdrawing his notebook and plucking his pencil from behind his ear, he jotted it down. 'It saves me the job of looking them up. I'm itching to know how much this must have set Halliwell back.'

'Have you finished ogling the place?'

Cantelli sighed with one last look around. 'Guess so.'

They headed for Bembridge, where they stopped for a late sandwich lunch in the café on the Duver overlooking the Solent before looking over Halliwell's boat. The wind was freshening even further, and dark clouds loomed in the west. Cantelli watched them warily.

Horton said he'd excuse Cantelli from going on board Halliwell's boat, but Cantelli declined. 'Don't want to be accused of not being able to do my job,' he said good-naturedly.

Horton unzipped the green canopy and climbed on board. Cantelli gingerly followed suit. There was a single forward-facing seat at the helm and Horton, sitting in it, inserted one of the keys into the instrumentation panel.

'For God's sake don't suggest taking it out,' Cantelli said alarmed.

'You'd be in safe hands, and there's enough petrol, the tank's a quarter full. But I'll spare you. There's no record of his last trip or any journey before that. But then he hadn't owned the boat long before he died.'

They descended to the main cabin. Horton said, 'This was where he was found, lying face down. He could have got up from the table, been gripped by a heart attack and collapsed. It was so sudden he could do nothing about it. Or perhaps he had been struggling to get to the helm to make a distress call. Have a rummage around, Barney, for any paperwork, while I lift some prints.' Horton found a few which could be those of Jason Arlett and his colleague from Ryde Inshore Rescue. He'd ask Elkins to take their fingerprints.

Cantelli reported there was no documentation. They alighted and Horton zipped up the canopy.

Cantelli studied the gathering clouds. 'Don't you think it's time to make for the ferry?'

The wind was certainly picking up speed. Horton was about to agree when his phone rang. It was Trueman with the news that the architect lived on the island and was at this moment engaged on a project at Seaview and would be happy to talk to them there.

'It's on the way to the ferry, and the storm won't get worse for hours yet,' Horton reassured.

Cantelli looked dubious.

'Trust me, I'm a sailor.'

'Yeah, and a policeman and we all know what they're like with the truth.'

'Speak for yourself,' Horton joked.

Ten minutes later Cantelli squeezed the car between a flatbed truck and a white van. There were two more vans parked in the gravel lane which was a dead end. The large detached house on their left was in the act of being completely re-modelled. The sound of hammering and loud music came from inside, and there were two men on the roof carefully removing tiles no doubt to be replaced once the house had been extended and refurbished. Cantelli asked one of the workmen where they could find Redcar.

'I'll get him for you.' A couple of minutes later a smallish round man in his late forties wearing a white hard hat over dark hair, and a high-vis jacket over casual clothes appeared. He greeted them pleasantly and curiously. Trueman had told the architect they wanted to talk to him about Cedric Halliwell and Beachwood House.

'Come through to the garden. It's quieter there, although this lot are knocking off any minute.'

And, as though on cue, the loud music suddenly stopped.

They followed him around the side of the house into a wide expanse of wild garden which gave on to a small sand and shingle bay where a woman and man were walking their dog. The wind was strengthening and the Portsmouth horizon had already disappeared in the gloom laden sky. Redcar invited them to sit on a wooden bench that afforded some shelter from the gusting wind from the west. Horton opened by asking when Redcar had met Cedric Halliwell.

'When he commissioned me to undertake the remodelling of the interior of Beachwood House, which was early March last year. He'd bought the property in February. I met him again during the refurbishment in mid-April and then finally on completion on the 28 June. A pleasant man, and a good client, not too demanding. Not like these.' He jerked his head at the house. 'Still, if they keep changing their minds, it's their money they're spending. He's a London banker and she's a top corporate lawyer in the City.'

'It's a big house,' Cantelli said, looking up at the three storey sprawling property. 'Do they have a large family?'

'No, it's just the two of them but they like to have house parties. This house, like the others along here, will only be used in August.'

A bit like Eames' mansion, thought Horton.

'Seems a waste,' Cantelli said sorrowfully. Horton guessed he was thinking of his five children and Charlotte in their semi-detached house on the eastern edge of Portsmouth, but Horton knew Cantelli wouldn't swap it for this. As long as he had his lovely wife and children all well and happy, Barney would have lived in Ben's log cabin.

Redcar was saying, 'Mr Halliwell knew exactly what he wanted, which is quite unusual. He was so clear on it that he could have practically drawn up the plans himself. Some of the rooms were remodelled, for example the old kitchen, pantry, utility room and a small room at the back of the house were all opened up to form one large kitchen and breakfast room. An en suite was added upstairs, other than that it was working with the existing structure.'

'Including the cellar.'

'How can I forget that?' Redcar smiled and widened his dark eyes. 'But that was all Mr Halliwell's doing. Again, he knew exactly what he wanted and who he wanted to build it, Simply Cellars, based in London. They stored Mr Halliwell's wine.'

This was good news. It meant they could tell them a lot more about Halliwell.

'Did he speak to you about his wine?'

'Only in the sense that he invested in it and paintings. He told me where his paintings were to hang so that the interior could be designed to suit them. But that was it. He was reserved. You couldn't get close to him, but then I only met him three times. And it wasn't my business to gossip but to get on with managing the project. I'm sure Dudley Coppens at Simply Cellars will be able to tell you more about Mr Halliwell.'

Horton hoped so. 'How did Mr Halliwell contact you initially?'

'By telephone.'

Horton nodded and Cantelli scribed.

Redcar continued, 'He said he'd looked me up on the internet and on the Royal Institute of British Architects website. He'd seen my work on my website and, because I lived on the island where he had bought a house, he thought I'd be ideal to assist him. We arranged to meet at Beachwood House at the beginning of March, and we walked through the house while he explained exactly what he wanted. He said he lived alone and that there would be no visitors to cater for, so he didn't require a guest suite or a children's room, and the kitchen design was to his specification.'

'Did he say why he had bought such a big house just for himself and in that location? It seems an odd thing to do,' Cantelli ventured.

'All he said was that he liked privacy, and I didn't pry. I got the impression he didn't want to discuss anything of a personal nature. I made a few suggestions to Mr Halliwell, especially concerning the exterior but he was adamant he wanted that untouched, likewise the gatehouse. He wanted everything done quickly, no delay and said he'd pay a premium for that. If I said I couldn't start the job for six months or get the builders then he'd go elsewhere. I drew up the designs, and he approved them.'

'How?'

'I sent pictures of the plans over to his mobile phone. I engaged the contractors, and we started working on the house in March, completing it in June.'

'But Mr Halliwell didn't move in until January.'

'I know. Bit odd that when he wanted it completed so quickly. Still, that was his business. He said I was to oversee the whole project without troubling him. He gave me free rein to appoint whoever I thought best for the job. He lived abroad, the Cayman Islands, but said he wasn't always there, he travelled a great deal. I was to call him if there were any issues which I couldn't resolve myself or any questions. He wasn't a man who went in for personal chit chat.'

And would Halliwell have been equally reticent with Simply Cellars? Possibly, but as they had stored his wine before the cellar at Beachwood House had been commissioned and built, Horton hoped not.

Redcar said, 'I also oversaw the purchase of the entire contents of the house except for the paintings, the wine, and the piano.'

Horton eyed him, puzzled. 'And the snooker table?'

'That too. Everything in the house was new, the furniture, bed linen, crockery, cutlery, appliances, towels, the lot.'

'Unusual wouldn't you say?'

'It does happen occasionally, especially if it is a holiday home or a property to let. I thought at first he intended to rent it out, but the cellar ruled that out. No one builds an expensive cellar for a tenant. I appointed an interior designer who worked closely with me on the internal decoration and the contents. Neither she nor the project manager met Mr Halliwell, everything was done via me. He paid handsomely, on time and no quibble. As I said earlier, I would like more clients like him. I was sorry to hear he'd died. I read about it in the local newspaper.'

Horton heard some vans starting up. The builders were leaving, and Cantelli looked anxiously at the sky as a few spots of rain fell. The strengthening wind was whipping up the green-blue sea, causing it to crash in an explosion of spray on the shore. Horton could taste the salt on his lips. As if reading his mind, Cantelli licked his and shifted uneasily.

Horton addressed Redcar. 'Did he mention the log cabin? The one in the bay beneath Beachwood House.'

'I saw it from the house and asked him about it, but he told me he didn't own it and that it was derelict because the land was given to landslips.'

'Did you see anyone living in it or anyone on the shore or cliffside while you were at Beachwood House?'

'No.'

Horton wondered whether the builders had. Cantelli, obviously on the same wavelength, asked if they could have the contact details of all the builders and the interior designer. Redcar said he would email all the information over. Looking puzzled he said, 'Why all the questions? Is there something suspicious about Mr Halliwell's death?'

Horton told him that a body had been found on the cliff just below Beachwood House and they were trying to establish if there was any connection between it and Mr Halliwell.

'Really! Who is it?'

'That's what we're hoping to discover. Do you still have the telephone number Mr Halliwell gave you?'

'Yes, but it won't be any good to you. It's no longer active. I tried it in September, three months after handing over the house to him, hoping I could persuade him to let me use it as a testimonial and example of my work. The line was dead. I had a feeling he wouldn't let me anyway. Well more than a feeling. There was a sort of determination about him. He had a very candid gaze, not hard exactly, but the steely kind that said don't mess with me. Firm jaw, iron grip. When the project was signed off, he said he knew where I was if he wanted me again. And even though he was delighted with the work, he wouldn't allow me to take any photographs of it and said I wasn't to include it in my portfolio. I thought he must have changed his phone company, and there was no need for him to give me his new number. So that was that.'

Redcar relayed the phone number from his phone address book, and Cantelli jotted it down. It wasn't the same number that Elkins had given him, the one that the Wakelins had for Halliwell. So obviously Halliwell had changed his phone and phone company between liaising with the architect and buying the motor cruiser. No crime in that. Another number for Trueman to check out. But this too might have been a pay-as-you-go account, which meant no phone records to obtain and scrutinize.

'And he gave no indication of why he wanted to live on the Isle of Wight?'

'None.'

Horton asked how Halliwell had settled his account.

'Through a bank in Guernsey. Morgans.'

'You have the details?'

'Yes, but they're in my office at home. I can email them to you.'

Cantelli gave Redcar a card with his mobile number and email address on it. The bank details would be the same as those on the documents Chilcott had given them, which Halliwell had used to purchase the boat and the wines from Wight Barn Wines, but it was always best to check.

Redcar ran a hand over his head and said with a little awkwardness, 'Do you think I'll be able to use the Beachwood House project now that he's dead? I know that sounds insensitive but the benefactor, or the new owner when the house is sold, might knock it about. They might even want an architect. Do you know who the benefactors are?'

'You can contact his executor, Peter Chilcott Solicitors.' Horton saw no harm in giving Redcar that information. 'Did you get any indication that Mr Halliwell was religious?'

'No,' Redcar answered.

'There was nothing in his belongings to indicate he was?'

'I didn't see his belongings. As I said, I handed the project over to him when it was complete and before he moved in.'

'Can you describe him to me?'

Redcar looked bemused by the question but said, 'He spoke quietly, without an accent but with a kind of force, the type that commands easily without having to shout, bully or flatter. I'd guess about early-sixties, silver-white hair, straight and thick, cut short, blue eyes, lean, expensively but casually dressed. Tag Heuer watch, gold signet ring. Confident. A bit taller than you, about six foot two.'

Horton's mind was racing. Cantelli had stopped chewing his gum, and his pencil had frozen over his notebook.

'Are you sure?' Horton said.

'Yes, why?'

Horton thought of the description that Chilcott and Nansen had given him of Halliwell, and of the one Jason Arlett had relayed to Elkins. Save for the Tag Heuer watch nothing else tallied, and there was no mention of a signet ring on the body or in the list of belongings that Chilcott had given him. 'Any distinguishing marks?'

Redcar was an architect with an eye for detail. He would have noticed if there had been anything. 'Well, yes, actually there was. There was some scarring on the back of his right hand, which went as far as his wrist. It might have gone further up his arm but I never saw him without a long sleeve shirt, jumper or sailing jacket.'

'Caused by?'

'I can't be sure, but it looked as though it was a burn and a severe enough one to leave permanent scarring.'

Horton's mind leapt to a fire in 1968 in which twenty-four men had died, including Zachary Benham. But then the fire in the Goldsmith Psychiatric Hospital wasn't the only fire in the world. But something else nudged at him. He tried to retrieve it... scars... burns... hands... *Hands are so important, don't you think? They don't lie.* Those were practically Dormand's last words to him on the abbey shore. Rory Mortimer had been wearing a ring in the photograph from 1967. Dormand had been wearing that ring when Horton had confronted him. He'd thought Dormand had been referring to the ring but maybe he hadn't.

He pushed the thoughts aside for re-examination later, for now, Redcar's final description had clinched one thing, and he saw from Cantelli's expression that he had also realized it; the man who had made his will with Peter Chilcott, the one who had purchased wines from Wight Barn Wines, and the man found dead on his boat by the Ryde Inshore Rescue team was not the same man who Colin Redcar had dealt with over the refurbishment of Beachwood House.

Thirteen

'Are you sure?' Uckfield said when Horton reported back to him in his office. Bliss had tagged along after seeing him enter the station. Cantelli had dropped him off at the entrance and Horton had despatched the sergeant home. There was nothing more that could be done that evening, and Cantelli was feeling a little rough after the stormy ferry crossing despite swallowing a couple more seasickness pills. Horton hoped he'd get home safely and wasn't too drowsy to drive. Cantelli had insisted he wasn't but said he would text Horton when he arrived home to let him know.

'Positive. The height and age are roughly the same but the rest doesn't tie up. Chilcott, Nansen and Arlett claim the Halliwell they saw had thinning grey hair, receding at the temples, and was of medium build with a lean lined face. And none of them mentioned the scarred hand – and before you say they might not have seen it or might have forgotten it, I phoned Nansen on the way back; he and Jennings, his manager, both confirm there was no scarring on the hand of their Cedric Halliwell. I've yet to check with Chilcott, and Elkins is going to confirm with Arlett tomorrow, but I've also called Dr Clayton. Yesterday I asked if she'd take a look at the autopsy reports of both Ben and Halliwell to see if anything struck her about their deaths possibly being suspicious. While she hasn't had time to study the reports yet, she looked up Halliwell's and confirmed the descriptions Nansen, Chilcott, Jennings and Arlett gave us and that there was no scarring on the hand.

'Cantelli will call Simply Cellars tomorrow morning and see if he can get hold of Dudley Coppens, the owner, although it being Saturday, Coppens might not be at work. I've lifted some fingerprints from the house and from Halliwell's boat, which I've sent over to the bureau. I've asked for them to be fast-tracked. Some of them might be Nansen's, Chilcott's and the art valuer, Felicity Ellwood, but we can quickly rule those out. I've asked Sergeant Norris to organize getting their prints, and Sergeant Elkins is getting the prints of the Ryde Inshore Rescue members who went on board Halliwell's boat.'

Bliss said, 'So which one is the real Cedric Halliwell? The man Redcar dealt with, or the one the wine master and lawyer met?'

Horton had been considering this on the ferry back and had discussed it with Cantelli in an attempt to divert the sergeant's attention from the rolling sea. Now he expressed one idea that had occurred to them. 'Perhaps the real Halliwell sent someone over posing as himself to liaise with the architect because he didn't want to return to the country and risk being here long enough to pay taxes. He did the same in late June when Redcar had finished the refurbishment. The man who liaised with Redcar either had a different passport or a fake one in Halliwell's name, although Redcar wouldn't have needed to see any passport, so it could simply have been the matter of this other man posing as Halliwell. He could have come from anywhere. He might even have been residing in this country so didn't need to come through passport control.'

Uckfield grunted acknowledgement that this could be possible. He mopped his brow with a large handkerchief. Horton thought he looked grey and unwell. Horton's phone bleeped. Quickly glancing at it, he saw it was Barney who had arrived home safely.

'There is a flaw in that theory though,' Horton continued. 'Because the real Halliwell didn't need to stay longer than a few days to commission Redcar or on the handover. There would have been no risk to him tax-wise. We might get a description from the Guernsey lawyers, Selwyns, who handled the purchase of Beachwood House on behalf of Halliwell and hold the deeds to the property. I've spoken to Inspector Guilbert on Guernsey, brought him up to speed with events and asked if he and his officers could interview Selwyns and talk to Morgan's bank, also to research if Halliwell had a property in Guernsey at any time. We might get more about Halliwell from the possessions he had shipped to Beachwood House; the paintings and the piano. I've already mentioned the wine. Both the piano and paintings must have been shipped by specialist removal companies, expert in handling such items. And Ms Ellwood might be able to tell us how, when and where some of the paintings were acquired.'

'Walters can follow up the piano removal companies tomorrow,'

Bliss said eagerly. 'His court case finished today. We got a conviction.'

That was good news, thought Horton. He said, 'Only if you authorize his overtime, along with Cantelli's.'

She dashed a glance at Uckfield who didn't seem to be taking things in. Bliss wouldn't want her budget blown, so she'd like Uckfield to sanction it and add it to the Major Crime Team's. It was, after all, Uckfield's case.

Horton said, 'And there's George Caws. His arrival at Wight Barn Wines might be purely coincidental but why then is his telephone number dead?'

'Because he is.' Uckfield stirred himself with an effort. 'No one's come forward yet with any information about the landslip corpse, and there's no one reported missing who fits the description.'

'They might not have noticed this person is missing,' Bliss posed.

'Trueman can't find any trace of Caws yet.'

'Somehow that doesn't surprise me,' Horton rejoined. 'Maybe Norris's officers will have something to report by Monday from the taxi companies.' Norris had called him while they'd been on the ferry to say that Chilcott had taken some clothes to the Red Cross charity shop in Shanklin – but no jewellery and certainly no Tag Heuer watch. Horton relayed this news to Bliss and Uckfield, adding, 'Norris's officers have made enquiries at all the other charity shops and jewellers in Shanklin, with the same result. No one's been asked to value or sell the watch. And I wouldn't be surprised if there were other items Chilcott helped himself to from Beachwood House, some expensive wine for example. But I can't see Chilcott letting us search his house or office without a warrant.'

'We'll get one if needed.' Uckfield rose, shakily. 'I'm going home.'

Horton eyed him with surprise. Yes, Uckfield could be abrupt, but he didn't seem interested in the case and was reluctant to take control.

Bliss scrambled up. 'Do you wish us to continue with enquiries tomorrow?'

'Can't see that the case warrants immediate activity. Monday will do.'

Horton wanted to protest but he could see there was no point, and Uckfield was right. Although the landslip corpse had been murdered, and that in itself warranted urgent action, it was looking increasingly possible that either Halliwell or Ben had killed him.

As Horton headed down the stairs with Bliss, he could see she was thinking that Uckfield seemed to be losing his grip on his work. Horton was convinced it was because he was unwell. Maybe it was the same with the Trehams robbery, which Dennings was overseeing. The incident room had been empty. Everyone save Uckfield had gone home.

Horton said, 'I'll call Cantelli and tell him not to come in. He can contact Simply Cellars on Monday. I'll see if I can get hold of the art expert and arrange a meeting for Monday. I'll also request a copy of the post-mortem on Halliwell.' He'd like to review it himself in addition to Gaye.

Bliss gave her approval. She asked about the sailing club arson.

'There's nothing new on it, as far as I'm aware, but there might be a report when I get back to my office.'

'Keep me informed, Inspector. I'm reporting to the chief personally on this.'

I bet you are, thought Horton. Still, if it saved the chief getting on his back, then he was grateful.

There was a message from DC Leonard to say that a canoe had been seen by a fisherman in the area before the fire had started. It was late for a lone canoeist to be out in the harbour, in the dark. Leonard said he was following it up. Horton rang through to Bliss on her mobile. Standing by his office window, he could see her hurrying to her sports car in the squally rain. She grabbed her phone, zapped open the car and said, 'Yes?'

He updated her, adding, 'A canoeist approaches slowly, silently and under the sailing club's CCTV camera's radar. He sets light to the boatyard in the dark by throwing a Molotov cocktail, which means he's fit and strong enough to propel the weapon. He also has good aim and steadiness, and is certainly knowledgeable about the harbour and tides, therefore, not your random arsonist. It was a targeted attack and for a reason.'

'That doesn't mean it was specifically directed at those three boats; the arsonist might have hoped the whole lot would be set ablaze.'

Horton agreed but added that it did mean the sailing club *was* the target. 'A disgruntled member or ex-member, or someone on the staff who had been dismissed; maybe even someone who'd failed to get a job there and thought that he should have done. It seems extreme action, I know, but if it is someone slightly unbalanced...'

'It sounds as though it could be an ex-serviceman with mental health issues,' Bliss pronounced. 'Get DC Leonard to look into it.'

Horton was sure he already was, but he rang him and left a message, espousing his ideas and those of Bliss.

He opened the folder that Chilcott had given them and found the telephone numbers for Felicity Ellwood – a landline and a mobile. The landline could be the gallery's number. Chilcott had said she had an art gallery based in Cowes. It was nearly eight-thirty. Too late to call her now.

He put in a request for the post-mortem on Cedric Halliwell to be emailed to him. The thought of the scarring on Halliwell's hand – or more precisely the Halliwell that Redcar had dealt with – ran through Horton's mind as he rode home in the wind and the rain. It stayed with him overnight along with the mortuary attendant's words on Ben: *there was some scarring on his back, possibly as a result of an accident, which had stripped away the skin, or it could have been caused by scalding, but that was all.* The autopsy report had stated there was damage to the epidermis on his arms, legs, neck and face, arthritis in his joints, some lung damage and old scarring on his back. How old? 1968? Had Ben and Halliwell been involved in that fire at the Goldsmith Psychiatric Hospital? But again he told himself that wasn't the only fire in the world, and he had no evidence or indication they were even connected with his investigation into Jennifer's disappearance. All he had was a man called Lomas.

Horton told himself there was no link to Jennifer's past. He was getting obsessed. Gaye had said that he looked worn down. Maybe she was right, and he was seeing connections where there were none. He didn't know for certain that the scarring on the hand of the man Redcar had dealt with was from a burn, and neither could he be sure that the scar on Ben's back had been caused by fire. Even if it had, the fire could have occurred anywhere and at any time in the past. He had to guard himself against taking all this personally. And with that in mind and Gaye's words ringing in his ears, he decided to go sailing over the weekend.

Fourteen

Two thoughts occurred to him overnight. One was the arson at the sailing club and the lone canoeist. The other was connected with his sailing trip that weekend.

On rising, he sent DC Leonard a text suggesting that the canoe might have been launched from the public slipway at the Hardway at Gosport, across the harbour from the sailing club. Leonard would get Gosport police to ask around for any sightings, and Horton said he'd also instruct Elkins and Ripley to make enquiries around the harbour for any canoe seen before the arson, or being launched at any of the other public slipways; the canoeist must have surveyed the territory before his attack.

That done, and after finishing his breakfast, he made the boat ready. It was a perfect day for sailing. The rain had ceased during the night and the wind had eased to that of a crisp April breeze. The forecast was for a chilly but clear day. His other thought had been that he could combine his sailing trip to Cowes with a visit to Ms Ellwood's art gallery. He didn't expect it to be open, or for her to be on the premises, but no harm in checking. So much for putting the case out of his mind, he thought with a wry smile.

He took his time crossing the Solent; he had no choice with the wind and tide, and he certainly wasn't going to cheat by putting on the engine until he had to, and then only as he was entering Cowes Harbour. Elkins called him on the crossing to say that he had received his text and would make enquiries in and around Portsmouth Harbour for the lone canoeist, and that he had also seen all the Ryde Inshore Rescue Team; they had an open day at their centre. He'd got prints from Jason Arlett and his colleague who had boarded Halliwell's boat and had sent them over to the fingerprint bureau.

After mooring up at East Cowes, and lunch at a waterside pub, Horton caught the small chain ferry across to West Cowes where he made his way through the winding narrow streets for the Bounty Art Gallery, wondering if he would find it open and Ms Ellwood inside.

The first was achieved and, as he stepped inside, the smell of varnish greeted him, along with a tall, casually but elegantly dressed woman in her mid-thirties wearing trousers, loafers and a tight fitting jumper that accentuated her shapely curves. Perhaps it was her smile – open and friendly – or her olive skin, or maybe the long curly black hair and lively dark-eyes that reminded him of Cantelli. He was convinced that, like Barney, she must have some Italian blood in her. He was delighted when she introduced herself as Felicity Ellwood. He thought it far too ordinary a name for someone so stunningly vibrant. She should have had a more musical name.

He commented on the spectacular paintings in the window of classic yachts in full sail, quickly adding that he wasn't in the market for buying them. He doubted he would ever be able to afford them. There was no price tag which meant they must be expensive. That didn't alter her attitude in the slightest. In fact, she smiled broadly and said, 'In Cowes people expect to see paintings of yachts and seascapes but it's not the only subject in which I specialize, far from it.'

He could see that from the other paintings around the gallery, some were urban landscapes of cities or towns which he couldn't identify. They were executed in clean almost clinical lines. Others were of an abstract nature that reflected the colours and movement of the sea. He showed his warrant card and explained he was keen to know more about the late Cedric Halliwell and his paintings.

Her dark eyes lit up. 'Stunning aren't they, and quite a find.' Then her expression became solemn as she recalled that Halliwell was dead and she was addressing a police officer. She pushed back her hair which sprang right back into its curls as though it had never been touched. 'Is there something suspicious about his death?' she asked, concerned.

'No, about his life,' he found himself answering.

'He was certainly something of a mystery and so are some of his paintings,' she added fervently with that open smile he found infectious.

'I don't want to hold you up but I would like to know more about them.'

'It will be my pleasure to tell you. I could talk about them for hours but then I'd be holding you up. You don't look much like a policeman, more a sailor,' she added, eyeing his sailing jacket. He felt amused by her critical and friendly gaze.

'I am. I sailed over from Portsmouth.'

Her shapely eyebrows shot up. 'Don't tell me police cutbacks have resulted in you being forced to use your own boats.'

'Give it time. I'm off duty, sort off.'

She laughed. 'And curious about the late Cedric Halliwell. Let me close the gallery.'

'I wouldn't dream –'

'Please, it gives me an excuse. I don't usually open on a Saturday afternoon anyway, unless by appointment. I'd have been gone by now if I hadn't been trying to catch up on some paperwork.'

Thank God for the paperwork, Horton thought, probably for the first time in his life.

'And I'd love to talk to you about Mr Halliwell's paintings and show off my knowledge or lack of it in the case of some of them,' she added, crossing to the door and turning the 'Open' sign to 'Closed'. 'It's a pity that I can't explain what I mean in front of them,' she said locking the door and turning back to him. 'It makes it much easier and I'd love to see them again, although I do have copies of them on my phone and computer, but it's not the same.'

'I have the keys to Beachwood House but no transport, unless we go by boat.'

'That would be fun but I've got my car outside.'

'Car it is then.'

'You might change your mind when you see it.'

Horton smiled. He liked her enthusiasm and easy manner. Like Gaye she had a straight-forward, no nonsense approach. He followed her through a workshop at the rear, where she grabbed a jacket. Noting him studying the contents of the workshop, she said, 'My real interest is restoration and painting. I have a studio at home.' She set the alarm, checked she had locked the door, and they struck out along the road of terraced houses.

'Where's home?' he asked.

'Niton. Not far from St Catherine's Lighthouse.'

The southernmost tip of the island. He knew it well. An important seamark along a rugged and spectacular coast. She suddenly halted alongside a maroon and cream Citroen 2CV.

'This is yours?' Horton asked surprised, although he didn't know what he had expected, a sports car maybe. But then on consideration, the vintage somewhat idiosyncratic classic French car seemed to go with her. Maybe she had French blood in her.

'Absolutely, gorgeous, isn't she?' Felicity said. 'Why are cars always female? She's a real classic, from 1988, low mileage and exceptionally well maintained. I travelled to Wales to buy her, three years ago. Modern cars are so boring, no personality at all,' she said unlocking it. 'Apologies if you have a state-of-the-art techno-whiz Audi or BMW, but somehow you don't look the sort.'

He climbed in, smiling. 'I'm not. I have a Harley Davidson.'

'Now why aren't I surprised?'

He didn't know. 'I haven't been in one of these for years.' It was a little cramped given his height but comfortable and smelt of leather and polish. He glanced at her hands as she placed them on the wheel.

'No, I'm not married,' she said, dashing him a glance.

She was sharp and observant.

'Never found the right man. I live with my father. What about you?' she asked, starting the car and pulling out.

'Divorced. One lovely daughter, nine years old, who I don't see enough of.'

'Why? Work?'

'I could say yes, but that's probably an excuse.'

'Difficult ex, eh?'

'You could say that. But it's partly my fault. I've let... Did you ever meet Mr Halliwell?'

She threw him a smile, acknowledging that he had changed the subject and that more personal probing was off limits. Again, he couldn't help thinking about Cantelli. He got the uncomfortable feeling, that like Barney, she could read him like a book. Maybe that was her artist's eye.

'Only through his paintings. What do you think of them? I take it you've seen them?'

'I have.'

'And?'

'Interesting.'

'Is that all?'

'No, perhaps not. With your eye I might see more of them.'

'And of their owner. What do you sail?'

'A small yacht which I also live on board in Portsmouth.'

Again, her dark-shaped eyebrows shot up, and she tossed him a glance. 'That takes some doing. It must be freezing in the winter.'

'I've got used to it. Do you sail?'

'Of course. I keep my boat in East Cowes, is that where you're moored?'

'Yes.'

'Then I'll show you mine if you show me yours when we get back.' He laughed.

She threw him a glance and smiled. After negotiating a busy junction, she said, 'Let me give you some of my background because I can see that you are about to ask me for it.'

Again she had pre-empted him.

'After my degree in the History of Art I worked for Sotheby's in London and then abroad but my father had an accident three years ago and, as I'm an island girl, I came home. I took over the gallery. My aim was to do more painting, only I don't get much opportunity for it. I'm kept busy with valuations.'

'Has Mr Chilcott given you many?'

'A few.'

'You don't like him?'

She shrugged. 'I don't really know him. I'm grateful for the work but I don't feel easy around him. I've done some insurance valuations for theft, both here on the island and on the mainland. And I go up to London occasionally to value, lecture and conduct research. It gives me the chance to catch up with friends as well as get my London adrenaline fix.'

'Does your father paint, Miss Ellwood?'

'Felice, please.'

'Italian!' Horton couldn't prevent himself from saying triumphantly.

'My mother. She wanted to call me Felice but my father wanted Felicity. They tossed a coin and dad won. The funny thing is he ended up calling me Felice too. I use both names depending on who I'm with and whether or not I like them. It's Felice if I like them Felicity if I don't.'

'I'm honoured.'

'So you should be, *Inspector*.'

'Andy.'

'Never Andrew?'

'Not for as long as I can remember.' Not even his mother had called him that but a couple of people he'd met while in care had, and he had hated them with a child's passion.

'Both my parents were artists,' Felice continued. 'My mother died ten years ago. I have some of my father's pictures in the gallery. The bright abstracts you might have noticed that capture the moods of the sea.'

'I did, and I liked them. Are any of your own in the gallery?'

'Not yet. Maybe soon.'

They fell to talking about sailing as she drove expertly through Shanklin, but he couldn't prise from her what kind of yacht she owned. Judging by her love of this vintage classic car, he thought her tastes might run to a more traditional yacht than modern like his own. Before he realized it they were turning on to the track that led to the footpath and the gatehouse.

Edging the Citroen carefully along the weed-strewn driveway, she said, 'Strange place this. You'd never think the inside was so contemporary and refurbished to such a high standard. It says something about your mystery man.'

'And that is?' he asked.

'A dual personality, maybe?'

No, thought Horton, two entirely different men. The man Redcar had met and the one the lawyer had drawn up a will for. Who was the real Cedric Halliwell?

She said, 'Clearly he was someone who wanted to keep people at arm's length, reclusive, the exterior tells of that. Excessively tidy, a bit OCD I'd say from the interior design; whereas his choice of some of his paintings indicate something different, a spiritual man with a taste for daring and adventure. A talented musician, if that piano is anything to judge by; artistic, from his eclectic taste in paintings, quiet and thoughtful because of where he choose to live, and perhaps secretive. Though what secrets he had to hide who knows, but you'd like to find out,' she said drawing to a halt and silencing the engine. 'And he was a shrewd investor with a taste in expensive wine, but was he a man who bought it to drink alone? Or was it purely an investment?'

She climbed out. Horton followed suit and extracted the keys.

'He was obviously comfortable with his own company and liked solitude,' she added thoughtfully.

'Can you throw any light on when and where he might have purchased the paintings?' Horton asked unlocking the door but not entering.

'Not at the moment, but I'm working on it. It's a pity there wasn't any paperwork but playing detective does make it interesting and fun, although frustrating at times, which I guess you'd know all about.'

'It's not much fun and mostly frustrating but it is challenging, as in this case. We've discovered a body in the landslip area below here. That death is suspicious.'

'And you think Mr Halliwell could have been involved with it?'

'It's just one possibility.' They stepped into the hall.

'As I said, an interesting man.' Her gaze swept over the abstract paintings in the hall and stayed there. 'As are these. They're by Jessie Balfour, an American who was hugely popular in the early to mid-nineteen fifties. She was one of a small group of American painters living in New York who seized the spotlight of artistic innovation which, until then, had been focused on Paris. Alongside the likes of Jackson Pollock they became known as the "Rebel Painters of the 1950s".' She turned her gaze back on Horton. 'Their art can be classified, if I can use that term, as Abstract Expressionism. It was in its heyday when, in 1956, Jackson Pollock was killed in a car accident. After that things started to change, not because of Pollock's death alone, but the political and social climate was shifting and a new generation of artists was beginning to emerge, more rooted in the wave of radicalism, the global student protests, the Cold War and communism.'

Horton thought of Jennifer and five of the men in that picture, members of the Radical Student Alliance, and Dr Quentin Amos's words – that Jennifer had been involved in the Alliance, helping to support and organize the protests.

As they entered the piano room, Felice continued, 'These two are

119

by an unknown French artist, Jacques Defour, who painted in the style of Henri Cadiou, a French realist painter and lithographer known for his work in trompe-l'oeil paintings. Cadiou died in 1989. We are seeing a resurgence in this style of work across Europe, Asia, North America and Canada, which will also make these highly popular and therefore will attract a good price. They're scenes of French life. Jacques Defour died in 1981 aged thirty two, drug overdose. These might be his only paintings, which again adds to their value. They are excellent.'

Horton could see that, just like Tim Jennings with his wine, Felice was passionate about her subject; enthusiasm shone in her eyes and rang in her voice. He felt his attraction for her deepening.

'Did Defour have any relatives?' he asked, as they crossed the hall into the drawing room.

'A wife and daughter. The wife died three years ago, but I managed to track down the daughter, she was only a year old when her father died. She said that her mother never spoke of Jacques being an artist and she wasn't aware of any paintings. Now these, as you can see, are urban landscapes.' She waved an arm at a number of paintings in the drawing room. Horton already knew there were a couple more by the same artist in the sitting room.

'They are scenes of London between the two World Wars, painted by Gilbert Morley, who, judging by the style, the period, and what I have gleaned from his background, was from the same school of art as the East London Group of painters, although his name isn't listed as being a member of the East London Group.'

'Why not?'

'Perhaps because he chose not to exhibit his work.'

'He could have just imitated the style.' That earned him a beaming smile, as though he'd passed a test. He felt ridiculously pleased by it.

'Sergeant Cantelli liked these. I work with him in CID.'

'Then he has good taste. Although I prefer others in this house, but we'll come to those in a moment. Which are your favourites?'

'The ones we'll come to in a moment.'

She inclined her head. 'To get back to these. The East London Group of artists were essentially working class, like Gilbert Morley who was a porter at Convent Garden. His paintings are evocative and, like the other artists in the East London Group, are scenes of life –

120

buildings, streets, markets – that reflect a way of life that has long since vanished. Because he, like the others, was working during the day, he had to find the time to paint, often in the evening, and he had to find the money for materials, which must have been incredibly difficult for him and many of the other artists in the group. But they were dedicated and highly talented.'

They moved into the sitting room. Felice continued, 'There is a great deal of interest in their work and a growing demand for it. Most of the East London Group's work is held privately, often by members of the artists' families. Gilbert Morley joined up at the commencement of the war in 1939 and died at Dunkirk. He wasn't married, but another family member could have been left his paintings and they subsequently ended up with Cedric Halliwell, but there is no way of knowing how. The value I've placed on Gilbert Morley's paintings could well triple at auction.'

Horton led the way back into the hall and up the stairs where the brightly coloured paintings in primary colours hung.

'Now these are stunning and by far my most favoured,' she declared excitedly.

'Mine too.'

'They have an abstract feel about them, but if you look hard you can discern the subject matter, an animal, a group of aboriginals around a fire, and this one,' she paused at the top of the stairs, 'a musical instrument.'

Horton peered at it and, with a start of surprise, realized he was looking at a harmonica. Nothing unusual in that save that such a musical instrument had been found on Ben's body.

'Is there a name on the harmonica?'

'You recognized the instrument,' she said amazed.

'I've seen one like it recently and only because you told me it was a musical instrument. I didn't look closely enough before.'

'There's no name but there is a small blob of white, a dash of red, and two blue stripes, all miniscule.'

'The Union Jack Flag?'

'I should have brought my magnifying glass for you to look through but hang on.' She reached for her phone, located the painting and enlarged it. 'There.'

He peered over her shoulder. Her hair smelt nice. An idea occurred to him based on what he remembered of the harmonica at the mortuary. It had been a Marine Band harmonica. That hadn't meant anything to him and yet these tiny colours, and the way they were arranged, reminded him of a Royal Marine Band member's uniform. Even if that was just his imagination the inclusion of such a musical instrument in one of these paintings indicated to him that the artist and Ben might have known one another, or that Halliwell had known Ben and asked the artist to include the harmonica in the painting. He didn't mention any of this to Felice.

She continued, 'These paintings are by an artist called Jethro Dinx, but I can't find any trace of him. No one I've spoken to in the business has heard of him. They're excellent and quite a find. See that one. It's of a group of aboriginals around a fire. The subject matter, the style, and his use of colour say that he was or is Australian, even though none of my enquiries so far have located him in that continent, either past or present.'

Horton thought of Gordon Eames who had died in Australia. Gordon Eames had not been a painter, as far as Horton was aware from what he'd read in the press about him, and from what he had had learned of his death while liaising with the Australian police in Nhulunbuy where Gordon had died. Besides, Australia was a huge continent with hundreds, maybe thousands of painters.

'Maybe he gave up painting or died young.'

'Possibly. There is no register of his birth or death in this country or in Australia. I've put out some feelers with my former colleagues in Sotheby's Australian and International Art departments in Sidney and Melbourne, so I might hear something from them. And I'm hoping that the picture framers can tell me more. They were framed in Stanmore in New South Wales so, again, another Australian connection. Dinx's technique reflects those of the artist, Ginger Riley Munduwalawala. Yes, it's quite mouthful,' she said, smiling at Horton's raised eyebrows. 'But a very musical sounding name. Munduwalawala was an extraordinarily talented and unique artist. He was born about 1936 in the bush in South East Arnhem Land, in the Northern Territory–'

'Where?' Horton said sharply.

'The Northern Territory,' she repeated looking puzzled. 'Why? Is something wrong?'

'No.' Just another connection, thought Horton, with a slightly quickening heartbeat. Gordon Eames' body had been found in the Northern Territory on Town Beach in Nhulunbuy off the Arafura Sea, on the Gove Peninsula in 1973, part of East Arnhem Land. 'Go on.'

'Munduwalawala was of the Marra people,' Felice said. 'He died in 2002. His art is a fusion of "Aboriginal" and "Contemporary".'

'So Halliwell needn't have paid a fortune for any of the pictures in this house.'

'No, and no one I've spoken to so far remembers a man called Cedric Halliwell in their gallery or auction house, but my contacts at all the major international auction houses are tracking back through their records to see if they have sold to Mr Halliwell at some time, or if they have handled the sale of any of these paintings with the exception of Dinx because, as I have already mentioned, no one recalls an artist of that name. I'll certainly let you know when I hear from them and the picture framers.'

'Did you speak to the abbot about the paintings? You know that the abbey has inherited all of the estate.'

'Yes, and I showed him photographs of them. He didn't recognize any of them or the artists' names, but then I didn't really expect him to. He also checked with the Brothers, volunteers, and staff and got the same result.'

Horton thought of George Caws who had visited Wight Barn Wines. 'Has anyone contacted you or come into your gallery asking about Mr Halliwell or any of the artists or paintings?'

'No.'

'Did you see anyone when you were at Beachwood House doing the valuation?'

'Only Ben.'

'You knew him?' Horton asked surprised.

'No, but I met him. I was in the garden looking for a footpath down to the bay when he emerged from the shrubbery. I told him why I was there, and we talked about the paintings. He said he hadn't seen them and knew nothing about any of them. He told me that wood carving was more in his line of work and Mr Halliwell had let him live in a cabin down in the bay.'

So Halliwell *did* know. Horton had suspected he must. He wondered if she knew that Ben was dead. He doubted it. He postponed telling her for a moment. 'Did Ben say anything about Cedric Halliwell?'

'Only that he knew the house would be put up for sale now that Mr Halliwell was dead and that he was living in the cabin on borrowed time.'

Did he mean he'd be evicted or had he a premonition or knowledge that he only had a short time left to live, wondered Horton?

'Did you go down to the cabin?'

'No. Ben said it was a fairly dangerous descent, the land being unstable, although I'd have liked to have gone to see his wood carvings, but I'd run out of time.'

'So has Ben. I'm sorry to say that Ben was found dead in his cabin eight days ago.'

'Oh, that's sad. Another death too! Suspicious?'

'I don't think so.'

'But you're not sure. There seems to be a lot of mystery surrounding these men.'

Horton silently agreed. As they descended the stairs, he said, 'Can you describe Ben to me?' He had only seen him in the mortuary and he thought her artist eye, like the architect's eye, might provide a good description, although in Ben's case not such a surprising answer as they'd got from Redcar.

She considered her response. Horton could see that she was visualizing the man. Eagerly, he awaited her description.

'He was deeply tanned with that ingrained bronze skin that looked as though he'd spent a lifetime in the open air. Abroad I would say, not in this country. His voice was gravelly, as though he'd once smoked, although I'd say if he did, he must have given up years ago because he looked too healthy to be a regular and recent smoker. He was well spoken, middle England, but there was something there, a hint of an accent. I couldn't detect its origin. Voices aren't my thing. Visual is more in my line.'

She paused in the hall looking thoughtful. After a moment she continued, 'His face was heavily lined, rugged, and he had very hypnotic blue eyes, the kind that see right through you and always have that hint of a smile in them, as though he knows something no one else does and certainly knows more about you than you do yourself. They were half mocking but in a warm and friendly way. His hands and arms were strong, as were his legs. He looked fit, not as though he worked out, but he had the fitness of someone who walks everywhere and does physical work. He was probably early sixties, wearing shorts and those brown leather sandals the monks at the abbey sometimes wear.'

Yes, Horton had seen them, and they were not unlike the ones he'd seen on Lomas, the beachcomber, back in October. He too had had that kind of ingrained tan Felice had just described, as though he'd also lived abroad. But her description of Ben was not Lomas. He hadn't expected it to be. Ben was decidedly the man in the mortuary. Horton recognized the description even without the hypnotic blue eyes and gravel voice, and the tan had been replaced by the pallor of death.

'Will that do?'

'Perfectly.'

'Then let's go and look at your boat.'

But as they climbed in her car her phone rang. A shadow crossed her face. 'I'll have to postpone that. My father's not well.'

'I'm sorry,' he said, keenly disappointed.

'So am I. I'll take you back to Cowes.'

'No, please don't. It will delay you. I can get a taxi. I'll take another look round here.'

'If you're sure.' She looked relieved.

'Positive.'

'I'll call you when I get any new information. Will you call me and keep me updated?'

'Yes.' He handed over his card and watched her drive away with a keen sense of disappointment that they hadn't been able to spend more time together. Maybe next time, he thought, hoping there would be one.

Fifteen

Monday

Over the weekend Horton thought a great deal about Felice. He called her mobile but, disappointingly, got her voice mail. He left a message to thank her for her help and said that he hoped her father would make a quick recovery. He wondered how the accident had affected him and what ailed him. Horton hoped it wasn't anything serious, but the shadow that had crossed her dark attractive face told him it was.

He spent some time on the internet looking up aboriginal paintings and the artist with the magical name, Munduwalawala of South East Arnhem Land, in the Northern Territory. He didn't learn much more about Munduwalawala, but he thought back to his enquiries with the Australian police in Nhulunbuy. The town had been relatively new in 1973, when Gordon Eames' body had been found and, although the area had been the traditional homeland of the Yolngu people for more than forty thousand years, it had expanded in the early 1970s after large bauxite deposits had been discovered on the Gove Peninsula in the 1950's. No one knew what Gordon had been doing there, or how he had arrived and ended up dead on the beach. It was suggested he had come in by boat, which he'd fallen from in a drugged stupor, and the boat had drifted and been lost at sea. There had been no post-mortem. Richard Eames had identified his brother, and the body had been privately flown to the UK to be laid in the family vault at their Wiltshire home.

Horton hadn't found any record of a Coroner's Inquest. As far as he could ascertain he only had the Eames' family's word that Gordon Eames had died of a drug overdose, and he didn't trust that one iota. Without proof, Gordon could have died of anything. He might not have died at all. But if Horton challenged Eames, he would just stonewall him.

Monday was a day of enquiries, reports and waiting. Uckfield came in late. Horton saw his car arrive from his office window and watched his squat figure gingerly haul itself out with a wince. He noted the absence of Uckfield's usual strident gait. He looked like a man twenty years older, bent and walking as though on glass. Horton felt concerned for him and, despite Uckfield's predictable short temper, Horton vowed to challenge him on his health.

Bliss was already in her office and as yet hadn't bothered Horton. Long may it last, he thought, as Walters ambled in and began to tackle the piano removers, a mammoth task, he reminded Horton. 'They could be located in the Cayman Islands where Halliwell lived.'

'Then try them first,' Horton re-joined. 'Then Guernsey where he had a bank account. Liaise with Inspector Guilbert.'

Walters put another doughnut in his mouth and fixed his eyes on his computer screen.

Cantelli put in a call to Simply Cellars and Horton, back in his office, read through the coroner's report on Halliwell, which had been emailed to him. As they had no medical records it was impossible to say whether there had been any existing health conditions that had led to his death. The pathologist had found some hardening of the arteries, some swelling of the brain, liver and kidneys, alcohol in the blood stream but not excessive, and no drugs. So that ruled out Elkins' view that Halliwell could have killed himself by a drug overdose. The conclusion was that Halliwell had suffered a coronary artery contraction, or severe spasm; in effect, a tightening of a coronary artery which, being alone on board his boat and unable to summon assistance, had led to a fatal heart attack. The spasm had cut off blood flow through the artery. It wasn't a common cause of a heart attack, but the pathologist had said that alcohol and the cold could have triggered the coronary spasm. The heating unit hadn't been on when the rescue crew had boarded the boat. The cause of death was determined as heart failure, as Chilcott had said. Horton checked the list of the items found on the dead man when he was taken to the mortuary and frowned.

He rang Norris and asked him to check the items PC Wetherton had found on Halliwell's body. Aside from the wallet with no credit or debit cards and only a small sum of money, Halliwell had been wearing a Tag Heuer watch but no ring as described by Redcar. They only had Jason Arlett's opinion of the Ryde Inshore Rescue team that the watch had been a genuine Tag Heuer. It had been listed as being removed from the body by the mortuary attendant, but how did the mortician know whether it was genuine or a fake? And why hadn't Chilcott mentioned it? Why not donate it to the charity shop along with Halliwell's clothes? Because he had known it was the real thing.

Horton called Gaye and was pleased when she answered.

'I've reviewed the post-mortem report on Ben,' she said before he could speak. 'There's nothing wrong with it that I can see, everything was fairly straightforward. Dilated cardiomyopathy – when the heart can't pump enough blood because its main pumping chamber, the left ventricle, is enlarged and weakened.'

As the mortician had informed Horton when he'd viewed the body. 'What causes it?'

'Could have been genetic, or an auto-immune disease where the normal immune response doesn't work properly, is over-active, and attacks the body's healthy cells and organs. Could be a viral infection, such as viral myocarditis, which can cause dilated cardiomyopathy because the virus doesn't clear from the heart. Exposure to toxins such as excessive alcohol and some drugs used in chemotherapy treatment can cause it, but not in Ben's case as there was no sign of cancer, and besides, that cause is rare. Pregnancy can also cause it, but I think we can rule that one out.'

Horton smiled. 'So nothing suspicious.'

'It looks that way.'

'But you're not sure?'

'It wasn't a forensic autopsy, so there could be something that was understandably missed by the pathologist.'

'I'd like to be certain,' Horton said, not that he had any idea of who would have killed Ben, save it being Lomas. 'I'll ask Uckfield if he'll authorize one.'

Gaye said she could conduct it Tuesday if he could rush through the paperwork. 'I've also examined Ben's wood carving tools,' she added, 'and none of them fit the pattern of the wound on the landslip corpse. But the killer could have ditched that particular tool in the sea.'

'Is a coronary artery spasm common? It's what Halliwell died of.'

'Yes, I saw that in the report, which I've also reviewed. There doesn't seem to be anything untoward about his death either. You're more likely to have these spasms if you have conditions that can affect the heart, such as high cholesterol or high blood pressure. Other things that can put someone at risk of coronary artery spasms are smoking, excess use of stimulants, such as cocaine and amphetamines, extreme stress, extreme cold, and alcohol withdrawal, but there was no medical evidence to say he was a drug user or an alcoholic.'

'He had an extensive and expensive cellar.'

'Complete with wine?'

'Yes.'

'Which bears out he wasn't an alcoholic unless the bottles were empty.'

'They weren't, at least not the ones I saw. I didn't go round checking them. But you're right. It seems as though they were bought as an investment. And not having Halliwell's medical records, we've no idea if he had high blood pressure or high cholesterol, or both.'

'His heart was pretty healthy, actually.'

'Could the spasm have been brought on deliberately by some other method?' he asked.

'It's possible. He could have been poisoned or forced to take an overdose, but that would show up during the autopsy and blood tests.'

'Not if there wasn't a full forensic autopsy.'

'No, but the pathologist would have seen other outward signs on the body showing evidence of poisoning. Or it could have been shock induced. That wouldn't show up in an autopsy.'

What kind of shock, wondered Horton? That Halliwell's criminal ways were about to be discovered or exposed *if* he had been a criminal?

Gaye asked if there was any further news on the sailing club arson.

'DC Leonard's on the trail of a night time lone canoeist who could have a penchant for Molotov cocktails and a good aim. A man with a grudge against sailors, or that sailing club, or particularly a grudge against Councillor Levy, the Chief Constable, or Venda Atkinson the latter of which you said earlier was highly unlikely.'

'It could be a woman with a grudge. We make competent canoeists and are renowned for our aim.'

'But arson is more a male thing.'

'Agreed, but it's not impossible for a woman to have committed this crime. Hell hath no fury and all that.'

'Jealous lover or wife?' She could be right. Both Levy and the chief were married, and perhaps one of them had been playing away and the lover, or wife, had taken drastic action. He rang Leonard and left a message on his phone, then he put the thoughts on hold while he went to fetch some sandwiches for them all.

He met Sergeant Warren in the canteen who broke the welcome news to him that two of his officers had caught the highway robbers up to their old tricks early that morning. The woman and older of the two men were, it turned out, known to the police for theft but not of the road kind.

'They usually go in for shoplifting and a spot of house burglary but thought they'd diversify. Anything more on the arson?'

Horton said no, to which Warren replied, 'That won't please the chief but then not much does. How about your landslip corpse?'

Horton briefly brought him up to speed as he paid for the sandwiches.

'PC Jennings happens to be into wood carving. I'll ask him about the tools used. He might come up with some ideas.'

Horton said he'd get Trueman to email over the photographs of the wound. He diverted to the incident suite. Trueman told him that the Land Registry had confirmed the boundary of Beachwood House went as far as the clifftop. Norris had earlier reported that the council could find no trace of any planning application for a log cabin. He had enquiries out for any builders or carpenters who had erected it, but Horton wasn't optimistic that anyone would come through on that. It might have been built by the previous owner. It didn't seem to matter much anyway. It had no bearing on the investigation. Ben had been in situ last May when he had approached the abbey, and Halliwell had known he had been living there. Horton crossed to Dennings who was scowling at the crime board on the Trehams robbery.

'Any progress?'

'Dead end,' grunted Dennings.

On the board were photographs of the stolen items – an emerald and diamond pendant necklace; a diamond clip brooch and bracelet; an Art Deco jade ring; a delicate diamond and sapphire bracelet with a matching heart-shaped diamond sapphire ring, and a Breguet marine date watch, the latter with a value of twenty thousand pounds.

Somewhat more expensive than Halliwell's Tag Heuer watch. And where was the ring that Redcar had seen? On the other Cedric Halliwell's hand, obviously, but why hadn't it been removed when he'd been killed? *If* he had been killed. After all Redcar's Halliwell could have been posing as him with the consent of the real Halliwell, who had died on board his boat.

Horton ventured, 'I take it that all of those items are the genuine thing and have been authenticated?' Judging by Dennings' expression, his question wasn't welcome.

'What do you take me for?' he snapped.

Horton didn't like to comment.

'The Trehams have valuation certifications and proof of purchase,' Dennings continued.

'Except for two pieces,' Horton said. 'Those. They haven't got any value beside them.' He indicated the pictures on the crime board of a diamond and sapphire bracelet and a matching heart-shaped diamond sapphire ring.

'That's because they're paste. Costume jewellery. Not real diamonds.'

Into Horton's mind came the song his mother had sung shortly before her disappearance: *Diamonds are a girl's best friend*. Had she been alluding to the brooch he remembered her wearing, or had there been a ring? He couldn't recall the latter but then he had only been ten. The brooch, he'd been shocked to see again as recently as last April, in a photograph of the late wife of former PC Adrian Stanley who had been sent to investigate Jennifer's disappearance. Horton had visited Stanley to see if he could throw any further light on his mother's disappearance, even though he'd read Stanley's sketchy report demonstrating a luck-lustre investigation, barely questioning anyone who had worked with Jennifer and only one neighbour. Horton believed that Stanley had stolen it but before he could question him, shortly after his visit, the former PC had died of a massive stroke and the picture Horton had seen had vanished. Stanley's son had told him there was no brooch in his father's belongings and no pictures of Mrs Stanley wearing it. If it had been paste then why had all evidence of it vanished?

He'd checked the national database of stolen art and antiques and the internet for any reference to the brooch – a blue diamond centrepiece with a pale pink stone beneath it and surrounding it, like petals, four clear diamonds – and had found none. He'd also asked a couple of jewellery experts he knew, again with nil result.

Dennings was saying, 'The scumbag thieves will get a nasty shock when they discover those two items are of crap value.'

'Why did the Trehams put them in the safe?'

'Because they were of sentimental value. They'd been given to Mrs Treham by her aunt shortly before the aunt died five months ago. The trail's cold. This case is going nowhere, which seems to be the same with your landslip corpse.'

Quite literally, thought Horton, knocking and entering Uckfield's office. He told a pale-skinned Uckfield that Dr Clayton could conduct a forensic post-mortem on Ben the following day if he authorized it. Horton expected Uckfield to refuse, or quibble about it, and had prepared himself for an argument, but Uckfield simply nodded and muttered something about sorting it out with Trueman.

Horton did so, postponing his questions to the Super on his health, on account that Uckfield's phone rang as he was about to do so. He asked Trueman to ring through to Dr Clayton to confirm it, and returned to CID, his mind mulling over what Dennings had told him. Had Dennings checked with jewellery experts that those two items really were paste? They must be though, because they hadn't been insured.

From the machine outside the office, he bought Walters and Cantelli tea and himself a black coffee. As he entered CID, Cantelli waved him over excitedly.

'I've finally managed to speak to Derek Coppens at Simply Cellars. He gave me the same description of Cedric Halliwell as Redcar, including the scarring on the hand, which means whoever Chilcott and Nansen dealt with was a phoney.'

'Not necessarily.'

'Well Coppens is convinced the man he dealt with is Halliwell. He was shocked to hear of his death. The last time he spoke to him was on the telephone last June. He asked if he was happy with the cellar and satisfied that all the wine they held for him had been safely transported there. The telephone number Coppens had for Halliwell is the same one Redcar had. Halliwell said he was completely satisfied. The last time Coppens saw Halliwell was in February, when he commissioned the bespoke cellar.'

'So who posed as Cedric Halliwell, took up residence in Beachwood House, made a will with Chilcott, and then ended up dead on the boat?' Horton handed out the sandwiches.

Cantelli indicated his Tupperware box containing his homemade ones. Walters leaned across and took the packet that Cantelli would have had, saying, 'Will the real Cedric Halliwell please stand up? Or maybe he's already lying down in the mortuary.'

'The landslip corpse?' Cantelli posed, tucking into a small square cheese and pickle sandwich. 'Could he be the man with the scarred hand, the Halliwell that both Coppens and Redcar dealt with?'

'If he is then there's no scarring left on the bones to confirm it,' Horton replied while wrestling with a particularly tough piece of meat that the packet said was ham; it tasted more like sandpaper. Not that he'd ever eaten the latter, just that this meat was so rough and chewy that he thought decorators must have been in the factory while it was being made and someone had slapped in a slice of sandpaper instead of ham. He threw it aside, wishing he'd plumped for something simple like cheese.

Cantelli sipped his tea and continued, 'Halliwell, the real one, stored his wine with Simply Cellars for fifteen years. He'd visit the warehouse once a year to inspect his wine. Not to drink it.'

'Seems pointless to me,' muttered Walters. 'Like looking at a hamburger and saying you'll keep it for a rainy day.'

'Hamburgers go off,' said Horton.

'So does wine.'

'Not this kind,' Cantelli said. 'I never knew there was so much to it. Storing wine is a serious business and a delicate operation, I've been told, but when you're handling thousands of pounds worth of property which could shatter in an instant and be wiped up with a dishcloth, you would have to be cautious. Give me bricks and mortar any day, and that's what Coppens' company has also done. They've invested in a state-of-the-art temperature controlled warehouse for storing the stuff, and charge their exclusive clientele for the privilege of keeping their wine there. According to Coppens there are only a handful of these especially equipped warehouses around the country. Theirs is just outside Guildford, which is why we don't know about it, because it's not on our patch. They look after about twenty five million pounds worth of their customers' wines, people who can't store it on their premises or who don't want to.'

Walters gave a low whistle. 'Blimey, that makes robbing the off licence look puny.'

'And Coppens says they have such tight security, including infrared alarms and twenty-four hour surveillance, that the thieves would need stamina, strength and intellect to even get within spitting distance of the warehouse.'

'Well, that rules out most of the scumbags on our patch,' Walters said and belched.

Horton agreed. Robbery on that scale meant the big boys, or inside knowledge, or both. He was momentarily distracted by thoughts of the Trehams jewellery robbery – carefully planned, executed and timed. Big Boys or an inside job?

'Coppens says all their staff are security vetted by a professional security company.'

'Not Mike Danby's, by any chance?' Horton asked, drinking his coffee, thinking of that expensive wine in Lord Eames' Isle of Wight cellar which Danby's company handled the security for.

'No. A company called Waterleighs based in London.' Cantelli referred to his notes. 'The serious wines, such as the Mouton 1961 and the Lafite 1945, are kept in special secure cages. Each case is bar tagged and labelled with unique identification numbers linked to the customer who owns it. Everything is on computer, which means we can check the wine which was stored by Coppens' company on behalf of Cedric Halliwell with those catalogued by Charles Nansen for probate purposes.'

'Good. And Nansen must know that, so I can't see him helping himself to a few bottles.'

'Maybe Chilcott will have thought the same,' but Cantelli sounded dubious. 'Coppens is emailing me the list. Though that doesn't mean if there is any wine missing it was pilfered by Chilcott. The real, or fraudulent Halliwell, might have drunk it after it was shipped to Beachwood House.'

'True.'

'Halliwell paid Simply Cellars from a Guernsey bank account, and the only address they had for him was care of that bank, Morgans. Coppens also said that it was because Halliwell travelled a lot, but he has no idea what he did for a living, *if* he worked. He knew nothing about Halliwell's personal circumstances or background. Said it wasn't their business.'

'Would have been if Halliwell had failed to pay, which he obviously didn't. Any hint that the wine they stored for him came from dubious sources?'

'None whatsoever, and you'd have thought I'd uttered a profanity when I suggested it. Coppens said they were instructed by Halliwell to liaise with the architect, Gary Redcar, over the building of the cellar. When it was finished, they moved all Halliwell's wine there. It wasn't simply a case of loading it onto a van either. The wine bottles had to be gently removed by hand and individually wrapped before being packed in hay-lined boxes to reduce the vibration during transport.'

'They must have waited for a calm day on the ferry then,' Horton said slightly tongue-in-cheek. 'Wouldn't want all that valuable cargo rolling around.'

Cantelli smiled. 'They then made sure the wine was safely installed and that the cellar was operating as it should before they left, and that was in May.'

Walters swallowed the last mouthful of his sandwich as Bliss marched in.

'On holiday are you?' she said scathingly, eyeing them.

'Cantelli's just been reporting on what Simply Cellars have told him about Halliwell,' Horton replied.

'And?'

Horton quickly relayed the gist of it.

'Write it up, Sergeant, and I'll tell Detective Superintendent Uckfield.'

I bet you will, thought Horton. Bliss would take the credit for it.

'Have you anything on piano removers yet, Walters?'

'No, Ma'am.'

'Then get on with it.'

Horton's mobile rang. It was Jane from the fingerprint bureau. He answered as Bliss hovered.

'We've got a match on the prints you lifted from Beachwood House and the boat,' Jane announced.

'You mean aside from Nansen's, Arlett and his colleague?'

'I don't have Mr Nansen's yet, but they are not Arlett's, and neither are they his colleague.'

'Then whose are they?' he asked, sitting forward. Cantelli eyed him keenly. Bliss frowned while Walters sniffed and put his eyes on the computer screen.

'They're the prints of a man called Michael Paignton.'

'Who the blazes is he? And why have we got them on file?' Horton asked, stunned.

'Because Paignton was convicted of the murder of Roger Salcombe in 1970.'

Sixteen

Three hours later, Horton, along with Cantelli, Bliss, Uckfield and Trueman were assembled in the incident suite. After the call from the bureau, Bliss had hot-footed it to Uckfield, and Trueman had been charged to get what he could on Michael Paignton from the case file, while Horton had read online all the press reports he could find on the trial and the obituaries on the murder victim, Roger Salcombe. He'd also called Inspector Guilbert in Guernsey and asked him to check for any records on a Michael Paignton. Guilbert said he was still awaiting information from the solicitors, Selwyns, who had handled the purchase of Beachwood House. He could confirm the bank account at Morgans in Halliwell's name, but he couldn't get a physical description of Halliwell from them. So far they'd drawn a blank on property owned by Halliwell, but he would continue enquiries and check out any registered in the name of Michael Paignton.

Horton now studied the photograph that Trueman had obtained from the case file and printed off. It was of a young man with fair features, wide frightened eyes and an angular jaw. He'd seen pictures of Paignton in the press reports but those had been taken so many years ago that it was difficult to see if he fitted the description of either of the two Halliwells. He said as much.

'He might be neither,' Uckfield grunted, mopping his brow with a large handkerchief. Horton thought the Super looked worse than he had that morning.

'His fingerprints are all over the house, and too many to have been merely a visitor. They're also on the boat. He has to be one of the Halliwells.'

Bliss said, 'Were any of his prints found in Ben's cabin?'

'No. And Ben's weren't found in Beachwood House. Neither did those I lifted match the prints of the landslip corpse, which Dr Clayton managed to obtain and sent over to the bureau. However, a more thorough examination of the house might find some and possibly hairs we could get DNA from.' Would Uckfield authorize that, Horton wondered?

Uckfield said, 'What do we know about Paignton?'

A fair amount, thought Horton. And what he had discovered had disturbed him. He'd learned with a shock that Paignton had been a student at the London School of Economics in 1967, the same time as Jennifer and the others in the photograph, and what's more, Paignton had been involved with the Radical Student Alliance. He must have known Jennifer. And he must have known Antony Dormand, Rory Mortimer, Zachary Benham, Timothy Wilson, James Royston and Gordon and Richard Eames. Horton's mind had raced at this new connection. How did the landslip corpse fit in, though? Who was he?

Horton was growing more convinced that this investigation had something to do with the men in that photograph of 1967, and with Jennifer's disappearance in 1978, and it wasn't simply an obsessive delusion. He felt a mixture of unease and excitement, along with a creeping sensation of foreboding. He wasn't, of course, going to mention any of this. He needed to see where this led first and even then, he debated whether he'd mention it. Maybe he wouldn't be given the chance to keep it quiet though. Any new developments in the investigation could take the matter out of his hands. A thought that filled him with dread. The last thing he wanted was his personal life paraded for all to examine. He put his full attention on Trueman while mentally holding his breath, waiting to see if the sergeant had uncovered anything he hadn't already read in the press reports.

'Michael Paignton was sentenced to twenty-two years for the murder of Roger Salcombe who was found stabbed in his flat in Kensington on 13 February 1970. Paignton was discovered crouching beside the body, holding a knife, covered in blood and out of his head on LSD. He served twenty years and was released early in 1990. There is no record of what happened to him after that. He hasn't paid UK tax or national insurance. He's never claimed benefits, and he doesn't show up on any electoral roll. He could have changed his name, left the country, or died and his body has never been identified, because there is no record of his death having been registered.'

'Which it wouldn't have been if he is the Cedric Halliwell found dead on the boat,' said Horton.

'Or the Halliwell with the scarred hand,' Bliss ventured.

Cantelli said, 'The Halliwell with the scarred hand could have been killed by Paignton or Ben and his body dumped at sea.'

'Hence the rapid purchase of the boat,' Horton added. 'But it being moored in Bembridge Marina would mean they'd have to transport the body there, which they could have done by using the boat in front of Ben's cabin. That has a powerful engine, and it's planed to make it go even faster,' he explained to Cantelli and Bliss's baffled looks. 'Or perhaps Ben and Paignton used it to dispose of Halliwell's body. Ben lived in the cabin and by all accounts led a simple life, but that doesn't mean he *was* simple.'

Trueman said, 'Why not live in the big house? Seems a funny place to shove your relatives and buddies, in a cabin on the beach.'

'Depends on what they're like.' Horton thought of his ex-in-laws. They would have certainly preferred to shove him in a cabin and as far away from their daughter and grandchild as was possible. 'Ben might have insisted on living there. Paignton knew he was there. You can see the cabin quite clearly from the study window in Beachwood House and right down into the bay through the binoculars. The two men knew each other. I'm certain of that.'

'Alright, let's get back to the point,' growled Uckfield. 'What have we got on Salcombe, the murder victim?'

Horton answered, 'From the press reports and obituaries, it's clear the case and subsequent trial caused a sensation because Salcombe was an eminent plastic surgeon. He was born in 1920 and was studying medicine when war broke out. He volunteered to work with the burns unit and was sent to Queen Victoria Hospital, East Grinstead in Sussex, thirty miles from London. A Plastic Surgery and Burns Unit had been established there in anticipation of expected air raids on a colossal scale and a mass influx of wounded servicemen. He worked there with the finest plastic surgeons in the world. After the war, he returned to his medical studies, continuing to specialize in burns and became one of the leading specialists in his field. At the time of his death he worked both within the National Health Service and as a private consultant with a clinic on Harley Street. He came from a wealthy Dorset family. His father was in the diplomatic service, his mother the daughter of a large engineering component manufacturer based in Yorkshire, who left her a considerable fortune. He was educated at Harrow and Cambridge.'

'And Michael Paignton's background?' asked Bliss.

'The only son of a bus driver and a machinist from the East End of London. His father was a Japanese prisoner-of-war who died in 1948, a year after Michael was born. He was raised by his mother who died the year Paignton went to the London School of Economics in 1967 to study politics.'

Two of the men in Horton's picture from 1967, Rory Mortimer and Zachary Benham, had also been studying politics. And there was also the fact that Salcombe had been a burns specialist and Zachary Benham had perished in a fire – or had he? Ben had scarring on his back, which could have been caused by burns, and the Halliwell who had met the architect and Coppens of Simply Cellars had scarring on his hands, which again could have been the result of a burn.

Cantelli said, 'So Paignton didn't have any family to help him when he came out of prison in 1990?'

'No.' And by then no friends either, thought Horton. If those six men in the 1967 photograph *had* been his friends. If the sixth man was Gordon Eames and not his brother, Richard, then all of them had died by the time of Paignton's release. Paignton might have known Richard Eames, but Horton couldn't see his Lordship helping an ex-convict. But Paignton *had* made for the Isle of Wight, his fingerprints were testimony to that, and it was where Eames had a property. It was also where Dormand had been posing as a monk at the abbey, and where Ben had been working on carving that bench seat, not to mention living in the log cabin beneath Beachwood House. Horton tried to tell himself to keep an open mind, but he was silently searching for more links in the chain he was mentally forging.

Trueman took up the story, 'Paignton had a previous conviction for criminal damage, while protesting with the Radical Student Alliance against the Vietnam War. There's no mention of any female or male partners, and nothing to indicate that Salcombe and Paignton were in a relationship. Paignton was twenty-seven years younger than Salcombe. The prosecution claimed Paignton went to Salcombe for money to buy drugs, and when Salcombe refused, he killed him.'

'How did they know one another?' Cantelli asked.

Horton relayed what he'd learned from the newspaper reports. 'The two men met in a pub and struck up a friendship. It was reported that Salcombe, after befriending the younger man, had been exploited by him, Paignton being a ruthless drug addict. But that could just be media talk. The truth could be miles away from that.'

Trueman interjected, 'I haven't got the trial notes but Paignton's statement in the case file says he met Salcombe in The Green Man in Wapping, long since demolished. The landlord said he'd seen Michael Paignton in the pub a few times, but he couldn't swear as to seeing Roger Salcombe there.'

'Hardly sounds like Salcombe's type of place,' said Uckfield.

Horton silently agreed. 'From the press reports it says that no one from Paignton's family and none of his friends were called to testify as to his character because his barrister thought it might prejudice his case further.'

Uckfield said, 'Either that or he knew Paignton was guilty and couldn't be bothered.'

'Paignton doesn't seem to have had a very good defence team,' Horton said, suspicions running round his head.

Cantelli said, 'Did he appeal?'

'Not as far as I can see from the press reports.'

'And not according to the case file,' added Trueman.

Why not, wondered Horton? Perhaps he simply gave up or his brain was too scrambled to think of it. 'Why didn't he get parole?' he asked.

Trueman answered, 'Because he always claimed he was innocent and he showed no remorse for what he'd done. His record of criminal damage didn't come out until after the verdict, but we all know a clever barrister can raise it and, once hinted at, even if it is struck off, it's firmly planted in the jury's mind.'

Horton said, 'And Paignton being a radical student probably didn't strike too sympathetic a figure in the box.'

'He *did* kill Salcombe,' Uckfield stressed.

'Did he though?' challenged Horton. 'Maybe he was framed.' The more he heard the less Horton liked this.

'Why?' snapped Uckfield.

'And by whom?' added Bliss.

'If I had the answer to both questions, we might be able to close the current investigation into the murder of the landslip corpse,' Horton smartly re-joined. There was a moment's silence in which Bliss opened her mouth to retort, then closed it. He continued, 'In 1970 the crime scene wouldn't have been as carefully preserved as it is now, and perhaps the real killer, *if* there was one other than Michael Paignton, was clever. He'd have had ample time to clean up after himself and incriminate Paignton, who was out of his mind on LSD.' And Horton thought of someone else who had been psychotic and so out of his mind on LSD that he had ended up being committed to a psychiatric hospital, where he had allegedly perished along with twenty three other men in a fire, Zachary Benham. 'Who called the police?'

Trueman answered, 'A friend of Salcombe's, George Patterlee, who was worried when Salcombe didn't show up for a meal that night as arranged. He called round just after eleven p.m., found the apartment door unlocked, Paignton crouching on the floor, spaced out, and beside him, the bloody figure of Salcombe. Paignton had the knife in his hand, he was covered with blood consistent with the stabbing.'

Bliss said, 'How did he get the LSD? Was he a habitual user?'

'He had no record of any drugs offence, and he claimed he had never taken any. The medical examination after his arrest confirmed that he wasn't a heroin addict, but it couldn't confirm whether or not he'd imbibed other drugs.'

Horton felt uneasy. This had the smell of a fit up. Surely he couldn't be the only one to see this? Did Uckfield scent it? If so, he showed no sign of it, though he was grimacing but not, Horton thought, because of the facts Trueman was laying before them. Uckfield was in pain.

Trueman said, 'The autopsy on Salcombe showed he wasn't a drug user and hadn't taken LSD or any other drug the night he died. Alcohol was found in his blood and two bottles of whisky at the scene of the crime were empty. One of the glasses had Paignton's prints on it, the other Salcombe's. Paignton couldn't say where he had got the drug. He firmly believed his drink was spiked, but no trace of a drug was found in either glass.'

No, it wouldn't have been. Someone had cleaned the scene, Horton could feel it in his gut. But why frame Paignton? Had he got on the wrong side of someone powerful? Had he discovered something dangerous? What though? Or was Paignton the scapegoat because Salcombe had to be eliminated? Salcombe was the one who knew too much, an eminent plastic surgeon… a specialist in burns… a fire at a psychiatric hospital two years before his death…

A cold shudder crept up Horton's spine. Was Salcombe's death the work of Antony Dormand, the man who had confessed to being a paid assassin? Had Dormand recently tracked Paignton to the Isle of Wight and killed him because Paignton knew the truth about that fire? But, no, Dormand couldn't have done; he died in October, three months before Halliwell had been found dead on his boat and before the landslip corpse had been killed. But as Cantelli had said, Halliwell with the scarred hand could have been killed any time before October and his body ditched at sea. Or perhaps Dormand hadn't died on that stormy night and had returned to kill. The flaw in that though was the fingerprints, Paignton's, which had been all over the house. That indicated that he had been living there more recently, and certainly after Dormand had taken out to sea. So the odds were that Halliwell, found dead on the boat on 1 February, had in reality been Paignton.

Bliss said, 'So Michael Paignton on his release from prison, left the country and assumed another name, Cedric Halliwell. He subsequently made a fortune, possibly illegally or by mixing with dubious company, lived in the Cayman Islands, had a bank account and solicitor in Guernsey, and then decided to buy a property on the Isle of Wight. Only he ended up dead on that boat. Someone from his past caught up with him.'

Trueman continued, 'Paignton couldn't remember what he had done or how he had got to Salcombe's apartment. No taxi driver came forward. A witness, Mrs Rosemary Shergold, saw Paignton entering the apartment at nine fifteen in the evening. There isn't a concierge service, or there wasn't in 1970, and neither was there a lift attendant. No one else in the apartment block saw Paignton or anyone else enter or leave at around that time. Rosemary Shergold had taken particular notice of Paignton because he didn't look the type who would normally be calling on anyone in the select apartments. He was, according to her statement, scruffily dressed and unshaven. He had a wild look about the eyes. He got in the lift, didn't speak to her and got out on the floor below. She saw him press the bell to Roger Salcombe's flat. She hadn't seen Paignton before. She heard raised voices at about nine forty-five but couldn't hear what was being said. She said that she had never heard a raised voice until that night, and neither had she seen anyone else visit Salcombe's apartment. She couldn't swear to the fact that it was Salcombe's voice and she hadn't heard Paignton speak. No one else in the apartments heard the argument. The owners of the apartment below Salcombe's were away, so there was only the apartment above his, which was Mrs Shergold's. She'd never had any cause to complain to Salcombe. He was a quiet, polite and distinguished gentleman. She knew he was an eminent plastic surgeon. She'd met him a few times in the lift and in the lobby, and they'd exchanged the usual greetings and spoken about the weather. She used to hear him playing the piano–'

'The piano?' Horton repeated sharply, causing everyone to look at him.

'Yes, why?'

Cantelli knew he was thinking about the expensive Yamaha piano in Beachwood House. But lots of people had pianos and some of them expensive ones. He asked Trueman if Paignton was a pianist.

'There's no mention of it in the case notes or his prison file, but then he'd hardly have been allowed to play a piano while inside.'

Cantelli said, 'He could have picked it up again after his release and bought that piano in Beachwood House. Walters is still working on tracing that.'

Trueman continued, 'The counsel for the prosecution was led by Sir Barry Drummond, a notable and respected barrister. He died eight years ago.'

Horton added, 'I read in the press that Salcombe's parents were dead. He had no brothers or sisters and he'd never married. He left his estate, which was considerable, to a medical research charity and the rehabilitation of victims of burns.' And Paignton had left his body to medical science.

Trueman said, 'Paignton was found guilty by a unanimous verdict and sentenced to twenty-two years.'

Cantelli said, 'What kind of weapon was used to kill Salcombe?'

'A serrated kitchen knife.'

'Who visited Paignton in prison?' asked Horton.

'Only those from the prison visiting system.'

Horton frowned as he considered this. It seemed unusual. His student friends had deserted him then.

'He spent most of his time in Parkhurst on the Isle of Wight after being transferred from Wormwood where he served the first three years of his sentence.'

'Why was he transferred?' asked Bliss.

'He was attacked and wounded in a fight at Wormwood, not of his instigation. The assault was vicious. No knives. Fists and feet. Paignton was hospitalized but we're not allowed access to his medical records, and even if we could get them under the Access to Health Records Act of 1990, we can only get information after 1991. After he was moved to Parkhurst, he was a model prisoner. Quiet, reserved, intelligent, did what he was told, took any opportunity he could to study, and he helped other prisoners with literacy skills. He was released on the 4 March 1990.'

'And finally returned to the live on the Isle of Wight, a place where he had spent seventeen years incarcerated,' mused Horton. 'Now that we know there were two Cedric Halliwells and one of them was Michael Paignton, it might make proving that will tricky. I'd like to re-interview Halliwell's executor, Chilcott, and break the news to him that his client is not who he thought he was. He also needs to be questioned about Halliwell's possessions, especially what happened to the Tag Heuer watch. We shall need access to all the paperwork he extracted from Beachwood House, although I can't see him handing them over without a warrant.'

Uckfield said, 'Then I'll get one. And you'd better break the bad news to the abbot because he and his monks might not be coming into a tidy inheritance after all.'

The briefing broke up. Tomorrow Horton would return to the island. Cantelli was relieved not to be detailed to go with him.

Seventeen

Tuesday

Chilcott looked worried when Horton entered his office just after one o'clock the next day. He looked even more perturbed when Horton broke the news to him that it appeared the Halliwell who had made the will was most probably an imposter. Horton had come accompanied by Sergeant Norris and a warrant. Norris had met him outside the lawyer's office. Horton had travelled on the ferry with his Harley.

'But you're not a hundred percent sure?' Chilcott said, blinking hard.

'Not until we have fully investigated the situation.' Horton saw no reason to tell Chilcott about Michael Paignton and the scarred hand on the other Halliwell. Not yet anyway. 'We're also checking how he accumulated his wealth. If it was acquired illegally then–'

'You don't have to spell it out to me, Inspector, I am a lawyer,' Chilcott snapped and ran a hand over his gelled hair. 'I'll have to tell the abbot.'

That would save Horton a job but he needed to speak to Dom Daniel Briar anyway. He wanted to ask him if he had ever heard of a man called Michael Paignton. Maybe by the time he got to the abbey, Chilcott would have broken the news to the abbot that the abbey might no longer be the legal benefactor. 'Everything will have to be frozen including any further work on the estate by yourself.'

'I realize that,' Chilcott replied with acidity, obviously annoyed that his nice fat fee was going down the drain.

'And we need all the documentation you took from the house and boat, and all the correspondence between you and other parties. I have a warrant.'

Chilcott puffed out his cheeks. 'If you must,' he tetchily replied, adding, 'where is the real Cedric Halliwell then if he wasn't the man who died on that boat?'

'That's what we are trying to establish.'

'Is he that body that was found in the landslip?'

'It's one possibility.'

'And he was killed by this imposter?'

'Possibly,' Horton said. 'We'd also like to know what happened to Mr Halliwell's possessions.'

'I told you, I gave them to the charity shop.'

'Including the watch.'

Chilcott squirmed. His eyes flicked to Norris. Chilcott knew they had checked. Bluff it out or admit it? His forehead was perspiring.

'No. I kept that. The abbot was quite happy about it,' he declared with an air of defiance.

'You know that we will check with him.'

'Then check away,' Chilcott replied.

'And we'll discover that you told Dom Daniel Briar it was just a cheap watch. Whereas it was Tag Heuer worth about six thousand pounds.'

'Is it? One watch is much the same as another to me.'

'That's bullshit and you know it.'

'Then prove it.'

'Maybe we will,' Horton said calmly, causing a flicker of alarm in the lawyer's eyes. Horton was convinced Chilcott had also helped himself to some of the wine in that cellar but proving that, as he and Cantelli had already discussed, could be difficult unless they found it in his house. Even then he could have claimed to have bought it and lost the receipts. And even if the wine was listed on the itinerary which Simply Cellars were sending over, that didn't mean that Halliwell hadn't drunk the missing wine after it had been transported to his cellar, or that the imposter, Paignton, hadn't drunk it.

Horton rose. 'Please give the Halliwell file to Sergeant Norris.'

Norris had instructions to keep hold of it at Newport Station until Horton could call to collect it. He left the solicitor looking exceedingly grumpy and made his way to the abbey. In the car park he tried Carina Musgrove's mobile number but again got her automated voicemail. He left a message saying who he was and asked her to call him. He said he wanted to go over the statement she had made on finding Ben's body. He reassured her that it was just routine and nothing to be concerned about.

He next rang the station. Walters reported that Cantelli had been called away by Bliss. He wasn't sure why. Walters said that no one in the UK had shipped a piano to Beachwood House, and he was still waiting to hear from the Cayman Islands and the Guernsey police if anyone there had carried out the specialist removal job.

'Surely there can't be many specialist piano removers in the Cayman Islands. Or Guernsey come to that. They're both small islands,' Horton said. 'Chase them up. No, hold on. Have you tried the UK companies who might have sold Halliwell that piano?'

'No.'

'Then get on to them. Halliwell or Paignton might have bought it more recently.'

'Do you know how many there are?' Walters said warily.

'No, but it's a top-of-the-range instrument so start with all the upmarket sellers.'

In the abbey bookshop Horton asked if he could see the abbot. When Dom Daniel Briar joined him, he waved aside Horton's apology for troubling him again. Horton quickly broke the news that the abbey might not be a benefactor of Halliwell's will. He explained why and that all matters were suspended while they investigated.

'I'm disappointed, of course, but also puzzled or perhaps not. The impostor might have viewed the bequest to us as atonement for his sins.'

A thought that Cantelli had originally expressed. Horton had wondered if Paignton had come to the abbey on his release from prison in 1990 and it was because of that he had decided to leave a fortune that he may or may not have legally possessed to the abbey.

'What I'm going to tell you now, I do so in confidence, Father, because we need your help, if you can give it.'

'You have it and my assurance of confidentiality.'

'Thank you. The man who posed as Cedric Halliwell and made the will was, we believe, Michael Paignton.' Horton watched the abbot's expression carefully and saw only bemusement. 'Does the name mean anything to you?'

'No. I'm sorry it doesn't.'

'You never heard Brother Norman mention him?'

The abbot looked surprised. 'No.'

Horton could see the abbot quickly trying to put the disappearance of Brother Norman in October with a dead man found on his boat in February posing as Halliwell and couldn't. Horton didn't blame him.

Dom Daniel Briar said, 'I can ask if anyone heard Brother Norman mention Michael Paignton.'

'Thank you. I also wondered if you could check through your records to see if Michael Paignton ever stayed here in your guest house around 1990.'

'Of course. Anything we can do to help.'

Horton asked him if Chilcott had requested he keep the watch that Halliwell had been found wearing on the boat. By the abbot's expression, Horton could see that Chilcott hadn't even mentioned it. That didn't surprise him.

Horton thanked the abbot and left. He didn't raise his hopes of receiving new information from the abbey, and neither did he from the house he was about to call on. He was certain that his Lordship wouldn't be at home. There didn't seem a lot of point in going there but as before, when he had gone on a whim in October from the abbey, he thought he would once more. Not that he expected history to repeat itself and Lomas to appear on Eames' private beach, not unless he was in the house or around Eames' grounds and spotted him on the surveillance equipment. Someone else might witness his arrival, though, especially if he made a point of trespassing again through Eames' private woods and down to the beach. Eames himself might have an alert linked to his laptop, phone or computer. And one of Danby's operatives might pick up his movements and report it back to Danby.

He turned off the main road just beyond Wootton and headed down the tree lined lane marked 'Private'. He wondered how long the landslip corpse would have lain undisturbed but for him stumbling over him. That had been a fluke. But for him the abbey would have got their inheritance and Chilcott his nice fat lawyer's fee. If those prints on the card Lomas had given him hadn't been identified as Ben's, he'd never have come to the island in the first place. The hand of fate can sometimes play funny buggers with people.

He pulled over at the edge of a field by a gate with a 'Keep Out' sign on it. In the middle of the field was a small group of stone buildings. The last time he had been here in October he had ignored the sign and made for the buildings. They hadn't been inhabited. The grass heading to them and around them had been wild and overgrown. It was the same now but with one slight difference. Perhaps the recent wind and rain had beaten it down. Two of the buildings were adjoined in the shape of an L, and another close by with a furnace was detached from them. It was derelict. He'd searched it in October and had found only earth and dirt. The same would still apply.

He turned his scrutiny on the other two buildings. Only the smallest of them boasted a roof, windows and doors. He recalled the strong, weathered oak door which had been secured with a fairly new padlock. There had been no evidence of anyone living there and there didn't seem to be any signs of life now.

He continued on his way. After a short distance he drew up at the large wooden gates set in the high brick wall, with security cameras mounted on the pillars. Removing his helmet, he silenced the Harley and pressed the intercom. There was no answer, as he had expected. He was about to turn away when a female voice crackled and, with a start, despite its slight distortion, it was one he recognized. This he hadn't expected.

'Come in, Inspector.'

The gate swung open and he had no option but to head up the gravel driveway to the house where, waiting on the threshold, was Agent Harriet Eames, Lord Richard Eames' daughter who worked for Europol. Was she here on holiday or connected with her work at Europol? He couldn't think what case she might be working on but then he wasn't privy to every criminal activity which went on in Hampshire. Besides, it was her house and none of his business what she was doing here. She must have been surprised to see him, although she didn't show it, or any curiosity as to why a detective she had worked with on a couple of investigations last summer should suddenly appear on her doorstep.

She was as immaculately made up as ever, wearing a white shirt tucked into tight-fitting jeans. Her shoulder length blonde hair was loose but her bright blue eyes looked tired, and there was a strain around her mouth and eyes that hadn't been there the last time he had seen her in August. She was also paler than he remembered. Perhaps she had been unwell or working too hard. Or perhaps she had been engaged on a particularly demanding and harrowing investigation for Europol that had left its mark on her and she needed some time off work to recover from it.

She invited him in and eagerly he stepped inside a roomy, beautifully decorated modern hall, with exquisite and probably valuable paintings of yachts on the walls. Felice would love them. Eames might even have bought some of them from her gallery in Cowes. 'I wondered if your father was at home.'

'He's not. Can I help at all?' Harriet asked, looking concerned.

Could she? He doubted it. Certainly not in connection with her father's possible involvement in Jennifer's past, but she might pass on a message to her father that would get Eames curious and maybe even worried that Horton was getting close to the truth. Or was he?

He said, 'I'm working on an investigation which could link to a man I met on your private beach here in October.'

There was a flash of surprise and bewilderment before her expression cleared and she said, 'Would you tell me about it over coffee, sir? I can ask my father to contact you.'

He should tell her to call him Andy. He felt uncomfortable about that when he suspected her father of abduction and murder. Still that was hardly her fault. 'Thanks, and it's Andy.'

She looked pleased.

He followed her through the hall to a large kitchen at the rear of the house. His pulse beat a little faster, not just because he was inside Eames' house, but because Harriet always made him feel that way. The kitchen was practically the size of a football pitch. She crossed to a coffee machine that looked so complicated he thought you probably needed a degree in engineering or artificial intelligence to operate it. Either Harriet Eames had both or she had honed her skill by making more coffee than a barista.

His gaze strayed to the immaculate grounds where, in the wall at the far end, he saw the wooden gate which he knew from his visit in October fronted on to the shore and pontoon where Eames kept his yacht during the sailing season. The yacht hadn't been there in October when he had met the beachcomber, Lomas. Horton wondered if it was now.

'This is a lovely house,' he said.

'Yes, it is.' But she spoke distractedly. Perhaps because she was busy operating the coffee machine. Then she said, 'This man you met on the beach in October, who was he?'

'He told me his name was Wyndham Lomas and that he was a beachcomber artist, but I've been unable to trace him.' He could see that the name didn't mean anything to her. 'I thought at first he might be connected with the body of the private investigator which was found on the beach, but he wasn't. Then I wondered if he could have been a guest in your house and could have come through that gate.' He nodded at it set in the wall.

'My father didn't mention anyone staying here.' She handed him his coffee. 'And no one could have got in here without an alert sounding on Mr Danby's and my father's security monitors.'

She didn't invite him to sit, not because she wanted rid of him, it was as though she was afraid to. There was a sense of awkwardness about her that he thought highly unusual. She had always appeared extremely confident. Maybe he made her nervous.

He continued, 'Could he have been renting one of the outbuildings?'

'No, they're derelict. How does he figure in your investigation?' She picked up her own coffee mug and took a sip from it.

'He gave me a business card, but it didn't have any address on it. I had that card checked for fingerprints and there was no match until last Wednesday with an unidentified man in the mortuary. I came over to identify him, thinking I would find Lomas, but it was a completely different man. One we only know by the name of Ben who was found dead in his cabin in Luccombe Bay by a woman called Carina Musgrove who had arrived by boat.'

She studied him so hard that he felt uneasy and concerned, not for himself but for her. He could see that something troubled her deeply. After a moment she said, 'I heard about the body found in the landslip there. Do you think it is this man called Lomas?'

'No. I think he could be the real Cedric Halliwell, the owner of the house above the bay, whereas the man found dead on his boat on 1 February posing as Cedric Halliwell was called Michael Paignton, convicted of murder in 1970 and released in 1990. It's possible that your father knew Michael Paignton.'

'How?' she asked shocked, then puzzled.

'Because Paignton could have been a close friend of Lord Eames' brother, and your uncle, Gordon.'

She looked thoughtful. 'Which is why you're here. You thought my father might know these men. But if he did, what can he tell you about them?'

Horton shrugged. He sipped his coffee; it was excellent, and she remembered how he took it: black, strong, no sugar.

'Lomas was sturdy, about six feet with a close-cropped greying beard and short grey hair. Do you recall seeing anyone like that around here?'

'No. I wasn't here in October.'

'I'd also like to know if a man called George Caws visited your father in January? Your father's name was given to Caws by Wight Barn Wines who supply Lord Eames with wine for his cellar. They also supplied Cedric Halliwell. We can't trace Caws, but we'd very much like to.'

'He hasn't mentioned any of these men to me, but then that is probably because he doesn't know them. I will ask him to call you.'

Would he though?

There was a moment's silence before she added, 'How is Sergeant Cantelli?'

'Fine.'

'And you?'

'Fine.'

She smiled. 'Still living on your boat?'

'Yes.' He didn't know what to say to her, and it seemed she was as equally tongue tied. He always felt awkward when dealing with her. It wasn't her fault who her father was, or that he despised him. But he wished he didn't like her so much. Quickly, he drained his coffee and said he'd better be leaving. She looked slightly taken aback at his abrupt exit but not disappointed. In fact, she looked relieved.

On his way back to the ferry, he wondered what Eames would make of his conversation with his daughter. Would Eames worry that he was getting closer to the truth behind Jennifer's disappearance, or would Lomas and Paignton prove to be dead ends because Eames and the intelligence services would ensure they were, or because they had nothing to do with Jennifer? Either that or he might end up being the dead end. Surely they wouldn't go to such extremes?

Would Eames phone him? Perhaps he would delegate that task to his daughter, telling her he had never heard of Lomas, Paignton or George Caws.

Horton collected the bulky file of paperwork from Sergeant Norris at Newport. Norris said he had checked the contents against the index to make sure it was all there. Chilcott hadn't had time or opportunity to remove anything because Norris had stood over him and his secretary.

Horton boarded the five o'clock sailing and had reached the entrance to Portsmouth harbour when his phone rang. It was Cantelli.

'I've got something, Andy,' he said excitedly. 'I know who the landslip victim is and if I were a betting man, I'd put my pension on it. It's not the real Cedric Halliwell but a man called Jerry Carswell.'

'And who the blazes is he?'

'I'll tell you when you get here.'

Eighteen

‘ I started by looking into wine thefts,’ Cantelli said to Horton and Walters. Bliss had left for a meeting and Cantelli said he hadn't had time to brief her on what he and Walters had discovered. Besides, Cantelli said, he'd wanted to tell Horton first. Horton with a black coffee in front of him listened eagerly.

‘I kept thinking of Nigel Tamar,’ Cantelli continued. ‘The wine fraudster who we know is not Caws because Tamar is younger, and he's done a bunk abroad. But I considered the fact that Caws could have been trying to pump Nansen for information of where valuable wines were held with the intention of stealing them.’

‘He wouldn't have been able to steal any from Lord Eames' property with Danby's high security system in place,’ Horton said. ‘I've paid a visit to his Lordship. He was not at home, but his daughter was. She asked after you.’

‘That was nice of her; but then she's a nice girl. Am I allowed to say that? Or am I'm being sexist or politically incorrect?’

‘Probably both,’ replied Walters.

Horton said, ‘I don't think Harriet would mind. She might even say you're a nice boy.’

Cantelli smiled. ‘Been a while since I've been called a boy.’

‘Probably even longer since you've been called ‘nice’ in this job,’ Walters muttered.

‘That's true enough. ‘Kind’ though, which is reward in itself sometimes. Is Harriet on holiday?’

‘She didn't say. I guess so. She said she'd ask her father if Caws had visited him, but I doubt he did.’ Horton made no mention of the fact he'd also talked to her about Lomas and Paignton.

‘I agree, because Cedric Halliwell at Beachwood House was a much better target.’ Cantelli swallowed some tea before continuing,

'Over the last four years there have been thefts of rare and valuable wines from four private investors, as well as two wine merchants, all of whom had purchased some rare vintages at auction. The same gang committed the crimes. Not on our patch but in London and Surrey. The modus operandi is that someone takes up a presence at the auction, watches who bids for the wine and then manages to overhear, or obtain from one of the officials, details of who has purchased it and where it has gone. Then they case out the joint and steal the wine. The perpetrators of those thefts have been caught and are currently serving time, so it's not our landslip corpse. But it made me wonder if someone else was playing the same game, i.e. George Caws, who was tracking down either Cedric Halliwell or Lord Eames, both of whom Nansen had mentioned to Caws. Either or both could have purchased rare wine at a recent auction.'

'I can't see Lord Eames doing his own bidding,' Horton said. 'He probably has a relationship with a vintner in London to do that for him. And the bidding is probably done by phone.'

'Mine and Walters thoughts exactly, and the same could be said for Halliwell but Caws could still have got the name of the buyer from the auction house. Walters and I spilt the list of auction houses who specialize in rare and vintage wines.'

'That's why I haven't got anything on the piano companies,' Walters quickly explained.

Cantelli continued, 'I struck lucky. I discovered that Cedric Halliwell had purchased some wine at an auction at Bonhams in London in December, and as you said, Andy, it was by telephone. The wine was shipped to Beachwood House on 7 January.'

'When Halliwell was in residence, or to be accurate the phoney Halliwell aka Michael Paignton.'

'Yes. Paignton posing as Halliwell already had access to all the real Halliwell's accounts. The wines are listed on the valuation report. One bottle of Moët & Chandon Champagne Cuvée Dom Pérignon 1975 vintage, which he paid just over a thousand pounds for and a Bordeaux Pétrus again 1975.'

'Obviously a good year.'

'An exceedingly good one, that bottle alone set Paignton or rather Halliwell – it was his money – back four thousand pounds. Paignton, posing as Halliwell, bid by telephone so the auctioneer couldn't give me his description, but when I asked her if anyone else had expressed an interest in those wines and regret at not getting them, or had been curious about who had purchased them, she said there had been one man. She remembered him well, a Mr George Caws. He was knowledgeable about wines, about sixty, slim, distinguished looking. A charming man who was most put out that the Champagne Cuvée Dom Pérignon and Bordeaux Pétrus had gone to someone else.'

'I bet he was. Did he bid for them?'

'Yes, but he knew he wouldn't get them. He knew exactly when to shake and nod his head.'

'I'm amazed she can remember him.'

'It's her business to remember names and faces, she said, when I questioned her on that. Besides, I think George Caws made quite an impression on her. Ms Passmore was concerned when I said we were trying to trace Caws. She told me that she would never divulge a client's details, and I believe her because, if she had, then Caws could have gone straight to Beachwood House without having to bother with Wight Barn Wines. But she admitted it was possible that Caws had learned that the wine had gone to someone living on the Isle of Wight. Caws set about tracing the client, in this case through the most reputable wine merchants on the island, Wight Barn Wines. Once he had the details, he called at Beachwood House using some guise to study it for the best opportunities for theft. Only when he got there, he found his old cellmate Michael Paignton.'

'Cellmate?' Horton's hand froze as he was about to take a drink.

'Yes. Caws, or that should be Jerry Carswell, served time in Parkhurst Prison.'

'Ah.' Horton swallowed his coffee as Cantelli continued:

'His most recent stretch was from 2002 until he was released last September and, before you say that has nothing to do with Paignton, the stretch he served before that was from 1985 to 1992 in Parkhurst. He should have served eleven years but was released on licence after seven. He was convicted for the theft of highly valuable vintage wines and aggravated burglary. He assaulted the owner who disturbed him in the act. Walters and I think that Carswell, on release this last time, was up to his old tricks again, only he got more than he bargained for. He ended up dead and buried on the cliffside.' Cantelli sat forward and eagerly continued, 'Carswell recognized his old cellmate even after twenty-five years. He knew he was on to a winner. He was talking to another ex-con like himself, one who was living in the lap of luxury. He had a hold over him, which he would exploit to the full. Paignton had something to hide. His prison record.'

'But from whom?' asked Horton. 'He didn't mix with anyone on the island. He lived like a recluse.'

'But he didn't want anyone to know about the wealth he'd stolen from the real Halliwell, hence the outside of his house looking decrepit while the inside was luxury. And he left his money to the abbey, probably as an atonement for his wicked ways.'

'So Paignton kills Jerry Carswell aka Caws and buries him on the cliffside, which means the time of death has to be before 1 February when Paignton was found dead on the boat. His death being from natural causes.'

Walters said, 'Ben could have killed Carswell.'

'That's possible, especially if a wood carving implement matches the wound in the victim's skull. Apparently, PC Jennings is a whiz at wood carving and Sergeant Warren's showing him pictures of the wound for his opinion. We need to get hold of Carswell's medical record. If he's had knee surgery and previously broken his leg in two places, as Dr Clayton found for the landslip corpse, then that could go some way to confirming your theory, which I'd say is highly probable. Gaye said the breaks were about twenty years old.'

'Someone inside might have helped break them,' Walters ventured.

'Possible, and we might get that from his prison record. Gaye's opinion was the knee surgery on the landslip corpse was conducted about fifteen years ago. So if it is Carswell then perhaps he had the knee op before his second prison stretch.'

Cantelli said, 'Carswell's last known address is a flat in Southampton. We can check it out. If he answers the door, then Walters and I are way off beam.'

'Only one way to find out,' Horton said, rising. 'Call on him tomorrow, while you, Walters, can get back on the piano trail. I'll update Uckfield.' Horton's phone rang on the way to the incident suite, and he was pleased to see it was Felice.

'I'm sorry about the weekend, Andy.'

'That's fine. How is your father?'

'A little better now, thank you. I've heard back from the picture framers in Australia. They said that the man they billed for framing the paintings was Cedric Halliwell.'

'He called in person?'

'They can't remember. They were framed fifteen years ago and stored at a specialist art depository in Sydney. I've checked with them. They were kept there until last July when they were shipped to Beachwood House.'

'Thanks.'

'Oh, and Andy, about showing you over my boat, maybe this weekend?'

'That would be great,' he answered with eagerness.

He met Uckfield at the bottom of the stairs, just leaving for home. The Super looked dreadful. His face was grey and creased up as though in pain, and he walked gingerly to the rear entrance.

'Are you alright, Steve?' Horton asked, seeing that Uckfield was far from alright.

'Fine,' Uckfield muttered. 'What do you want?'

Horton fell into step beside him, relaying what Cantelli and Walters had discovered. He wondered how much was sinking in. Uckfield was distracted and breathing heavily. 'I'd like to request access to Carswell's prison record,' Horton said.

'OK,' Uckfield managed to mutter through gritted teeth as they reached his car.

Horton was even more worried but, before he could say anything, Uckfield emitted a loud cry, swore vehemently and clutched the right side of his body.

'Steve!' Horton stepped forward.

'I'm fine,' Uckfield snarled, breathlessly. 'It's this ruddy stomach bug, it just won't shift.'

'Maybe you should see a doctor.'

'Waste of time.'

'Would you like me to drive you home?'

'Stop bloody fussing.' Uckfield, with an effort tried to pull himself up. He made to open the door, swayed and was suddenly on the ground, clearly in a great deal of agony. Horton shouted to a uniformed officer who was crossing to the station rear entrance. 'An ambulance! Quick!' Then to Uckfield he said, 'It's OK, Steve, despite what you say you're seeing a doctor now!'

'Thank Christ for that,' Uckfield hissed and passed out.

Nineteen

' Burst appendix,' Horton relayed to Cantelli on the phone from the hospital the following morning. After going in the ambulance with Uckfield the previous night, Horton had stayed until Alison – Uckfield's wife – had arrived along with her father, the former Chief Constable, who had told him curtly and ungratefully he was no longer needed. Horton had never much cared for Reg Dyer and disliked him even more since he had chosen to believe the false claims of gross misconduct against him that had sealed the end of his marriage and scuppered his promotion chances. This morning before heading for work Horton had made for the hospital and enquired about Uckfield's health.

'There was a risk of peritonitis, but they say he's going to be OK.'

'Well that's a relief,' Cantelli said with feeling. Horton could hear a voice in the background. Cantelli continued, 'That's Walters. He says, knowing the Super, he'll still want to run the investigation from his sick bed.'

'The Assistant Chief Constable will have other ideas and you have one guess who Dean will put in charge.'

'Bliss,' announced Cantelli. 'Not sure DI Dennings will be pleased about that.'

'Not sure any of us will be, but she is the senior officer so we'll have to grin and bear it and try and keep out of her ponytail as much as possible. And, if I'm not mistaken, that's her now on the phone I can hear ringing in the background. You'd better update her about Jerry Carswell. Tell her I'll be back shortly. I'm just going to see if I can have a word with Dr Clayton.'

He was pleased to find Gaye in her office. 'Just writing up the report on Ben's autopsy,' she said, 'but I'm glad you're here because I was about to call you.' She waved him into a seat in her cramped office.

'That's not the sole reason I'm here.' He told her about Uckfield.

'Poor man. I'll look in on him.'

'He'll think you're sizing him up for an autopsy.'

She smiled. 'I can't imagine him being the best patient in the world.'

No. But then Horton knew he wouldn't be either. He'd hate it, but sometimes, sadly, you weren't given any choice. 'I think Bliss will be put in charge of the investigation. Did you find anything new from your autopsy on Ben?' he keenly asked.

'My examination yielded the same results as the other pathologist. Ben died of natural causes.'

'Oh.'

'But …'

'You're not sure?' he asked eagerly.

She fell silent for a moment. Then, 'There are one or two things that I thought interesting, hence my thoughts of calling you.'

Horton eyed the petite, freckled, fair-skinned woman across the desk. 'Go on.'

'First I'd like to know why you think he was murdered. And don't tell me it was a gut feeling because I thought the days when coppers went by instinct were banned.'

'That doesn't stop us having them.'

'Or acting on them.'

'And getting a roasting for it,' he added with a wry smile. 'But sometimes it's all we have to go on. And this is one of those situations, along with the facts that we have a murdered man found on the cliffside, an impostor living in the house above it who also died alone on board a boat off the coast of Ryde, and another man who is missing – probably also dead – the real Cedric Halliwell. That's enough to make any detective's antennae twitch.'

'Well, I'm with you as far as instinct goes, and I really shouldn't say that being a woman of science, but then doctors can sometimes work on instinct too and this is one of those cases.'

His pulse beat a little faster in anticipation of what he might learn.

She said, 'All the evidence points to Ben having died of natural causes, which were as the first autopsy found, dilated cardiomyopathy, which can be inherited, or it could have been caused by a viral infection, alcoholism or drugs. But there are some things about Ben that make me wonder. I have put the facts in my report but not speculations.' She sat back and considered him for a moment before continuing, 'The chest had already been cut open from the first autopsy, but only the heart had been removed and examined and, as that was determined as the cause of death, it was put back in and none of the other organs were removed.'

Horton repressed a shudder.

'I took samples of blood, cerebrospinal fluid and tissue samples from the organs after removing them. I found some swelling of the liver and fairly extensive liver damage, which suggests that, at some time, Ben was a heavy drinker. There was also evidence of musculoskeletal damage, which, from my examination, I would determine was caused by an accident rather than inherited. Probably incurred over thirty years ago.' She picked up her mug of coffee. 'I'm sorry, I didn't offer you one.'

But Horton waved that aside as he was anxious to hear her findings.

After taking a draught she continued, 'I examined the body in minute detail, including under the fingernails, the hair and genitals, but as the body had already been washed for the first autopsy I didn't expect to find anything save any possible pin pricks that might tell us if Ben was a drug user or had been injected. I also looked for scars, moles and tattoos. I found no evidence he had been injected, no tattoos but several moles, some that were clearly squamous cell and basal cell carcinomas, others gave indications of melanoma. There was considerable damage to the epidermis, particularly on his arms, legs, neck and face. I've taken tissue samples for analysis. I would say that he had lived and worked for some time in a hot climate and certainly hadn't bothered with sun screen. His hands were strong and well-weathered. There was evidence of arthritis in the thumb and forefinger joints. The skin on the soles of his feet was rough and hardened.'

Horton sat, reflecting. He was beginning to wonder.

'There was evidence of lung damage that could indicate he was a heavy smoker, except that I saw no evidence of nicotine staining on his fingers, which is not conclusive in itself that he didn't smoke heavily, but there is the possibility that the lung tissue damage could have been caused by occupational means.'

'Such as working with hazardous chemicals?'

'Possibly, though not for a considerable period otherwise there would have been more damage than was evident. But it could have been exposure to asbestos or some other chemical agent. We should get more from the tissue analysis. I also found that the brain, liver and kidneys were enlarged. I looked deeper into his eyes. Sorry, being a bit flippant there.'

'No need to apologize to me,' Horton said, knowing that black humour was often the only way those in his job and other emergency service personnel, including the medical profession, dealt with death on a regular and often daily basis. He also knew that some pathologists and undertakers had an even darker sense of humour that only fellow professionals would understand.

'I found nothing untoward, but I have taken samples of the fluid behind the eyes.'

'Did you expect to find something?' he asked, picking up on the intonation of her voice.

'I considered the possibility of carbon monoxide poisoning.'

'The silent killer.'

'Yes.'

'Which can happen in boats,' Horton added, thinking of the motor cruiser with Paignton dead on board.

'Yes, with faulty heating and ventilation or faulty cooking equipment. There was no evidence of it in the liver or the blood.'

And would the pathologist who conducted the autopsy on Paignton have looked for such evidence or taken samples of eye fluid? Horton thought not. And he didn't think the boat had been checked for a leak either.

'I also considered nitrogen dioxide poisoning which can occur in the same way as carbon monoxide poisoning through the inhalation of the gas,' Gaye was saying. 'We've seen it used, sadly, many times with car exhausts. Inhalation of high concentrations can rapidly cause burns, spasms, swelling of tissues in the throat, upper airway obstruction, and death. It can lead to tachycardia, a dilated heart –'

'As in Ben's case with his heart failure?' Horton quickly

interjected.

'Yes. Nitrogen poisoning can lead to chest congestion, and circulatory collapse. I found no evidence of burns or swelling of the tissue of the throat but that doesn't rule out the possibility of nitrogen poisoning. If done slowly and well there are no signs of it in an autopsy. It's a favoured means of suicide in some countries.'

'Such as?'

'Canada, Australia, Sweden. There is something else of interest though, not connected with the cause of death, but it made me think of you.' She paused not for effect, or to marshal her thoughts, but Horton sensed that what she was about to say was of a delicate matter. He was intrigued.

'I found scarring on Ben's back.'

'The original post-mortem found that.'

'Yes, but what the pathologist didn't say was that the scarring is consistent with Ben having been burnt in a fire, and it is old scarring. At least *forty* years old.'

Horton felt a jolt of excitement. His speculations had been correct then.

'It made me think of what we previously discussed about the fire at the Goldsmith Psychiatric Hospital in 1968,' she continued. 'But of course, just because Ben had scarring, doesn't mean to say he was in *that* fire. In fact, he can't have been because all the patients in that ward died because of the locked door. And I've no reason whatsoever to believe that Ben was there.'

But did Horton? He'd already considered it, and now he was growing convinced that Ben could be Zachary Benham and that Halliwell could also have been in that fire. *Hands are so important, don't you think? They don't lie.* Dormand's words. Then there was what he had recently learned about the murder of Roger Salcombe and of Michael Paignton.

'Andy, what is it?' she asked worried, as he remained silent, staring at her intently but not really seeing her. He was seeing the events of over forty years ago.

Abruptly, he pulled himself together and told her what they had discovered about Michael Paignton and the murder of the burns specialist, Roger Salcombe. Of the scar tissue on the real Halliwell's hand, adding that Paignton had been studying at the London School of

Economics at the same time as Zachary Benham who had died in that fire at the Goldsmith Psychiatric Hospital. She listened without interrupting.

When he finished, she said quietly, 'Benham aka Ben. Maybe he didn't die. Maybe someone got him out and got his hand burnt as a result.'

Exactly what Horton had been thinking. He said, 'I'm convinced that Paignton was framed for the murder of Roger Salcombe. The evidence against Paignton is so flimsy I'm amazed the case ever got to court and even more astounded that he got convicted.' But Horton knew the reason for both; someone had seen to it that Salcombe and Paignton were silenced. About what though? And why not silence Halliwell? Because he had gone on the run? Because he had gone abroad to a hot climate and one where he had met an aboriginal painter in the Northern Territory, Australia. And that was where Gordon Eames had died in 1973.

He said, 'Paignton had never touched drugs in his life and yet he was spaced out on LSD when they found him crouched over the body of Salcombe. Perhaps whoever gave him the drug thought it would kill him, or scramble his brains, which it did for a while but not long enough. In prison, when he recovered, he started to rock the boat by claiming he was innocent and swiftly got badly beaten and was moved to Parkhurst. He learned his lesson: keep your mouth shut or else.'

'But –

'He couldn't remember how he had got the drugs, from whom, and where and how he had ended up in Salcombe's flat, a man he claimed not to know. The landlord of The Green Man said Paignton drank in the pub, which he did, but he couldn't remember Salcombe.'

Gaye looked intently at him.

'No witness statements were taken from those in the apartments, except for one woman who was in the lift with Paignton. And what's the betting there was more forensic evidence in that apartment that wasn't even taken? I think when Paignton recovered from his overdose of LSD he realized who the killer was and, on his release from prison, set out to find him. He did too. Cedric Halliwell.'

'So how does Ben, or that is Zachary Benham, fit into this? *If* they are one of the same.'

Gaye didn't know about the photograph from 1967 or how it was connected to Jennifer's disappearance or Lord Eames, and Horton wasn't going to tell her yet. Maybe he never would. He'd already gone further than he had ever thought possible relaying information about Benham, but Gaye had already known of the fire.

'Either Ben found Halliwell for Paignton or Paignton teamed up with Ben to track down Halliwell. Halliwell could have set that hospital fire and got his hand burnt as a result, and it was Michael Paignton who rescued Benham from the fire. Or maybe Halliwell rescued Ben and they both managed to get out alive.' But Horton knew the latter didn't tie in with his theories about Paignton believing Halliwell to be Salcombe's killer and his need for revenge for being framed. Why would Ben help Paignton kill Halliwell if Halliwell had been his rescuer? Perhaps he hadn't assisted him, and Paignton had murdered Halliwell alone, told Ben that Halliwell was dead and allowed him to live on in the cabin, and Ben was content with that.

Thoughtfully, Gaye said, 'Ben's scar tissue is on his back but not his legs, so it indicates that he wasn't standing at the time of the fire. He could have been sitting in a hard-backed chair with the fire behind him, but it's impossible after all this time to see if there is a pattern in the scar tissue. Alternatively, he could have been lying down and the fire was under him but not under his entire body, otherwise there would be scarring on the legs and shoulders. If he was on a bed then I'd have said that the mattress, comprised of highly combustible material, would have resulted in far more extensive burns and most probably death. The same applies if he was lying on a sofa and the fire was close by. He could have realized there was a fire, rolled off the bed, staggered about and got caught in the flames. Or perhaps he was lying on a wooden bench with the fire under him, although, again, wood being highly combustible means he might not have survived, unless someone had the presence of mind to snatch him from the jaws of the flames. Or it could have been an iron bed with no mattress just springs. The mattress could have been removed and used to start or fan the fire. Ben could have been drugged and fell or was placed on that bed.'

Horton knew as well as Gaye that this was all conjecture. He wished to God he had some facts to light the way.

Gaye continued, 'I said before that it was common practise in the nineteen sixties to drug mentally ill patients to give the staff an easy night. Smoke inhalation would certainly have damaged his throat and lungs and, as I said, I found evidence of lung damage. Maybe someone pulled him off the bench or bed in time, but not quick enough to prevent the flames from reaching the skin of his back. Whoever it was could have thrown a blanket or towel around him, rolled him on the ground to smother the flames, then quickly picked him up and carried him out.'

'Locking the door behind him and leaving those other men to die,' Horton said solemnly. That took a cold-blooded killer.

Gaye remained silent.

Horton rapidly thought back to his final conversation with Dormand on the beach behind the abbey in October. Dormand had said he had killed Rory Mortimer because he was a traitor, as were Royston and Wilson, selling secrets to the Russians. Horton had asked, "And Zachary Benham? Was he selling secrets?" Dormand had said not, and that Benham had been trying to unearth them and died doing so. Horton's response to that had been, "In a psychiatric hospital? What was he doing there?" Dormand said he didn't know but he suspected someone would very much like to know, even after all these years. Who was that someone? Andrew Ducale? Was that why Ducale had planted the photograph on Horton's boat and left him to make his enquiries? But that didn't make sense.

Gaye's voice finally broke through his thoughts. 'The extent of Ben's scarring means he would have been hospitalised, and if Halliwell's scarring on his hands was intense, he would also have needed medical treatment. The burns would have needed regular dressing changes, which would have been painful, so Ben and Halliwell would have been prescribed pain relief, not just when changing the dressings but at other times during the rehabilitation. And when discharged, Ben would have had to return regularly to hospital as an outpatient for dressing changes. Ben likely experienced nightmares and flashbacks. Maybe he was given professional help to overcome these, or perhaps he turned to drink to try and forget his ordeal and cope with the trauma. If the latter, then at some point he realized that wasn't working and gave it up because he'd have been dead long before now of cirrhosis of the liver.'

'Someone could have helped him overcome his drink problem.' Horton wondered if that someone had been Paignton or Halliwell.

'Ben would also have needed specialist care to avoid serious and debilitating contractures,' Gaye continued. 'I'd say he got that help. The musculoskeletal deformities I mentioned could have been partly caused by the contractures as a result of the burn injuries, but the position of them, the shoulder region, makes me say not. Scar management for post-burn injury is a long and often painful process; it is not something that can be carried out for a few weeks and then abandoned. It has to be continued for many months to avoid complications. Judging by the scar tissue on Ben's body, I would say his treatment was well-managed and on-going. In fact, it looks as though it was excellent.'

'Perhaps both Ben and Halliwell got that treatment from a top burns specialist, Roger Salcombe.'

Following his train of thought, Gaye said, 'If they did survive that fire in Woking at the psychiatric hospital and someone didn't want that known, then they could have been treated at a private clinic or an exclusive nursing home with a specialized consultant overseeing it, especially if money was no object, or if secrecy was the reason for it. The medical team would need to have been thoroughly reliable though.'

But had they been? Horton's mind was working on overdrive as several thoughts occurred to him. 'No questions were asked until Salcombe discovered the reason for their injuries and that all those men in that ward had been murdered. He decided to speak out but was killed, and Michael Paignton was framed for it because Benham must have told Paignton what had really happened. If Paignton was not the man who rescued him.'

'Or Halliwell could have told Michael Paignton.'

Of course! He'd been assuming that Paignton had killed Halliwell for revenge and to take over his estate and wealth, but what if it was the opposite. Halliwell and Paignton were friends and Halliwell had wanted Paignton to have his estate. He might have bequeathed it to him and then died, naturally, but Paignton needed to protect his and Ben's identity. Halliwell's body was taken out on the dinghy and disposed of in the Solent and then Paignton assumed Halliwell's identity, and he and Ben were quite happy until Carswell showed up. One of them had killed Carswell.

Gaye said, 'The medical team must have cared for Ben and

possibly Halliwell until they were able to be travel.'

'Abroad.'

'If they travelled first class no one would have been impertinent enough to ask questions. The cabin crew could have been told that it was too traumatic for the patients to even think about the fire. And it depends where the scarring was. Ben's wouldn't have been visible and Halliwell's could easily have been hidden.'

And this had been before Paignton had been framed for murder in 1970. Perhaps a private plane had been hired to take the patient and his rescuer, Halliwell, abroad, and as far away from England as it was possible to get. To the other side of the world in fact, where another medical team could give them on-going out-patient care, until it was time for them to move on. Gaye had said Ben had probably lived and worked in a hot climate. Horton thought of Gordon Eames allegedly dying on an Australian beach in 1973, of those pictures in Halliwell's house by an unknown Australian artist and their aboriginal leanings, of the bauxite mine in Nhulunbuy, a town with an aboriginal community. And there was damage to Ben's lungs which could have been caused by occupational means such as working in a bauxite mine.

And finally, he thought of Cedric Halliwell, a man with knowledge of fine wines, a musician, a man who understood art and architecture. An educated, well-spoken man who knew what he wanted and how to get it. A man who knew the sea, who had an account in the Cayman Islands and in Guernsey where he had possibly lived, where the Eames family had spent their holidays and sailed with the Ducales. A man who had come to live on the Isle of Wight where Lord Eames owned a property. And Horton knew that Cedric Halliwell must, in reality be, Gordon Eames.

Twenty

Instead of heading down into the city and work, Horton turned left out of the hospital and climbed the hill that overlooked Portsmouth where he pulled into a layby and silenced the Harley. He gazed down on the city shrouded in a fog. Removing his helmet, he caught the sound of the foghorns out to sea booming over the rooftops and the tower blocks of the densely populated city.

His head was spinning with what he and Gaye had discussed. Was he right about Halliwell being Gordon Eames? He had no proof of anything, only a feeling and suppositions, and they weren't nearly enough. Even now he began to doubt his earlier conviction. Gordon had died, his body had been identified by his brother, flown home and put in the family vault on their estate in Wiltshire.

Just because Ben had burn scars and so too did Halliwell, it didn't mean either man had got them in that fire at the Goldsmith Psychiatric hospital. He just wanted the pieces to fit. In fact, the more he thought about it the more uncertain he became.

Gaye said she would put the scarring in her report but there would be no mention of what they had discussed. It was all conjecture anyway. And she was correct. The landslip corpse wasn't conjecture though. He had been murdered, but his killer might never be brought to justice because he was already dead, either Ben or Paignton, or perhaps they had both conspired to kill him.

He returned to the station and the incident suite wondering how Cantelli was getting on in Southampton on the trail of Jerry Carswell. Horton crossed to Trueman. Bliss was in the office next to Uckfield's and on the phone.

'At least she hasn't taken over the Super's office,' Trueman muttered.

'Give her time.'

Trueman said he was checking with the Red Jet car ferry to see if Carswell had booked on a Southampton to Cowes ferry in his own name or the alias of Caws. 'He doesn't hold a driver's licence in either name. Nor is there any vehicle registered to him. Norris's officers are still trying to find the taxi company and driver who took him and Paignton to Wight Barn Wines. How's the Super?'

'Out of danger.'

'Then let's hope he's soon out of hospital and back here,' Trueman said with feeling and a nod in Bliss's direction. 'At least Uckfield lets you get on with it. She's like a jack in the box, popping out every few minutes to see if anything new has come in on either case, the landslip corpse and the Trehams robbery.'

'And has it on the latter?'

Trueman shook his head. 'Dennings and Marsden are re-interviewing Victoria Treham, hoping to prise out more information.'

'Has anyone checked with experts that those two items which Victoria Treham claims to be paste really are paste?'

'Yes. No one recognizes them but without actually handling them they say it's difficult to confirm if they are real diamonds and sapphires, but why would the Trehams lie about them only being costume jewellery?'

'Why didn't the dogs bark? OK, so they were allegedly drugged.'

'You think they weren't?' Bliss said sharply.

Horton started and spun round. He hadn't seen her emerge, and Trueman hadn't either otherwise he would have indicated by a nod or raise of eyebrows that she was on the loose. His expression now said, see didn't I tell you. Horton thought Bliss was getting very stealthy.

'I don't know. I'm not on the case but it doesn't smell right.'

Bliss opened her mouth, probably to retort that his sense of smell had nothing to do with collecting evidence and capturing the culprits, but Horton swiftly continued, 'I said to Superintendent Uckfield and DI Dennings that it might be an inside job, and I still think that's possible. The paste jewellery was either there because of its sentimental value and nothing to do with the robbery or...' He paused as a few thoughts jolted into place, not just about the Trehams jewellery but about Jennifer's brooch.

'Or.'

'It was what the thieves were really after.'

'That doesn't make sense,' she snapped.

'It does if those two items were more valuable than the Trehams thought. Or they might have considerable value to someone other than the Trehams.' Just like Jennifer's brooch, thought Horton. PC Stanley had stolen it without any idea of its value, either monetary or sentimental, but someone had gone to a lot of trouble to make sure the brooch and all evidence of its existence had vanished.

He said, 'We should ask a real expert.'

'We already have,' Bliss smartly re-joined.

'I mean one on the inside. Oliver Vernon. He's one of the country's leading jewellery historians.'

'Only he's not around.'

'Winchester Prison isn't far and, as I put him there a year ago, I'd like to ask him what he thinks of the Trehams collection.' And of a certain brooch, he added silently.

Bliss looked dubious.

Horton pressed on, 'It could give us a new lead or at least some new ides to explore that Superintendent Uckfield hadn't considered.' Horton knew that would win her over. Her eyes flashed at the thought that she might get a breakthrough in a case she'd only just taken over.

'Very well.'

After she left, Trueman muttered, 'You wouldn't like me to go with you, I suppose? I can ride pillion on your Harley.'

Horton smiled and hurried out before Bliss could change her mind.

It took him slightly longer than he anticipated to reach Winchester as the fog had caused two traffic accidents on the motorway. At the prison he went through the routine security checks and was shown into a bland private room that smelt of disinfectant and paint. He tried to shut out the sound of doors locking and his fear of being shut in, a legacy of a bitter and cruel experience at one of the shit-holes of a children's home in which he'd been incarcerated. He concentrated on why he was here.

The door opened, and a man in his mid-forties was ushered in by a prison officer who nodded at Horton and closed the door behind him. Horton knew they were on camera.

Vernon was thinner than Horton recalled from the last time he'd seen him in the dock, although he'd never run to fat. The once intelligent and friendly blue eyes were now mistrustful and dull. The close-cropped fair beard had gone, revealing a pointed chin, making his face narrower, longer and gaunter, but Horton had no sympathy to spare for a killer and a crook.

'I've come for advice,' he said.

'Try Sotheby's or Christies,' Vernon replied, taking the seat opposite Horton across the table.

'Already have, and Bonhams, but this stuff is special and you are an expert in historic art, jewellery and gemstones.'

'*Was*, Detective Inspector Horton. Amazingly there's no call for such talent in these salubrious surroundings.' He waved his thin arm around the bland beige room. His voice was slightly camp. Horton knew it was an act.

'The Treham robbery.'

A light flickered behind Vernon's eyes, although his expression gave nothing away.

'You've heard about it?' Horton asked.

'No.'

That was a lie. Horton extracted his mobile and scrolled to the photographs of the stolen items. The Trehams had been advised by their insurance company to catalogue the jewellery in that way, with the exception of two; the costume jewellery. That photograph was of Victoria Treham wearing them, which Trueman had cropped so as not to show the wearer. It was the same pictures Horton had seen on the crime board.

'These are some of the items which were stolen,' Horton said, thinking, now let's see how good you are.

Vernon's eyes flicked down and then up. 'Why should I help you?'

'Because I'm asking nicely.'

Vernon snorted.

'And I've brought you these.' Horton reached down and put the items on the table.

'I don't smoke, and I don't eat chocolate.'

'But you can trade both.'

'Is that all I get?'

'Depends how good you are at providing information. Tell me about these.' He indicated the picture of a necklace and a stunning brooch.

Vernon shrugged his narrow shoulders. 'An emerald and diamond pendant necklace and a diamond clip brooch, circa 1930, both by Hennell.'

'Who's he?' Horton asked. He'd seen the name on the crime board along with the estimated value but knew little else.

'Hennell of Bond Street founded by David Hennell in 1736 originally made fashionable silverware for the nobility and landed gentry. His son, Robert, turned to jewellery-making in the late eighteenth century. By the twentieth century Hennells was *the* British jeweller. During the Art Deco period, Hennell was known for jewels of superlative quality, like those. The brooch should fetch anything in the region of a hundred and fifty thousand pounds, and the necklace about two hundred thousand, probably more. Am I right?'

'Spot on. But then you must have heard these have been stolen.'

'No. I'm just good at my job–my old job. Even without seeing the real thing I know what they are.'

And that was just what Horton wanted to hear. 'And this diamond bracelet?' He showed another photograph.

'A Harry Winstone piece,' Vernon answered with only a glance at it. 'Harry Winstone died in 1978, aged 82. Some of the World's most important gems passed through his hands, including an emerald cut diamond sourced for the Duchess of Windsor, and a 241-carat rough that became the 69.42-carat Taylor-Burton diamond. Difficult to say how much that would fetch at auction, *if* it was legally auctioned. Hundreds of thousands of pounds.'

'And if illegally bought?'

Vernon again shrugged. 'Possibly the same, maybe even more. Depends who wants it and how badly they want it. That is an Art Deco jade ring,' he said, as Horton showed him the next picture. 'The price depends on the rarity and quality of the jade. Possibly forty thousand pounds, if it's good.'

'And the watch?'

'Nice piece.'

Horton thought so too.

'A Breguet marine date watch, eighteen-carat white gold on a wave motive. Value about twenty thousand pounds.'

Horton wondered if Chilcott had got rid of the Tag Heuer he'd stolen from Halliwell's estate after their recent interview. Vernon's assessment and valuation of the items was almost spot on with the expert from the auction house who had also valued the pieces for insurance purposes eighteen months ago. Now for the items Horton was really interested in and which the Trehams claimed was paste.

'And these?'

Vernon remained silent as he studied the intricate and delicate diamond and sapphire bracelet and the heart-shaped diamond sapphire ring in the picture. A flush suffused his pale prison cheeks. Footsteps echoed in the corridor. A door slammed, and keys rattled. Horton took a breath. He felt the sweat beginning to prick his back but thankfully not his brow. He didn't want his discomfort to show for Vernon to gloat over but, as he watched the former jewellery historian study the pictures, he concluded that Vernon wouldn't have noticed if he'd been in the throes of a heart attack, so completely focused was he on the jewellery. The silence seemed to stretch on forever, and when Horton thought he might have to break it, Vernon looked up. His eyes gleamed.

'They're part of the collection of the Princess Catherine Yourievsky, the daughter of Tsar Alexander II. She fled Russia before the communist revolution with her second husband, Prince Serge Obolensky.'

Horton was surprised and sceptical. He knew the princess's story because she had ended up living on Hayling Island a few miles east of Portsmouth across Langstone Harbour. She had been buried in St Peter's churchyard in 1959. 'Are you sure? I thought she died penniless.'

'Apparently she did. And I'm sure.'

'How?'

'It's not every day I get the chance to look at something so beautiful, and exciting.'

'More so than the other items you've just seen?'

'Infinitely.' Then cockily he said, 'Your experts didn't identify them?'

No. 'They might be fake.'

'They might, but I doubt it.'

Horton didn't believe Vernon was lying, in fact he was more convinced than ever that he had come to the right source. It would take someone like Vernon, who knew everything there was to know about historic pieces of jewellery, discovered and missing, and what the jewellery acquiring underworld were after, to recognize something like this. Had the robbers known it too?

'You said part of the princess's collection. She sold other items?'

'A diamond and sapphire necklace, a tiara and a diamond brooch.'

'Who bought them?'

'I wasn't around then,' he said somewhat cynically.

Horton raised his eyebrows. 'But you'll know nevertheless.'

'All I know is that the collection was split. The tiara, necklace and brooch were sold to an unnamed collector and have never been seen since.'

'But the auction house will have records of who bought them.'

'If *they* sold them, which I doubt. The princess and her husband could have negotiated a private deal, as they obviously did with these. How did they end up in the Trehams collection?'

Horton told him that an aunt had given them to Victoria Treham five months ago, shortly before her death.

'So no provenance from the aunt, unless they're keeping quiet about that. Not that it would bother some,' Vernon said.

Just like the wine in Beachwood House and the paintings. They would find buyers with or without provenance. 'How valuable are they?' Horton asked.

'More than all these other things put together.'

'That much!'

'Yes.'

That made Horton even more certain this must have been what the thieves were after. Several theories were running through his mind. 'Who would want them?' he asked.

'Perhaps a Russian would like them back?'

'Anyone in mind?'

'Take your pick. Any of the Russian oligarchs.'

It was a thought, and one Horton didn't think Uckfield would be pleased to hear, only he wouldn't hear it now on his sick bed.

'But if I was you, Inspector, I'd look closer to home for your robbers.'

'Meaning?' Horton knew exactly what Vernon was alluding to.

'Perhaps someone is not as well off as they purport to be.'

'They are. We've looked into it.'

'Then perhaps one of them, Mr or Mrs Treham, wants to provide a secret income for later.'

One of the theories that had already struck Horton. 'Divorce?'

'A nice little nest egg tucked away, not part of the divorce settlement, to sell on later. Those items will fetch a lot even when sold underground.'

Horton pushed the cigarettes and chocolates across the table. As Vernon reached out for them, Horton held on to them. He hesitated for just a fraction. 'What do you know about a brooch, blue diamond centre, pink diamond beneath it and white diamonds surrounding it, like petals?'

Vernon's brow furrowed. 'Is it also part of the Trehams robbery?'

'You recognize it?'

'I might.'

'Stop hedging, Vernon,' Horton snapped, his pulse racing a little faster. He could see that Vernon had recognized the description. 'Tell me what you know.'

'In exchange for what? And don't say more chocolates and cigarettes. I want more than that.'

'Such as?'

'Unlimited and private access to the internet, and permission to write my book.'

'On?'

'The lost historic jewellery of the world.'

Horton raised his eyebrows. 'Such as the princess's pieces?'

'That and others.'

Horton felt a frisson of excitement. 'The brooch I've just described?'

'Possibly,' Vernon replied slyly.

Horton scraped back his chair. 'I'm not here to bargain with you.'

'The Portsmouth Blue.'

Horton remained still. 'And?'

'Do I get what I requested?'

'I'll put in a word.'

'I think you owe me more than that, seeing as I've also given you information on the princess's jewellery.'

Horton gave a curt nod and waited almost breathlessly. Would Vernon tell or would he hold out until he had what he demanded? But from the glimmer in his eyes, Horton could see that Vernon couldn't resist displaying his knowledge.

Twenty-one

The fog was thicker than ever and showed no sign of lifting as Horton returned to the station. On his journey back, he considered what Vernon had told him. He had no reason to doubt him, he was the best jewellery historian in Europe, possibly the world. Besides, it fitted with the mystery over the brooch's disappearance and what he had suspected about it and its theft from Stanley.

The Portsmouth Blue, as it had become known because of its remarkable blue diamond centrepiece, had been owned by Charles II. He had given it to one of his faithful Royalists as a reward for his loyalty to the Crown during the English Civil War when Charles returned to the throne in 1660 two years after the death of Oliver Cromwell. It had been mined in India and kept in that same family for centuries. It had never been sold, either legitimately or underground, and had rarely been seen. The last time being on 28 June 1838, at Queen Victoria's Coronation.

Horton had asked the name of the Royalist it had been given to, though he'd no need to. He had already guessed. Vernon confirmed it. Viscount Lord Eames.

Someone in the Eames family had given that brooch to Jennifer. And someone in that same family had taken it back when they had discovered it had ended up with PC Adrian Stanley. When had Jennifer been given the brooch? *Diamonds are a girl's best friend.* She'd been singing that song shortly before her disappearance, so it had to be around that time.

But why give such a priceless heirloom to Jennifer in the first place? Had it been a token of love? A pretty expensive one at that! Maybe someone had stolen it from the Eames family and given it to Jennifer. Horton considered only one man could have done that, the errant son, Gordon, who had died in 1973. Or had he? Not if he was Cedric Halliwell, as Horton had previously conjectured. Had Gordon been Jennifer's *ghost* and entered that casino in 1978, causing her to go pale and leave the gaming table, according to her colleague, Susan Nash?

He pushed aside his personal thoughts and made his way to the incident suite. Dennings was in with Bliss. Seeing him enter, Bliss sprang up and, with Dennings following her, met him as he reached Trueman's desk.

'What did you get from Oliver Vernon?' she asked.

Horton relayed what Vernon had told him about the princess's jewels. They listened in silence.

'How reliable is Vernon?' Bliss queried.

'Very.'

'So it wasn't an inside job after all,' Dennings declared cockily.

'It could be if divorce is on the cards, and one of them wanted to make sure they could keep hold of the princess's jewellery and sell it underground later without having to declare and share it.'

'Has there been any hint of marital discord?' Bliss shot at Dennings.

'No.'

Horton continued, 'Or it could be a family member who thought the princess's jewellery shouldn't have gone to Victoria Treham. Perhaps someone else had been promised it and knew the true value of the items. Or maybe a friend of the Trehams saw and recognized the jewels for what they were. The person who approached the dogs was able to drug them, so it must have been someone familiar with the house and who the dogs trusted, and that could only be a relative or a friend.'

'Why not the vet?' quipped Dennings sarcastically.

'If he or she is having an affair with either Victoria or Maurice Treham then maybe it was.'

Bliss sucked in her breath and directed her beady eye at Dennings. 'We start again. I want every relative detailed and interviewed. I want a list of friends who regularly visited the Trehams, and I want to know how sound that marriage is. Are either of them having an affair? And talk to the vet.'

Dennings made to speak when PC Jennings entered. His eyes

alighting on Horton, he hurried forward.

'It's about the body found at Luccombe Bay,' he said, his gaze flicking between Bliss and Horton. 'I'm something of an expert at woodcarving, Ma'am, and I was asked by Sergeant Warren if the shape and pattern of the head wound matched any wood carving tools. It does.'

'Go on,' Bliss commanded when Jennings paused. Not out of nervousness or even modesty, Horton thought with a suppressed smile, but for effect.

'In my opinion, the small round head wound was made by a chisel, and then the skull was smashed in with a solid and heavy brass-head mallet, which might also have been used to ram the chisel into the skull, particularly if the victim was unconscious.'

'Let's hope the poor blighter was,' muttered Trueman.

'Amen to that,' agreed Horton. 'Neither were found in Ben's cabin. Would he have used such tools? I take it you've seen pictures of some of his woodcarvings?'

'I have, and they're amazing. He was exceptionally talented, and yes, he most certainly would have had a chisel and a mallet.'

Bliss said, 'He must have buried them or tossed them in the sea. It sounds as though Ben is the killer and then died of natural causes.'

Horton said, 'Someone else could have taken and used his tools.'

'You mean Michael Paignton.' Bliss then addressed PC Jennings, 'Have you got pictures of these tools?'

'Yes.' Jennings reached for his phone.

'Send them to Inspector Horton. Get them over to Dr Clayton, Inspector, and ask her expert opinion. Trueman, Dennings, my office.' She jerked her head and strode off, leaving them to follow her swinging ponytail. Horton sent the images to Gaye's email, thanked PC Jennings and made for CID. There was no sign of Walters. Horton suspected he was in the canteen, and Cantelli was still out following up Carswell. He again put in a call to Carina Musgrove, and again got her automated voice mail. She was an elusive lady. And she hadn't returned his earlier call. He wondered why. Did she know more about Ben than she had divulged in her statement? Or perhaps she didn't want to get involved. She might have left the area. The mobile number was the only one she had given. He called Sergeant Norris on the island.

'I was about to call you, Inspector,' Norris said. 'We've just managed to trace the taxi company and the driver who took George Caws to Wight Barn Wines. He picked up the fare at the Red Jet ferry at West Cowes.'

'The foot passenger service then.'

'Yes. The driver took him straight to Wight Barn Wines where he went for a walk while Caws went inside. He then drove Caws to Shanklin and dropped him off outside St Blasius' Church. Nothing further after that.'

'Did Caws say anything to the driver other than give directions?'

'Only that he was over from the mainland on business. The driver said he quickly got the message that he didn't want to chat.'

'Did he catch the train or the bus from Shanklin to Ryde?'

'We're making enquiries.'

'Is there a bus from Shanklin to Cowes?'

'Checking that too.'

'How far is it from St Blasius Church to Beachwood House?'

'Just over a mile I'd say, maybe a mile and a half. It's uphill then along the coastal footpath.'

Horton asked him to get a local constable to call on Ms Musgrove tomorrow at her cottage. 'If she isn't there, see if her boat is and talk to any neighbours to discover when she might return.' Horton suspected that the neighbours might not be able to help as the other four cottages in that row were probably also holiday homes and unoccupied at this time of the year.

He headed for the canteen where he found Walters finishing off a pudding, which, according to the menu board, was jam roly-poly with custard. He was engrossed in a newspaper spread out before him. Horton bought a coffee and some sandwiches and took the seat opposite the corpulent detective constable.

'You want to read this, guv, it's all about Agent Eames' lot.'

'Europol.'

'No, her family.'

'It's the sports pages,' Horton said looking down at the pictures of horses, a large racing yacht and Lord Richard Eames' lean fair smiling face holding up a massive cup.

'It's the only bit of the papers worth reading. Her father's horses seem to win everything. Must ask her for a few tips when I next see her.'

'I doubt you'll get any. I don't think she's interested in horse racing.' But he knew she was into yacht racing because he'd seen her racing at Cowes in August. He relayed what Norris had told him.

'Do you think Caws went straight to Beachwood House after paying a visit to Wight Barn Wines?' asked Walters.

'It's probable given that he was dropped off by the taxi nearby.'

'Wouldn't he have looked a bit odd walking on a country footpath dressed in a suit?'

'Not if he was wearing an overcoat, which he'd left in the taxi while in Wight Barn Wines. It was January and cold, and there probably weren't many walkers about to notice him. It's also a very secluded area. His first job would be to case the joint. On arrival he found a derelict gatehouse, neglected grounds and a large dilapidated manor house. Maybe he thought the owner was elderly and vulnerable and licked his lips with glee. Or perhaps he thought that Nansen had given him the wrong information, or he'd got the wrong Beachwood House.' Horton bit into his sandwich. 'He walked up the driveway. He'll check anyway. The door is opened by none other than his old fellow prisoner, Michael Paignton.'

'Do you think he ever left there and returned to collect his blackmail money?'

Horton saw Cantelli's car swing into the car park. 'Paignton could have invited Carswell in, knowing what his game would be. He might even have shown him the cellar and offered to cut him in. Perhaps Carswell decided he didn't want to return to Southampton, probably to a shabby bedsit, when he could live in comfort at Beachwood House. Paignton agreed. He got a message to Ben and they killed and buried him.' Horton finished his sandwich. 'Can I read that?' He indicated the article on the Eames family.

'Be my guest.'

Horton quickly did so. It didn't tell him anything more than he already knew and had researched. Richard Eames had inherited the estates, title and family wealth on his father, Viscount William James Eames' death in 1979 when he'd been swept overboard from his yacht off the coast of France in a tragic accident. His body had been recovered. Lady Marsha, William Eames wife, had died the year before in November of a sudden and unexpected heart attack. The double tragedy had projected the only surviving son, Richard, into managing his father's estates, businesses and sporting enterprises, which he'd done with considerable success, building on William Eames' triumphs in yacht racing, horse racing and the business world. He was also an ambassador abroad for British businesses involved in many trade missions. The man could do no wrong, Horton thought with bitterness. There was a brief mention of his two sons running successful business enterprises, a wife who was a much sought after interior designer to the rich and famous, and a daughter who worked in Europe, but no mention of where or what she was doing, and certainly no mention of the black sheep of the family, Gordon.

Cantelli plonked himself down opposite Horton. 'I hope Bliss doesn't fancy a cup of tea, because she'll have a fit if she finds her CID team in the canteen. Talking of which I'm gagging for a cuppa.'

Horton rose and fetched it.

On his return, Cantelli said, 'Carswell was last seen in January by a neighbour as he was leaving his flat. The neighbour can't remember the exact day but the timing fits with when Carswell called on Nansen on 14 January. No one has seen him since.'

'So he could have been killed on that first and only visit,' Walters said.

Cantelli said, 'I also visited the letting agent, after getting the details from the neighbour. The agent says his rent is due on 1 May. I don't think his tenant is going to be around to pay it. The agent accompanied me back to the flat with the keys. I found literature lying around about wine and forthcoming auctions, the address of Wight Barn Wines and the times of the Red Jet ferry from Southampton to Cowes.'

'That's pretty conclusive then. Carswell was posing as George Caws, but it doesn't necessarily mean his is the body in the landslip.'

'Ah, but there's more,' Cantelli grinned and took a long draught of his tea before continuing. The canteen was practically empty now. 'There was no computer, or mobile phone in the flat. The latter of which was probably dumped in the sea, after he was killed. There were a few clothes and some stale food. I found some bank statements with little in the account. No regular work by the looks of it. I headed to the nearest medical surgery and asked if Carswell was registered with them. He is, or he was. The receptionist referred me to the

Practice Manager who is married to a police officer. She couldn't divulge any medical details, but I told her about the body and who we suspected it was, and she confirmed that Carswell had knee replacement surgery fifteen years ago on his left knee.'

'That more or less clinches it.'

'She doesn't know who the next of kin is.'

'I'd better tell Bliss.' Horton rose and Walters followed suit. Cantelli swallowed the rest of his tea and scrambled up after them. On the way out, Walters said, 'Oh, I almost forgot, I've tracked down that piano in Beachwood House. It was bought new in September and shipped direct to Beachwood House.'

'Someone must have visited the showroom and tried it out.'

'No. It was purchased over the phone and paid for by bank transfer.'

'From a bank in Guernsey no doubt.'

'Yes, Morgans. And the account was in the name of Cedric Halliwell. But I also discovered something else. I got digging on the computer, checking out the local clubs and schools where Paignton was raised in the East End of London. I found a couple of press reports going back to when he was a child about him winning local music competitions. You know the kind of thing, local child from a working class background destined for the Albert Hall type of story. He was enormously talented apparently, something of a genius on the keyboard.'

'Yet he chose to study politics at the London School of Economics.'

'Maybe he suffered from burn out. Perhaps his mother and teachers pushed him too hard and he thought sod this for a game of soldiers, I'm not being a pianist.'

Possibly, thought Horton heading up the stairs to the incident suite. Instead Paignton had ended up being convicted for murder.

Horton reported back to Bliss, who said she'd request access to Carswell's medical records. She also said that the prison had confirmed he was incarcerated at the same time as Michael Paignton and in the same cell block, so their theory seemed to be panning out. And the prints Dr Clayton had managed to take from the corpse were currently being checked with those of Jerry Carswell. Bliss was confident they would match, so was Horton.

'It looks as though we have our motive and our killer, or killers,' she triumphantly declared. 'But as both are deceased, we can't prosecute. Once we have fingerprint verification, the investigation will be closed and you and Sergeant Cantelli can assist with the Trehams robbery. DC Walters can liaise with DC Leonard and assist in the arson investigation.'

It was to be expected, thought Horton. He said, 'Sergeant Elkins and PC Ripley are asking around the harbours, sailing and yacht clubs for sightings of anyone launching a canoe in the harbour on the day and night in question, or on the days before it. It's a process of elimination and will take time.'

'That's why Walters can assist,' Bliss smartly re-joined. 'It could speed things up.'

If anyone could get that kind of information, then Dai Elkins would. He knew the harbour, the area around it and the people who used and worked in it. Horton was confident he'd pick up some intelligence that could lead them to the arsonist and said as much before Bliss dismissed him and told him to write up his reports.

He did so, forcing his mind to focus on what Vernon had told him about the Trehams jewellery, and not the brooch and his personal quest. He hoped to spend some time later sifting through everything he had learned, not just over the last week but over the last eighteen months since embarking on his mission to discover what had really happened to Jennifer. But his mind kept wandering. Brother Norman at the abbey had been Antony Dormand. If Ben really was Zachary Benham, then which of the men in that photograph from 1967 had been Cedric Halliwell? Maybe none of them. Michael Paignton could have taken the photograph, because Horton was certain he wasn't the sixth man in it. Halliwell could have been Gordon Eames, as Horton had already considered, but if so, why would Paignton and Ben contrive to kill him and dispose of his body? Maybe they hadn't. Perhaps Halliwell had died a natural death, they'd covered it up and Paignton had seen it as an opportunity to take over his identity and wealth. Perhaps they had done so, not for fraudulent purposes, but because they didn't want any questions asked. Revealing Halliwell's death could mean revealing his true identity, and if that was Gordon Eames then Richard Eames wouldn't want that known. Perhaps Richard was in on this too and had helped to cover up Cedric

Halliwell's death. Or perhaps none of these men – Halliwell, Paignton and Ben – had anything whatsoever to do with Jennifer.

He was interrupted several times by calls, and when he had finished his report and dealt with his urgent emails it was twenty past six and his phone rang yet again. This time it was Gaye to confirm that the pattern of the wounds fitted the wood carving tools PC Jennings had mentioned. Horton phoned Bliss who said it further confirmed that Ben had killed Carswell, aided and abetted by Paignton, and both had then died from natural causes. It was possible but convenient voiced Horton, adding, 'It doesn't answer how the real Cedric Halliwell accumulated his wealth.'

'Not our problem, Inspector,' she smartly replied. 'It's ACC Dean's decision if he wishes to pass that over to fraud. Paignton and Ben were obviously crooks, they latched on to Halliwell and, after extracting from him all his personal information, killed him, ditched his body in the sea, and Paignton took up residence in Beachwood House while Ben preferred to rough it in the log cabin. The fingerprint bureau has just confirmed they have a match on the landslip corpse with that of Jerry Carswell so from tomorrow you and your team are reassigned, as I instructed earlier.'

Horton relayed this to Cantelli and Walters and told them to knock off home before Bliss changed her mind and got them working that evening. They didn't need telling twice. Horton took his own advice but instead of heading for his boat he made for the hospital to visit Uckfield. The fog was thicker than ever. He pulled into the car park, silenced the Harley and removed his helmet. As he did, his mobile rang. He was in two minds whether to answer it, then seeing who the caller was did so eagerly. It was Harriet Eames.

'My father turned up at the house this afternoon. I asked him if George Caws had visited him. He hasn't.'

As Horton had expected because Caws' first and last visit, as it transpired, had been to Beachwood House. He told her about George Caws being Jerry Carswell and the theory of his death as espoused by Bliss. She listened in silence. Then in a doubtful tone, said, 'And you believe that?'

Horton didn't answer the question. Instead, he said, 'Wyndham Lomas. Does your father know him?'

There was a short pause. He heard a tannoy announcement in the background, although he couldn't make out what it said. She obviously wasn't at home so no chance of her father overhearing the conversation. 'He's never heard of him and he doesn't recognize the description,' she said. 'And neither does he know a Michael Paignton or Cedric Halliwell.'

But Horton caught a note of hesitation in her voice.

He said with some disbelief, 'He didn't recall Paignton being convicted of the murder of Roger Salcombe in 1970?'

'No, he was at Cambridge then.'

'But you asked your father if Paignton had been a close friend of his brother, Gordon?'

There followed another short silence. 'Yes.'

'And?'

'He said he had no idea.'

'But you don't believe him.'

Again, a pause. Then, as though on impulse, she quickly said, 'Can you meet me? There's something I need to tell you.'

It was his turn to keep silent, not for effect, but because his mind was rapidly thinking. What was it she needed to tell him? Something her father had said? Or perhaps Eames had betrayed himself by his reaction when she had put Horton's questions to him, and she was curious? Or could this be a trap? Had Eames asked her to lure him somewhere? But he couldn't see Harriet being used by anyone. Not even her father? No.

'Where?' If her phone was tapped, then her father would know the location of their rendezvous.

'Southampton airport. I'm fog bound. I'm returning to The Hague. I haven't checked in yet. I'll meet you in the terminal.'

'I'll be there in thirty minutes.'

Twenty-two

He found Harriet with an anxious look on her fair face and a rucksack at her feet. Her expression lifted a little as she spotted him, and then quickly clouded over. Horton couldn't see anyone taking any special notice of her or him, but if Richard Eames had had his daughter tailed, or asked her to arrange the rendezvous, then Horton knew whoever it was would be good enough not to be conspicuous. There was an awkwardness about her that he'd seen a hint of before on the Isle of Wight. She looked drained and seemed edgy.

'Let's go outside?' she said, as he drew level.

They struck out, away from the waiting buses and their queues of people until they had a corner of the building to themselves. The fog wrapped its damp tentacles around them, curling the ends of her long fair hair.

'I've been recalled, and I suspect it has something to do with my father. And with Ben.'

That brought him up sharply. His mind spun. 'Ben?'

She took a breath. 'I found his body.'

The air seemed to reel. My God, that was totally unexpected. 'You're Carina Musgrove?'

'Yes. And don't say I can be charged for impersonation, because you know I can't.'

He was finding this difficult to take in while trying to interpret the implications of her words. 'You were working undercover?'

'Yes.'

'Then Ben is, or was, wanted internationally?'

She continued, 'Everything I said in my statement was true.'

'Except for your name, and you omitted several facts,' he sharply re-joined. 'Did your father know?'

'Not until I told him. As soon as he arrived, he started in on you. He knew you had visited the house because he must have seen you on the security monitors.'

And Eames would have seen that his daughter was already in residence and had invited him in. That would have been enough to make him hurry there from wherever he had been.

'Practically the first thing he did was ask me what you had wanted, even before I mentioned those names you gave me. I said you'd asked me about George Caws, Wyndham Lomas and Michael Paignton. He wanted to know what I'd told you, which was nothing because, of course, I'd never heard of them, but I told him your enquiries were in connection with Ben after which I had to tell him about Ben and why I was there. He was annoyed and even though he denied knowing any of those men, I could tell he was lying. Then he told me that it was best if I didn't see you again.'

Horton raised his eyebrows.

'I asked him why. He said something about you being a police officer whose career was unlikely to go anywhere.'

Horton's stomach tightened at the threat, but he made no comment.

'I told him that maybe you didn't want your career to go anywhere and asked him what he meant anyway. He said there were things about you that it was best for me not to know. What those were, he wouldn't say. I was livid with him for treating me like a child. I said I'm thirty-four not sixteen and I'd seen many things in law enforcement that had appalled, shocked and distressed me, and I could never believe you capable of any crime.'

He silently thanked her for that.

'Shortly after I'd told him about Ben, I had a phone call from my boss at The Hague recalling me, saying that the investigation into Ben's death is no longer our remit and there is nothing to investigate.'

'And you believe your father influenced the recall?'

'I'm sure he did, although I don't know how he arranged it. Perhaps being a peer of realm carries weight,' she said with bitterness.

But Horton knew exactly how Eames could have arranged it, with his influence in the intelligence services. Eames must have been furious that he'd not been told his daughter had been sent over to investigate Ben. A slip up? Or had someone engineered all this? Horton was beginning to think the latter because it was too neat. And he had an idea who that person was.

He could see how angry and hurt she was. She had been determined to make her own way in the world, and in her career, without the advantages of privilege, but she had been thwarted. Horton knew that the truth behind Cedric Halliwell, Michael Paignton and Ben would never be investigated, let alone be revealed. There was no case to answer except Jerry Carswell's murder, and that had already been put down to Ben and Paignton, which was probably the truth anyway. He had several questions to ask her and rapidly tried to arrange them into some kind of order.

'Why did you leave the cottage at Bonchurch and return to your father's house?'

'Because by then you were on the island, and the landslip corpse had been found. I didn't know anything about his body being there and neither did anyone else. It was quite a shock. But that meant my identity as Carina Musgrove was compromised. I went to our house. I was surprised when you arrived, even though I knew you were investigating the death.'

'You needn't have let me in.'

'I was curious, as are all police officers, or we should be.' She gave a faint smile. 'And why shouldn't I have invited you in? You didn't know I had been undercover. Besides, I enjoy your company.'

He also enjoyed hers, but he wouldn't tell her that. There was too much history to make anything more than an acquaintance possible. The fog eddied around them. The airport was eerily silent for a change, with no flights in and out.

'What was your assignment, or can't you tell me?' Horton said, wondering if she would claim she was under orders not to reveal it.

But she took a breath and said, 'I was told that Cedric Halliwell and a man he was friendly with, were wanted for robbery. The theft of valuable diamonds.'

'Then you recognized the name when I mentioned it. You were good. I'd never have guessed. Who told you this?' Horton sharply asked, knowing that the reason she'd been given was a lie. And he could see that she also suspected it now but not at the time of her assignment.

'My boss, and don't ask me where that information came from because I don't know.'

Maybe she didn't but Horton did. From MI5, but not Lord Eames it seemed, because Harriet had said her father had been genuinely surprised and irritated to find her on the investigation. So the orders had come from someone else and were not shared with Eames.

Quickly, she continued, as if eager to get it off her chest. 'Halliwell and Ben had been traced to the Isle of Wight. As I knew the island, I was asked to get more information on them, to see if I could get friendly with them. Before I arrived, the news came through that Halliwell had been found dead on his boat off Ryde and that there were no suspicious circumstances. But there was still Ben who was living in a cabin on the shore. I was instructed to make his acquaintance. I did, but he didn't reveal anything about himself or Cedric Halliwell, and I had no idea that Michael Paignton had assumed Halliwell's ID. There are two things that perhaps I shouldn't be telling you, but I will.'

'Why?' Horton's pulse raced.

'It involves you, and I don't believe my father when he says you are mixed up in criminal activity.' She took a breath and continued, 'My father asked if we'd gone into the garden, down to the shore or to the boat. I said we only went into the kitchen where we had coffee.'

'The boat is on the pontoon then?'

'Yes. The other thing I think you should know is that I saw someone with Ben.'

Horton felt a thrill of excitement.

'It was only once and from a distance, but the two men were talking and seemed to know one another well. Then they both went inside the cabin.'

'You put this in your report?'

'To my boss, yes, but not in my statement to Sergeant Norris's officers.'

Then Eames would have asked to see it after Harriet had asked him about Caws, Lomas and Paignton.

'It was a week before Ben died. I was on the small motorboat I had hired for the purpose of making Ben's acquaintance.'

It couldn't have been Jerry Carswell or Michael Paignton, and neither could it have been Antony Dormand because they were all dead by then. But Horton knew who it was.

'He was sturdily built, tall, about your height, short cropped grey hair, tanned, dressed casually, early sixties late fifties.'

Lomas. Here was proof that Ben had known Lomas. And what was the betting that Lomas knew Cedric Halliwell and Michael Paignton? Was Lomas still around or had he cleared out after his meeting with Ben? Had he killed Ben by some method that had made it look like natural causes? But if Lomas hadn't cleared out, then there was only one place he could be.

'And you told your father this?'

'No, I told my boss at The Hague.'

'Who told your father?'

'Possibly. I don't know. Andy, what has all this got to do with him?' she anxiously asked.

Even if he decided to tell her, he didn't know where to start.

When he remained silent, she persisted. 'Please. I need to know.'

How much did he trust her? Had she been detailed to tell him all this and, as soon as his back was turned, she'd call in to her father? Did it matter now if she did? Swiftly, he decided it didn't.

'Your father and his brother, Gordon, along with Ben and Paignton knew my mother, and they knew what happened to her and why she disappeared in 1978. Your father doesn't want me to discover the truth.'

She looked stunned and confused. 'But why not? I didn't know about your mother.'

'You're not meant to. There's more, Harriet, but I can't tell you.'

She nodded solemnly. 'What are you going to do?'

'Talk to your father. No, Harriet, you can't come. I have to do this alone.'

'I... Will you tell me what happens? Whatever it is, I need to know.'

Did she already know? Had she guessed? Had she overheard Richard Eames talking to his not-so-dead brother, Gordon? Her expression said not; she was troubled and bewildered.

'I can't make that sort of promise.'

'No, I suppose not.'

He watched her go, then made for the Red Jet ferry terminal and the Isle of Wight.

Twenty-three

Horton rode slowly down the same narrow deserted country lane just beyond Wootton as he had in October and, more recently, when he'd found Harriet at the house. The tarmacked road gave way to a gravel track. The trees closed in on either side of him and within seconds he was pulling up in front of the solid grey stone wall and the pair of sturdy wooden gates, behind which were more trees and the house. This time, he didn't alight and neither did he press the intercom. Someone would see he was here.

He swung the Harley round and returned along the track until he came to the fields now on his right and a track on his left which he took, heading north towards the sea. After about a third of a mile the track petered out and in front of him was a dense wood. He silenced the engine. There were no public footpaths here. A sign bordering the woods told him they were 'Private' and that 'Trespassers would be prosecuted'. Ignoring it, as he had in October, he climbed the low fence and trekked through the undergrowth until he came out onto a shingle shore with a small inlet to his right that led up to more trees. That inlet was where Horton thought Lomas had come from after taking a small boat up there and mooring it up on the shore out of sight, screened by the trees.

He struck out to his left where the shore widened. A high wall came into view on his left with the Solent on his right, except that, in the fog, he could see nothing save a vague shadow of a yacht at the end of the pontoon.

The foghorns sounded as he made his way towards the yacht, his heart beating fast, his body as tense as steel. He thought of that foggy day in November 1978 when Jennifer had left their home, never to return. Would the same fate await him?

There was a dim light on board, as he had expected. Had the man on board been forewarned that he would come? Would there be two men on the boat waiting for him? Harriet could have telephoned her father to say he was on his way. Her phone could be tapped and her meeting with him known. Or maybe Richard Eames had known that Harriet would call Horton and tell him she had been warned off him. Richard Eames could easily guess his next move. Horton didn't think he had been tailed, but he realized a tracking device could have been planted on his Harley. He hadn't checked for one. The device could have been there for some time. Eames would know exactly where he was and what he had been doing. His appearance at the gates of the house would also have shown up on the monitors, not that Eames would have needed that if his Harley had been fitted with a tracking device. Now all Eames had to do was slip out of the house, leave the grounds by the door in the wall, and climb on to the pontoon and his yacht, knowing Horton would be drawn to that dim light like a moth to a candle. Horton's heart thumped against his chest. This could be where it ended for him.

He climbed on board. The man at the helm turned to face him. Horton found himself confronting not Richard Eames but Wyndham Lomas, as he had half expected. He could hear no other sound, but were they alone? Richard Eames could be down in one of the cabins, silent, still and waiting.

Lomas had abandoned the shorts and sandals for a sailing jacket over a polo shirt and chinos. Rapidly Horton re-thought what he had learned over the last few days and months. His eyes went to Lomas's left hand, yet he knew he wouldn't find what he sought as Dormand's words raced through his mind, *Hands are so important, don't you think? They don't lie.* Horton had believed that Dormand had been referring to the ring that Mortimer had been wearing in the photograph from 1967, but that was only partly it, because Horton saw that he had meant Mortimer's burned hands.

Lomas said, 'Looking for burns scars? You won't find them.'

Tersely, Horton replied, 'I know. They were on Rory Mortimer's hand. He changed his identity some years ago to Cedric Halliwell. He rescued Zachary Benham from that fire, where you put him after pumping him full of LSD, but unlike Michael Paignton, Zachary wasn't framed for murder; he was meant to die. You started that fire,

Gordon Eames. You are Gordon Eames, aren't you? Don't bother to deny it.' Horton could see he was right. 'Twenty-three men died in that fire. Why did so many men have to be sacrificed in order to kill one? How could you lock that door and let all those innocent men die?'

His gut churned with anger and disgust at the thought that this man, who he believed was Jennifer's ghost and possibly his father, was a mass murderer. Would Gordon let him live? Would he kill his own son? Yes, if what Horton believed was true. Gordon Eames, the wild child of Viscount William James Eames, was without compassion. What was the death of one more man to him? It was of no account that he was his own flesh and blood. Gordon had abandoned him as a child, and he'd killed his lover, Jennifer.

'I didn't start that fire or lock those men in and leave them to die.'

Horton studied him carefully. The grey eyes that returned his stare were steady and convincing, and in them Horton thought he detected pain. Or was that what he wanted to see? It looked and sounded like the truth. But was this man simply a skilful liar?

'Then who did?' he asked.

'You've already got the answer to that question. The hand.'

'Halliwell, his real name, Rory Mortimer?'

'Yes, and he got his hand burned as a result. He believed that Zach was inside, but he wasn't, and I didn't rescue him.'

Horton searched Gordon's face, his mind working swiftly. It didn't take him long. 'Zach was never there. But the burns on his back?'

'From another fire in Australia in 1973 when he was working at the bauxite mine in Nhulunbuy.'

Horton began to put together the pieces of what he'd discovered. 'That was how he and you were traced to Australia?'

'Yes. Although we'd taken up new identities, Zach's fingerprints were taken after that fire because his papers were missing, and I wasn't around to stop them doing it. They were matched against criminal records. Not that Zach had been convicted, but he had been arrested during the Vietnam protests in the UK, and it was made certain that his prints stayed on file in case he surfaced somewhere and started to get his memory back.'

'They didn't show up when I had that card you gave me checked with the fingerprint bureau. The fingerprints only matched when Ben, that is Zach showed up in the mortuary, and his prints were taken there because there was no ID for him.'

'His prints were not on the usual records.'

Of course. Horton should have known. 'The intelligence services files. But how did you get Zach's prints on that card?'

'He had handled the card, so too had I, but very carefully up until that point. When I gave it to you, your fingerprints went over mine, therefore only yours and Bens' showed up. I was curious to see what happened. I thought you might destroy the card, or have it checked. If no one came for Ben, then I knew he and Michael were safe.'

'Who authorized the release of Ben's prints?' Who had wanted him to go to the mortuary to see if he could ID the corpse, knowing he couldn't and, consequently, would start probing? Not Richard Eames. That would have been the last thing he wanted. Or was it? After all, it had drawn him here, alone, in the fog. Admittedly Richard Eames wasn't here – unless he was hiding below – but Horton didn't think so. He'd be here soon enough though and was probably observing and listening in on them. Would Richard help his brother kill him just as he helped Gordon kill and dispose of Jennifer? Gordon might not be a mass murderer, but he was still a killer.

But if the prints had been switched to *stop* Horton probing, then someone knew he had been given that card in October, and that he had asked for a match from the fingerprint bureau. Again, he came back to Richard Eames. He'd have seen him on his security monitors in October, here on the beach, and witnessed him meeting Gordon. Richard Eames had made sure that Danby and his staff didn't witness that. Eames would guess that he would ask for a match and make sure there wasn't one, certainly not to his brother who was supposed to be dead. Richard Eames had thought that was the end of that trail but someone else had released Zachary's prints when the body had been found in the cabin, and Horton thought he knew who that was. Andrew Ducale, the man who had left the photograph on his boat and set him off on this quest.

Horton said, 'So in 1973 when Ben's prints were matched in Australia, Mortimer was sent there to silence you and him. But again, you got Ben away and faked your own death.'

'Someone died, and Richard identified the body as being mine. There probably wasn't much of it left having been on the beach for so long.'

'There would have been fingerprints and dental records.'

'Perhaps Richard was just glad to have me officially declared dead. It suited us both.'

Horton's mind was racing. There was so much he didn't understand. 'Why wasn't Zach in the Goldsmith Psychiatric hospital?'

'When I found him in 1968 in his bedsit, out of his head on LSD, I knew that someone had given it to him without his knowledge. He'd taken some before, yes, but he was not an addict. And this was enough to have killed him, or at the least make him insane. Thankfully it didn't, by some miracle. His life was in danger. I knew that someone had killed Tim Wilson after visiting our estate in Wiltshire and that James Royston's overdose hadn't been accidental. But I didn't know who was behind it. It had to be one of us; Mortimer, Dormand or Paignton. We were all involved in the Radical Student Alliance with our cell being known as the Radical Six. After I found Zach, I called for a private ambulance and put it about that Zach had been committed to the Goldsmith Psychiatric Hospital after losing his mind because of the LSD. In reality, I got him into a private clinic in the New Forest and then across to the abbey on the Isle of Wight by a private boat I hired. I didn't know that twenty-three men would be killed as a result. I should have done, though.'

Again, Horton saw the anger in his eyes but this time there was a weariness about them, or perhaps sadness. Horton had asked the abbot if he or his Brothers had known Ben, but Gordon was talking about 1968, and Dom Daniel Briar hadn't been the abbot then. One or more of the Brothers had probably been there at that time. They might recall a young man suffering from a drug overdose, but probably hadn't connected it with the woodcarving Ben of recent days. And even if they had, they might not have said for fear of betraying a confidence.

Gordon said, 'I stayed with Zach at the abbey and eventually when Zach was better, we left for Australia. He was never completely cured. He had memory problems and hallucinations. He would become paranoid when he was upset or under stress, at other times he seemed perfectly OK. One of the monks in the abbey encouraged him to try wood carving, and he excelled at it. It also helped ease his mind. It calmed him down. It was while I was at the abbey that I learned about the fire. Then, in February, I read that Michael had been arrested for the murder of Roger Salcombe while out of his mind on LSD. I knew he'd been framed and that whoever had done it was the same person who had tried to kill Zach. Salcombe was a burns specialist and a friend of my father's from the war. I discovered later that Michael had read about the Goldsmith Hospital fire in the newspapers. He knew that it had been started deliberately. Like me, he worked out that it must be one of two men, Dormand or Mortimer. Mortimer was missing from college. Michael began to ask around about him, who had seen him, when, where? No one had, but Dormand was in college so Michael reasoned that either Dormand had killed Mortimer and his body hadn't been discovered, or Mortimer had started the fire and was in hiding because he had been injured doing so. He contacted the local hospitals, but no one called Mortimer had been taken in for burns. So he researched burns consultant specialists and found Roger Salcombe.

'He went to see him at his private clinic and told him of his suspicions; that a man he could be treating for burns could be the same man who had killed those twenty three men in the Goldsmith Hospital fire. Salcombe might not have had any idea that was how Mortimer had got his burns. He could have been spun a complete lie. Worried, Salcombe confided in the wrong man.'

Gordon took a breath and moved closer to the helm. The fog wafted around the boat. 'Salcombe and Paignton were dealt with. Paignton didn't die but, by the time his brain returned to something like normal, he was banged up in Wormwood. When he tried to say what had happened, it was made quite clear to him that next time if he opened his mouth, he wouldn't be so lucky as to live. He was moved to Parkhurst Prison on the Isle of Wight. He kept quiet and served his time.'

'And when he came out of prison you looked after him.'

'I got him a new identity. I was, by then, good at it. I knew people who would help me. Michael came to live with me and Ben in Australia. He took what jobs he could. We supported each other, me with my paintings –

'You're Jethro Dinx?' *A beachcomber artist.* Not of these shores, thought Horton, recalling those paintings in Beachwood House of Australian shores.

'Yes. Ben with his wood carving and other jobs in between when the needs demanded it. Michael's one aim was to find Rory Mortimer, who we eventually discovered had re-invented himself as Cedric Halliwell.'

'You found him through his knowledge of wines.'

'That was our intention, but as it happened Mortimer found me, only he didn't recognize me as Gordon Eames. After all, he thought I was dead.'

'The paintings.'

'I had an exhibition in Darwin at the same time that Mortimer had stopped over there to attend a wine auction. He had business interests in the Far East, both dubious and legitimate. There was an auction of some rare and vintage wines in Darwin which he thought he might as well take in, being in that part of the world. Michael had also learned of this. You see, Michael had studied wines in prison because he knew how Mortimer, even back in 1967 when we were all young, was a wine connoisseur. It was something of a joke with us all, drinking wine wasn't as fashionable as it is now.'

'And Michael had a good teacher in Jerry Carswell, a fellow inmate.'

'Yes. Michael worked hard and saved hard. Soon he had enough to start bidding for wines at the lower end of the market. He also managed to track down a couple of rare wines. He bought cheaply, put them into auction and made a good profit. Word began to get around that he was something of an expert. He had a good eye and nose for investment. He always kept a watch on the auctions of fine and rare wine in the UK, Australia, America and Paris. He researched who was buying and selling. He came up with a number of regular buyers, one of whom was a Cedric Halliwell, and when an auction came up in Darwin, Michael went, not expecting Halliwell to be there in person, and not knowing at that time if he was really Rory Mortimer. But he thought he might learn more about the top wine investors. He recognized Mortimer instantly.'

'Because of his scarred hand.'

'That and his distinctive ring.'

The ring that Horton thought Dormand had been alluding to on the shore of the abbey that night in October. *Hands are so important.*

'Mortimer didn't recognize Paignton no more than he did me when he found me in Nhulunbuy. He never met Ben, and he never discovered that Michael and I previously knew one another. Michael deliberately cultivated Mortimer or, I should say, Halliwell's friendship. They had wine in common. He gained Halliwell's complete confidence.'

'As a lover?'

'No. Although Mortimer never married and wasn't interested in women, he wasn't homosexual either. He was just one of those neutral or asexual men. Michael became Halliwell's personal assistant, secretary, and confidante. He'd flag up the wine auctions, identify those rare and vintage wines which would make good investments, scout for them, track them down in private ownership, do deals and bid at auctions on Halliwell's behalf. We were all getting older, Halliwell included, and his mind wasn't as sharp as it used to be, but Michael's was razor sharp.'

'Dementia?'

'Possibly the early stages. Michael would also source art for Halliwell to purchase as an investment and advised on other financial matters.'

'Gaining access to Halliwell's property and account, until he was ready to take over and live as Cedric Halliwell.'

'And get what he was owed.'

'Was it Michael's idea to purchase Beachwood House?'

'Yes. He found the property, which, as you know, is isolated. It had a cabin in a bay inaccessible to the public, unless someone got nosy by boat, which they didn't.'

'Not until Carina Musgrove turned up.' Did Gordon know it was Harriet? Horton guessed his brother would have told him by now, unless he had known before.

'Yes, but by then it didn't matter. It was perfect for Ben who wanted a simple lifestyle. Michael easily persuaded Halliwell to purchase Beachwood House as an ideal retreat. By that time, Halliwell was more than happy to let me, as one of his favourite artists, take up occupation in the cabin in the bay, along with Ben, who I told him was my companion. The house was refurbished over the spring and summer.'

'Halliwell instigated that. He met with the architect and the wine people who designed and built that cellar for him. He seemed pretty astute then.'

'He was also briefed and prompted by Michael. We all returned to the UK in June. I bought a small boat for Ben and myself to use.'

'The one I saw on the shore by the cabin and the one you used to motor round to here in October when I met you on the shore.'

'Yes.'

'Then Michael Paignton killed Mortimer aka Halliwell.'

'No. He didn't have to.' Gordon Eames smiled. 'Michael wouldn't kill anyone. Even though he'd spent twenty years behind bars for a killing he hadn't committed, and he could have thought he might as well do time for one he did.'

'Then who did? And why come here to the Isle of Wight to do so?' asked Horton.

Gordon Eames made no reply. Horton rapidly thought. He came up with three answers. Because Richard Eames had a property here but then he had properties in Wiltshire and Scotland, not to mention others around the world. Because Michael Paignton had served time at the prison on the Isle of Wight, but then he'd hardly wish to return to a place that held bad memories for him. Because Antony Dormand was at the abbey posing as a monk. Horton's mind flashed back to his conversation with Dormand in October.

'The beachcomber I saw on the shore on Friday. Who is he, Dormand? Is it Rory Mortimer? The sixth man in the photograph?'

'No, he's dead.'

'How can you be sure?'

'I killed him.'

Horton had thought Dormand had meant in 1968, but now he realized he had meant far more recently than that. It was the reason Paignton had persuaded Mortimer to buy Beachwood House. It was the reason Gordon Eames and Zachary Benham had returned here. To make sure that Dormand killed Rory Mortimer.

The forlorn cry of the foghorns pierced the silence of the cabin. Gordon Eames' expression remained impassive, his body still and upright. 'You've worked it out,' he spoke quietly, calmly.

Horton had. Keeping his tone neutral, even though his heart and mind were racing, he said, 'Ben approached the abbey knowing that Dormand was there as Brother Norman. It wasn't just to sell his wood carvings, that was a bonus, the real purpose was to make sure that Dormand recognized him. And to make doubly certain of that, you took Ben's boat on to the shore behind the abbey where you met

Dormand. You told him where he could find Mortimer. But why did you think Dormand would kill Mortimer for you?'

'Because Antony Dormand hated Mortimer almost as much as Michael hated Mortimer. Not at first but later when he came to realize how much Mortimer and his master had deceived him.'

'His master?'

The foghorns sounded almost continually. The air was chill yet suffocating. Horton found it difficult to breathe.

Wearily now, Gordon continued, 'In the sixties we were all part of what we thought was a social, political and cultural revolution. I know, awfully *Sergeant Pepper's Lonely Heart Club Band.* Part of that was a commitment to the communist cause. What we didn't know was that Mortimer was committed to the opposite, as far away from communism as you could get. He was a fascist, as was his master, who was working for British Intelligence. It was Mortimer who killed Timothy Wilson and James Royston.'

'But –'

'Dormand told you *he* did, but he was about to take his own life and Mortimer was dead by then. He saw no need to tell you the truth. It wasn't his place to anyway and it would take too long to explain. He told you he had killed Timothy and James because they were traitors, selling secrets to the Russians as Zach had been. But they had no secrets to sell, not that type anyway. Yes, there were riots and demonstrations and plans to disrupt as many public services as possible, and that's all it was. But Mortimer was clever, manipulative and murderous. He was also in the pay of one man, someone who was a committed fascist and had been long before 1939 and all through the war, working for both the British and the Nazis.'

Horton didn't hide his surprise. He had thought Gordon was talking about Richard Eames being this 'master', but Richard hadn't been born then. Before he could comment though, Gordon continued:

'Someone who still believed that the only way forward was the far right. And I discovered who that was. Naively, I confronted him, just as Salcombe had done. His old friend,' he added with bitterness. 'I was twenty-two, invincible and stupid. I told him we would make the story public. I didn't care about the consequences, only I hadn't foreseen that those consequences would be murder. I should have done. He knew he had to kill us to make sure his secret stayed that way. Tim was killed in 1969, James in 1970, Zach was almost killed in 1968, and Salcombe was killed in 1970 when Michael should also have died. Instead, he was convicted of murder. Mortimer would have killed Dormand except that Dormand went missing after James Royson's death. At first, we thought it was because he was distraught. Antony Dormand and James Royston were lovers. But after the attempt on Zach's life, I wondered if Antony had also been dealt with until he surfaced as a monk in Italy where I had travelled for an exhibition of my work two years ago and came across him while I was staying at their guest house.'

'He really was a Benedictine monk then,' Horton said surprised.

'Yes, although I'm not sure he believed in God. He shut himself off from the world once James died and he sort of got used to it. He liked the peace and solitude. He was soothed by the chants, the prayers and the routine. We had a great deal to talk about.'

'Why did you return to Portsmouth in 1978?' Horton asked, his heart beating fast, his mind racing to assimilate all he was learning.

Gordon Eames remained silent for a moment. He shifted and leaned back against the helm. 'It was a mistake. We all make them, but I didn't know at the time the implications of that decision. I was an idiot. I read about my mother's death in the newspapers.'

Horton recalled reading the article in Walters' newspaper earlier of Lady Marsha's death in November 1978, a sudden and unexpected heart attack, and the Viscount's tragic accident on his yacht the year after off the coast of France.

Gordon was saying, 'I thought about it over and over. I felt sick at the thought that they would all be at her funeral and everyone would be sympathetic to my father who'd be looking suitably upset and dignified. In the same article, I read about myself. How I'd been a great disappointment to the family, how I'd blackened its name and tarnished its reputation with drug abuse, criminal behaviour and communist leanings, and how I had died alone in a drugged stupor on an Australian beach. God knows what I thought I was going to do but before I could reason it out, I'd packed a rucksack and was on a flight to England. And even though I had a new identity and passport, my father knew where I was. In fact, I didn't find out until afterwards that he never believed I was dead. Richard had told him he'd identified a body he believed to be mine, but maybe our father got it out of

205

Richard that he'd done that so I could just carry on with my new life.'

'And Richard knew your new name?'

'Not that I was Jethro Dinx, because I only assumed that after 1978. But he knew the name I had been living under in Australia before that. I flew out of Australia on that passport, and my father knew that, as he did when I had arrived in England. He gave instructions that I was not to be stopped.'

And a Viscount had influence enough to do that, Horton thought. Nobility could pull strings and rank.

Gordon said, 'I had three days to kick my heels before the funeral. And three days to cool off. I stayed in Portsmouth where I'd spent some time in my misspent youth. I went to the casino amongst other places and found Jennifer there. I had no idea she was working there. She recognized me. I left almost immediately but she came after me. We couldn't talk for long; she would be missed. She never mentioned she had a child, although I could see that something was troubling her. I told her that I lived in Australia and asked her to leave with me. She said she didn't want to travel under her own name but didn't say why. She said she would tell me everything later. That was enough for me. I said I would get her out without a passport and then could obtain another for her under a new ID. We agreed to meet at Albert Johnson Quay in four days, after the funeral, where we could pick up a cargo boat to some foreign port and then another ship on to another port, and so make our way to Australia. But I changed my mind about going to the funeral. I never went. I just wanted to get out of the country. I had the impression I was being followed, and I thought that when Jennifer and I were talking outside by the pier we were being watched.'

'Then why did you wait that long to meet her?' Horton asked angrily.

'Because I needed time to make arrangements to get us abroad. She didn't know I intended for her to leave with me on that same day we'd arranged to meet. I didn't want her to bring any personal belongings or pack a bag and draw attention to the fact she was leaving. Remember, at that stage I didn't know of your existence. She never showed up. I didn't know where she lived. I couldn't ask in the casino because that would have drawn attention to myself and her. The boat was about to leave. I had to clear out.'

'Leaving her to die,' Horton said with disgust. His father was a coward. He didn't for a moment believe that Gordon Eames hadn't known about him. 'So you left the country,' he said scathingly. 'How do I know you didn't kill Jennifer or the others?'

'Because I would hardly spare Zach and help Michael if I had done so.'

That rang true. With his chest tight, his head spinning, Horton said, 'Jennifer kept the rendezvous but instead of you, she met your brother, Richard. You'd contacted him and asked him for money in exchange for clearing out and keeping silent over the fact that he had falsely identified your body. He agreed. Richard lured Jennifer away and killed her.' It was as Horton had always suspected; Richard Eames was a murderer.

Gordon Eames took a deep breath. The sea mist swept into the boat. Horton could hear the foghorns of the ferries and cargo ships in the Solent.

'It wasn't Richard who met her, but a man who would do anything to protect the fact that he was a traitor and always had been. Who thought Hitler should have won the war and who, after the war, still believed our country would be better served by extreme right wing policies. The same man who had made sure his old friend Salcombe died, along with all of us in the Radical Alliance save his puppet, Mortimer. He wouldn't have spared me, and he didn't spare Jennifer.'

Horton's head spun as he concluded who Gordon Eames was referring to. 'You're saying your father, the Viscount, was responsible for those deaths and Jennifer's?' he said incredulously.

Gordon moved closer to the helm.

'How long have you known this?' Horton demanded, unsure he could believe what he was hearing.

But Gordon didn't answer him directly. 'Richard's sin was turning a blind eye to it and helping to cover it up. Mine was running away from it. Life is messy. People cock up. We make bad decisions and have to live with them. Richard and I remained silent, even when people died. Yes, my father, the Viscount William James Eames, was the master, a traitor and a killer. Protecting his secret for the sake of his family and the country, as he saw it, from socialism and communism, at any cost.'

Horton was finding this difficult to take in. He stared, dazed, at Gordon Eames. 'Your father *ordered* Jennifer to be killed.'

'No. My father met her after she'd been seen with me and told her that I had sent a message to say that the place and day she was to meet me had been changed to three days' time, not four, and at the quayside at The Camber at Old Portsmouth.'

Could Horton believe this? 'And she went? Just like that?'

'Yes, because she had no reason to think anything suspicious. He had told her she and I had his blessing. That I knew she had a child but not who the father was, and that he would never say.'

Horton felt the pontoon rock. Gordon Eames seemed not to notice, but he must have sensed the movement and knew what it meant.

'Why would she agree to meet your father? And how did he know about me?'

'Because Viscount William James Eames is your father,' Gordon said evenly.

Twenty-four

'It's true.'

The figure who stepped on to the boat was the man Horton despised. The man he had held responsible for Jennifer's death. Richard Eames. And here was his brother, Gordon, telling Horton they were step brothers. And that their father had killed Jennifer. No, it couldn't be true. Horton stared at them, aghast. His body stiffened.

'What happened?' he asked, his voice taut with emotion.

Gordon answered, 'She boarded our father's yacht at the Camber believing I was on board. Before then, when he had met her to change the rendezvous place and time, he'd given her a valuable family heirloom, a brooch.'

'The Portsmouth Blue.'

'Yes. He told her it was his gift to her and me, and he was happy for her to make a new life with me. He did so for two reasons. One to make her believe he was sincere, and secondly, he knew that if I had told her about his treachery and murder, she would refuse the brooch. She didn't. So far, he was safe. But he couldn't take the risk of her going with me and finding out about him. He had to make sure it stayed that way.'

'You knew your father killed Jennifer and you did nothing. You let me rot in a children's home. Neither of you helped me. You are both accessories to Jennifer's abduction and murder,' Horton hotly declared.

Richard Eames answered, 'But you'll never charge us.'

'Don't be so sure,' Horton rounded on him, but he knew Richard Eames was right. The last thing he wanted was to have his heritage paraded for all in the Hampshire police and the wider world to know. His father, a Viscount, a fascist traitor during the war, Mortimer's paymaster, a killer. Now he knew why their flat had been searched, why everything was seized after Jennifer's disappearance. It was to remove anything incriminating such as letters, photographs, diaries that might have betrayed an affair with Viscount William James Eames. And to retrieve the brooch, but PC Stanley had got there first not knowing its heritage and true value.

Angrily, Horton continued, not waiting for an answer, 'You think you're protected because of who you are. Both of you have colluded in and covered up murders – Jennifer's, Timothy Wilson, James Royston, not to mention those men in the psychiatric hospital fire.'

'Where's your evidence?' Richard said. 'Gordon's hardly likely to make a statement, and I certainly won't. It's all a fabrication of your imagination.'

Horton tensed. His fists clenched. He'd dearly love to smash it into Richard Eames' over-confident lean face. His eyes flicked between the two men standing at the crowded helm. It was all he could do to restrain himself from lashing out. Violence would get him nowhere, although it might make him feel better in the short term.

Richard Eames was right, damn him. Getting evidence was another hurdle, aside from not wanting his past made public. He had no evidence that William Eames had killed Jennifer. There was no Antony Dormand or Rory Mortimer to confess to the murders they had committed, and no bodies to find. Dormand had probably killed Mortimer outside Ben's cabin, with either Ben, Gordon Eames or Michael Paignton having lured Mortimer, aka Halliwell, down there. Had Ben, Gordon and Michael Paignton witnessed the murder? Two of the three were dead, and the third would never tell. Dormand, having killed Mortimer, had ditched his body in the sea just as William Eames had done with Jennifer's. There were no witnesses, and Horton would never get a confession from either of these two.

He felt nauseous and disgusted. He was angry that Ducale had left him the picture which had set him off on this quest. But, even through his anger, his brain told him his quest had begun before then, with the charred remains of a body found on a burnt out boat in a marina, which had led him to a Portsmouth vicar who had kept track of his career in past copies of the local newspaper. It had been that discovery which had sparked curiosity about his mother's disappearance, which he had managed to relegate to the back of his mind for years. Now he wished he had never discovered the truth.

'What now? You kill me too, to silence me?' he said tersely.

Richard answered, 'Why should we do that? You're unlikely to tell anyone.'

He was right. He didn't want anyone to know he was the bastard son of a Viscount and one who had been a traitor during the war, a right wing fascist all his life, and a murderer. No one was who they claimed to be. Nothing was how he had believed it. Secrets, lies and deception was what Dr Quentin Amos had said in his urine smelling flat in Woking before dying, and after telling him the names of five of the men in the picture from 1967. And the lies and deception would continue. These two would never betray their father and their family name. And Horton would never speak of this.

Horton addressed Gordon, 'You colluded in murdering Mortimer.'

'Murdering a murderer, yes. Paignton deserved justice, and he was never going to get it any other way. Dormand killed Mortimer in October. And sadly, Michael died on his boat in February.'

'But not of natural causes.' Horton's glance fell on Richard.

Richard Eames drew his lips together in a tight line. Gordon looked bewildered. He glanced at his brother, and a dark expression crossed his face.

'Carbon monoxide poisoning,' Horton said. 'His ventilator was faulty. Easy to fix for someone who knows about boats. The canopy was in place and zipped up. It was a cold foggy day.' Horton didn't know for a fact that the heating ventilator was faulty, it had never been tested, and he didn't care. He wanted to sew distrust and suspicion amongst these two.

In a quiet voice that held more menace than an angry one, Gordon addressed his brother, 'Is that true, Richard? Did you kill Michael?'

But Horton harshly interjected, 'You don't expect a habitual liar to tell you the truth!' He scoffed.

Richard said, 'Of course I didn't.'

But Horton could see that Gordon didn't believe him. Good. He addressed Gordon, 'Richard couldn't let Paignton live because he knew that the orders to frame him for murder hadn't solely come from your father, although Mortimer believed they had. In fact, father and son colluded to kill Salcombe and frame Paignton, and when Paignton recovered his memory in prison he asked to appeal against his conviction. He had new information. He was forcibly persuaded to keep quiet. You saw to that,' Horton tossed at Richard. 'How did you know where to find Paignton?'

'I didn't.'

But it was bluff. 'Then I'll answer my own question. After Mortimer was killed by Dormand in October, Paignton flew back out to the Cayman Islands using the identity that Gordon had created for him.' That was a guess, but Horton could see he was correct, and he could check if Gordon ever gave him the name that Paignton had assumed while living his new life. 'Paignton already had access to Halliwell's accounts having worked as his secretary, and he had the authority to tidy up Halliwell's affairs. This he did. He also had Halliwell's passport. He altered his appearance to look as much like Halliwell as he could. They were of the same build, height and colouring, and the passport picture was almost ten years old. It worked, no one queried it. He flew back to the UK on Halliwell's passport on 4 January.

'He visited Wight Barn Wines on 10 January where he purchased some expensive wines. That was foolish of him, but he couldn't stay hidden forever and he knew a great deal about vintage wine, as you told me,' Horton directed at Gordon. 'But Paignton didn't account for Jerry Carswell, an old cellmate, finding him and recognizing him. Paignton also made his will with Chilcott in something of a hurry. Perhaps he knew his days were numbered, not for health reasons but that someone might discover who he really was and would make sure he remained permanently silent. After all, Carswell had traced him. And Carswell was the link, the catalyst that led you to Paignton.' Horton scrutinized Richard Eames' lean fair features. The man gave nothing away. Horton hadn't expected him to, but Gordon's study of his brother told Horton that doubts were turning into realization that he was telling the truth.

Richard took a few steps in Horton's direction. Was he armed, Horton wondered? Would Richard shoot him? There would be no one here to see it, only his brother, Gordon, and he wouldn't tell. The fog would muffle the sound, not that there was anyone within hearing distance anyway.

Forcing his voice to remain calm while his heart pounded and his senses were on full alert, Horton continued. He kept his eyes on Richard. 'Charles Nansen at Wight Barn Wines told Carswell that there were two excellent cellars on the island and two men who owned bottles of Domaine de la Romanée-Conti, you and Halliwell. You had a telephone call from Charles Nansen who was apologetic over letting it slip to someone who had visited him. The man who had called on him, George Caws, was keen to purchase some privately, and Nansen said he had given Caws your name and that of Cedric Halliwell who lived at Beachwood House on the island.'

Richard Eames was still trying to look superior and unconcerned but harshly Gordon said, 'Go on,' when Horton paused.

Addressing first Gordon, Horton said, 'Richard asked Nansen when he had last seen Halliwell, and he was told that he'd visited Wight Barn Wines on 10 January. Richard knew that wasn't possible because Halliwell was dead. Dormand had told him in October, or maybe it was you who told your brother when you were on this shore as Wyndham Lomas, at the same time as I was.'

Horton turned to Richard, 'So who was this Halliwell at Beachwood House? You had to know. But you didn't want to make it official. You called at Beachwood House and found Michael Paignton. He recognized you and vice versa. Paignton could reveal you and your father's parts in Salcombe's death, and the deaths of Royston and Wilson. As well as the fact that you knew your father had given Mortimer orders to set that fire at the Goldsmith Psychiatric Hospital killing twenty-three men, while Ben had never been there because of Gordon. But you easily persuaded Paignton that no one would believe him. After all, he was a previously convicted murderer, and now he had stolen another man's identity and was living under false pretences. You told Paignton that you would claim he had killed the real Cedric Halliwell in order to steal from him. Paignton knew it was pointless. No one would listen to him. Why should they when they hadn't before? Paignton also knew that Ben had killed Jerry Carswell to protect him, so he was an accessory to murder.'

Studying Richard Eames steadily, with a cold heart, Horton said, 'You killed Michael Paignton, not physically but mentally. He bought a boat as rapidly as he could, one that he paid cash for and could have within a few days. No boat survey, no fuss. And on 1 February – a cold and misty day – he took it out after sabotaging the heater and ventilator. He committed suicide.'

Gordon eyed his brother with a contempt. In a quiet, deadly tone, he said, 'Even to the end you haunted Michael. Just for the sake of the family honour.'

Richard remained silent. His fist clenched in his right jacket pocket.

Gordon addressed Horton, 'Ben worshipped Michael, and he could see that Michael was disturbed about something. He thought it was Carswell who was threatening to reveal his secret and his past unless he gave him a vast sum of money. And to a degree, it was, but neither he nor I knew my brother had paid Michael a *visit*.' Gordon left no doubt as to what he thought of his brother as he spoke that word. 'Ben killed Carswell and buried the body on the cliff. But when Michael discovered what he'd done, he became even more dejected. When Michael died, the energy and light went from Ben. He kept hoping that it was a mistake and that Michael would return. But, as the days and weeks dragged on, he came to realize that he wouldn't. I found his body.'

'And cleaned up after it.'

'Yes. I destroyed the suicide bag containing Nitrogen which Ben had used to put over his mouth. It's a method of death that is perhaps better known in Australia than over here.'

Exactly what Gaye had told him after she'd conducted the autopsy on Ben, *if done slowly and well there are no signs of it in an autopsy. It's a favoured means of suicide in some countries...Canada, Australia, Sweden.*

Gordon expanded, 'Helium was the popular substance to begin with, but Australian officials started to control sales of helium to stop the rise in suicides. It's been replaced by nitrogen canisters, such as those used for carbonating beer. It's quite simple and effective. I removed all evidence of it, and of me being there. You never picked up my prints from that cabin.'

'No. But you couldn't report the death because that would have meant answering some awkward questions, but neither could you leave him there to rot away, as Jerry Carswell would, buried on the cliffside. So you asked someone to help you.'

Richard Eames shifted position. His body tensed.

Horton continued, 'You contacted an old friend of your brother's. You knew how to reach him through his aunt in Guernsey because her nursing home bills are paid by that man, her nephew, Andrew Ducale. All you had to do was tell Violet Ducale that you needed help and where Andrew could reach you.'

At last Horton caught a flicker of unease in Richard Eames' eyes.

As the sound of the foghorns grew more frequent, and the fog thickened and chilled him through to his bones, Horton resumed, 'Ducale obliged by making sure that Europol despatched your niece, Harriet, to the island.'

Richard's mouth opened to comment but snapped shut again.

Gordon said, 'I didn't know who he would send, and I never for a moment expected it to be Harriet. I didn't want her to get mixed up in the family's sordid secrets.'

'And neither did her father but Ducale had other ideas. She was told to keep under surveillance a man who lived in a log cabin in Luccombe Bay who was wanted in connection with the theft of valuable diamonds involving a Cedric Halliwell, who lived above the bay. She was booked into a cottage at Bonchurch, given a cover story of being a geologist keen on fossil hunting and a boat. She met Ben once before he died. Two days afterwards she found him dead. She called in to her boss and asked what she should do. She was told to report it and leave before the police arrived, and then to show up at her father's house as though she had a few days holiday. When she read about the other body being found on the cliff and I showed up here at the house with questions for her father, she grew concerned and puzzled and you didn't much like that, Richard. You warned her off. But she's a grown woman and can make up her own mind. She has no idea that her father is a killer.'

Richard Eames stepped forward. 'You –'

Horton said, 'She was recalled to The Hague by her boss, who was given instructions to do so.' But not, as Harriet and he had thought, by her father. By Ducale. 'But like you say, Eames, there is no one left who can corroborate any of this, unless Gordon decides to come clean and tell all. Somehow, I don't think he will. The family will close ranks, the service will protect you, just as it's always done.'

Horton was sick of them. His heart and his head ached with anger and hatred which coursed through his veins. He didn't want to feel like this. There was no justice for Jennifer or for him. He had to get away from them. The air was corrosive.

He turned, brushed past Richard Eames and climbed off the boat. He'd seen the hand Richard Eames had kept in his sailing jacket pocket tighten. As he stood for a moment on the pontoon with the fog eddying around him, he wondered if this was when the bullet would come, Richard would shoot him in the back. He didn't want to die, but neither would he grovel, plead or fight them.

Slowly, his body taut with tension, he walked the length of the pontoon, mentally counting the steps, waiting for the loud retort, the sharp pain, then oblivion. These could be his last seconds on earth and his head was filled of his darling daughter, Emma. No more would he see her, hold her and hear her childish laughter. He'd come to the end of the pontoon, perhaps to the end of his life. He stepped down on to the pebbled shore and then a loud retort rang out.

He spun round. He was still alive. Unmistakably a gun had been fired. He froze for a few seconds then leapt on to the pontoon and ran the length of it, his pulse racing, his blood pounding in his ear, his chest heaving. What the hell would be find? What had happened? Had Richard killed his brother? Was the next bullet intended for Horton, or had that gunshot been fired into the air to make him turn back so that Richard could kill him face to face? But the sound of a boat's engine came to him in the clinging fog and, as he reached the end of the pontoon, he saw it swing out to sea and the shadow of a man at the helm. Richard or Gordon? He couldn't tell.

He shouted to it. No answer came, only the revving of the engine greeted his call. Again, he hailed it, but his voice was swallowed in the mist and gloom as the foghorns boomed. The water lapped against the wooden struts of the pontoon. Reaching for his torch he switched it on and scoured the black murky sea, holding his breath. There was no body. The boat's engine grew fainter, but it stayed with Horton long after the boat had disappeared and lingered with him all the long way home.

Twenty-five

The marina was silent. The fog clung to the boats turning them into ghostly hulks. As Horton punched in the security code and walked the length of the pontoon to his boat, he knew it wasn't the weather that was making him shiver but a coldness inside him. He drew up sharply. The hatch to his boat was open and he certainly hadn't left it that way. He stiffened, then his heart sank. If it was Detective Chief Superintendent Sawyer of the Intelligence Directorate after that brooch, the Portsmouth Blue, the information of which he could have picked up via prison intelligence, Horton would tell him to piss off. He certainly wasn't going to tell him a single thing. But, as he descended into the cabin, the man who was waiting for him was the man who had left the photograph. Andrew Ducale. He should have guessed Ducale would show up now.

'Your timing is perfect,' Horton said sourly, studying the fit-looking man in his mid-sixties who held his gaze steadily with steely grey eyes.

'There are some things we need to discuss.'

Horton remembered the well-modulated authoritative voice from when they had first met last June. Was that really less than a year ago? It felt like an age. From the moment they had met, Horton had known that Ducale was a man who could command, and people would follow without question. He bore little resemblance in looks to his twin sister, Horton's foster mother, Eileen, save there was a determination about the set of the chin.

He took a breath and nodded, forcing himself to relax. After all, there was still a great deal he didn't know, and questions had run through his troubled mind on the ferry home. Opening the fridge, he said, 'Drink?'

'No. Thank you.'

Horton extracted a bottle of water and, only after taking a long drink from it, did he take the seat opposite the silver-haired, muscular man sitting behind the galley table. 'Jennifer worked for you.'

'Yes, that is she worked for MI5. I was her liaison officer. My sister, Eileen, also worked for MI5.'

Horton felt only a small surprise because he had begun to suspect it. Eileen had left no photographs of herself save a couple of just her and Bernard at their wedding. She had never spoken of her past and no relatives or friends had come to her funeral, only neighbours and those associated with her in her final years. She had worked for the civil service in the naval dockyard when he had lived with her and Bernard, and before then had worked in the tax office in Belfast during the Troubles as a secretary, but that was just a cover for her real role of gathering and passing on intelligence.

Ducale was saying, 'Eileen recruited Jennifer when they were both working in the typing pool for the Ministry of Defence in London.'

Dormand had been right then when he'd told Horton that Jennifer had worked for the intelligence services. 'Eileen never once mentioned that she had known my mother,' Horton said with bitterness. 'Why not?' he demanded, feeling a stab of betrayal against his foster mother for not confiding in him. All those years and someone close to him could have revealed more about his mother.

'You know why.'

'Because of the Eames' family,' he said scornfully.

'Because she was bound by the Official Secrets Act.'

'She could at least have said she knew her.'

'And you would have asked questions which she couldn't answer, because some she didn't have the answers to, and others she was unable to. Eileen recognized that Jennifer was highly intelligent and that she was frustrated her intelligence wasn't being utilized. She also craved excitement and action. She was patriotic and she wasn't afraid of danger, although she grew more cautious after you were born.'

'Eileen knew who my father was?'

'No. But I did. It wasn't until I returned to the UK from the Far East in 1982 though that I discovered Jennifer was missing and that you had been taken into care. No one looked out for you or protected you because William Eames saw to it that your existence was kept a secret. Likewise, her disappearance was only briefly investigated. It was hushed up because of her background, and you weren't given any special treatment because that would have been questioned and that was the last thing William Eames wanted. William knew where she was, but she didn't pose any danger to him then because she knew nothing about his secret affiliations and betrayals. Everything was dealt with quietly and effectively. But I managed to get permission to take you from social services and hand you over to my sister and her husband to raise. They were more than happy to do so, and it wasn't guilt Eileen felt because she had recruited Jennifer. She genuinely cared for Jennifer, and for you. She couldn't have children of her own. She was with Jennifer when you were born, and she helped your mother while they were both living in London.'

'And you expect me to believe that Jennifer never confided to Eileen who my father was?' Horton said incredulously.

'Yes. Because they were both working for the same organisation. They knew the rules and even if they decided to abandon them, which neither did, Eileen didn't know what work Jennifer was assigned to and vice versa. When you were five, Jennifer was moved to Portsmouth. Eileen was sent to Belfast where she worked in the tax office while assisting in gathering intelligence on both the Irish Republican Army and the National Unionist Party. It's where she met Bernard, who, as you know, was an RAF police officer and was shot by the IRA while patrolling the airfield at RAF Aldergrove. He was wounded in the shoulder and taken to the Royal Naval Hospital Haslar, Gosport in 1978, but Eileen didn't return to live in Portsmouth until some months later. She thought Jennifer had left Portsmouth of her own free will until I told her what had happened.'

'I saw you give Bernard a tin containing what you had of Jennifer's. You were the man on the motorbike who was talking to Bernard when I came home early from school that day.'

'Yes. As you know there wasn't much in it. Just some pictures of Jennifer and your birth certificate, which were given over to social services and filed on the request of MI5. I got them released and the authority to hand them to Bernard after you'd been living with him and Eileen for a while.'

All of which had been burnt when a villain had torched Horton's previous small boat. But the Portsmouth Blue had been missing from that tin because PC Adrian Stanley had already taken it.

'I knew you'd be safe with Bernard and Eileen, and you were. You also had no desire to probe into your mother's background until fifteen months ago when your interest was sparked by a case you were working on. You discovered that Jennifer had met up with a diamond thief while working in the casino, and it was him that it was believed she had run away with, abandoning you.'

'And Detective Chief Superintendent Sawyer was sent to probe how much I knew about the Portsmouth Blue.'

'He didn't know about that, or about Jennifer being employed by MI5. He was investigating the thefts of diamonds masterminded by an international crook codenamed Zeus who, as it turned out, was not the diamond smuggler Jennifer had met at the casino as you know. After that investigation you accessed the missing persons report on her. There was an alert on anything connected with Jennifer Horton and I was informed. Richard Eames was also notified. He, as you rightly suspected, works for MI5. Then last April you called on the police officer who was sent to investigate her disappearance, PC Adrian Stanley.'

'How did you know that?' When Ducale didn't answer, Horton swiftly continued, 'You had me under surveillance. I didn't notice.'

'I'd have been disappointed if you had.'

'And my phone at work? Is that tapped?'

'No, and neither is your mobile.'

Horton wasn't so sure about that. He said, 'You called on Stanley after my visit.'

'Yes, but too late. Richard had got there before me, not that he told me that. Stanley was unconscious.'

'And Richard's visit to Stanley, immediately after mine, caused him enough distress to trigger that stroke.'

'It appears so. Richard had to leave quickly. He didn't have time to search the flat or retrieve that photograph, which Stanley must have put away after he noticed you looking at it. Richard tried again when Stanley was in the hospital. And he succeeded. He found the brooch in Stanley's flat and he sent an operative to the hospital to retrieve any photographs Stanley's son might have taken there for his father, and into the son's house to see if there were any further pictures to remove.'

Horton withdrew the much thumbed black and white photograph

and placed it on the table. 'Why did you give this to me?'

'It's a long answer, but I'll do my best to explain. As you've discovered, Richard Eames works for MI5. He has access to a great many people in high places and picks up lots of intelligence. Unlike his father, Richard does not have extreme right wing leanings but he does have an acute sense of family, and was keen to make sure his father's murky past was never discovered. He had no knowledge of it at the time he was recruited along with me when we were at Cambridge, although he came to learn of it after the series of deaths of the Radical Six and his brother's disappearance. I recommended my sister, Eileen, and, as I said, she in turn recruited Jennifer. Jennifer got a job as a typist at the London School of Economics, where it was known there was an active communist cell but not who was behind it. Her job was to infiltrate that cell and feed information to me. She discovered that one of the most active members wasn't a student but a young man who was the leader of the group, who lived in a squat in London, Gordon Eames. She obviously had no idea exactly who he was at that stage, or his background. I passed that information on, which in turn ended up with Viscount William Eames who was much higher up the chain than I was. William asked to meet Jennifer. He needed to know more about his son's involvement, a son he was already estranged from. Jennifer and William met, and they began an affair.'

Horton took a swig of water.

'William Eames was charming. She was flattered. He told her to get all the information she could on the Radical Six at the London School of Economics, which included Michael Paignton. Gordon was on the outside because he wasn't a student there, but it should have been the radical seven, or not because Rory Mortimer was a plant, a fact Jennifer had no knowledge of. That was William's insurance. Mortimer, who had the same political leanings as William, was in fact working for William Eames' secret fascist organisation. He was also gathering information. A belt and braces job except that Mortimer was not MI5. That picture was taken by Michael Paignton, as you probably worked out.' Horton had. 'But Jennifer's camera was used to take it.'

'There were others on the film?' Horton asked.

'Yes. Taken after and before that one. There were pictures of them preparing for the demos and at the demos, some of them violent. There were two photographs in particular of the group, including Gordon Eames meeting with George Belton, a known double agent, who was later imprisoned but managed to break out of jail, obviously with some help. From whom, it was never known, or at least it wasn't made known, but that's another story and doesn't concern you or Jennifer. Unexpectedly, Jennifer fell in love with Gordon Eames and he with her. But how could she tell him she was betraying him to MI5 and his father at that? She was bound by the Official Secrets Act. Then she discovered she was pregnant not by Gordon but by his father.'

'How could she be so sure of that?' It had been one of the questions that had been burning in his brain on the ferry home. He had taken the Eames' brothers word that he was the late Viscount's son.

'Because Gordon Eames was infertile, and he'd told her that. He'd had mumps badly as a teenager and, when an eighteen year old girl claimed he was the father of her child, it was medically determined to be impossible.'

Horton took another swig of water as though to rid the Eames family from his mouth. He thought of the gun shot he'd heard and the two men on that boat. Which of them was dead? Did he hope they both were? Did that make him as bad as them? He didn't like the fact that his mother had been sleeping with father and son at the same time. But who the hell was he to judge? He had wanted her to be perfect, but he knew she wasn't. No one was.

'William Eames told her that he could never openly admit to being the father or to their affair. It would compromise his cover. She was bound by the Official Secrets Act and the media would love it, if they ever found out. It was also the last thing Jennifer wanted exposed. She would lose Gordon. William said he would arrange for a private abortion. As you know abortion was legalized in 1967.'

And even if it hadn't been, Horton knew that William Eames would have found a medic to do it.

'It was a tough call for Jennifer. No one except William and I knew she was pregnant. She thought that if she went through with the abortion, she could be free to go with Gordon and put everything behind her. But while Jennifer had been gathering information on Gordon and the Radical Six, Gordon had been making his own enquiries and digging deep into his father's past. In fact, he'd started building information on his father, whom he hated long before 1967. He'd spoken to people who had known his father, former employees who had been sacked or suffered an accident, and to their relatives, and began to see just how deep his father's treachery and betrayal went. He was disgusted by it and cared nothing for the family name. He faced his father with it.'

'As he told me. You know that I've just come from them, on Richard's boat on the island?'

Ducale nodded. 'Gordon told his father he would go public. Foolish, but he was young and believed in his cause. William asked Mortimer if Gordon had spoken about his past. Mortimer said he had and that he'd told all of them in the Radical Six.'

'Had he?'

'No. Mortimer was protecting his own back. He didn't want his fascist leanings paraded in public, or to be associated with William Eames if it all came out, and Mortimer knew how determined and committed Gordon was. Mortimer knew that if he said they all knew the secret they would be dealt with.'

No wonder Mortimer was hated. Horton took a deep breath. 'Gordon was meant to die in that fire. William was prepared to kill his son.'

'Yes, with Mortimer's help. William had no time or love for Gordon. William was a self-centred, arrogant, opinionated man with a sociopathic nature that made him believe he was right on every occasion and superior to others. And Gordon was a communist whom William despised as much as the gypsies and Jews.'

Horton was appalled that some of the blood that had run through that man also ran through him. His gut twisted at the thought of it, his body ached with tension. He tried to tell himself that he was also his mother's son, that he must have inherited some of her genes, all of them he sincerely hoped. He said, 'Mortimer drugged Zachary Benham. The rest Gordon has told me.' His head throbbed with the knowledge of what he had learned.

'Jennifer was told that both Gordon and Zachary had died in the fire, which was what was believed. Despite William's wishes, Jennifer went ahead with the pregnancy, which showed how strong willed she was.'

Horton knew that must have been a tough call because illegitimacy was a stigma back then. Unmarried mothers were ostracised. It was a totally different world now. And it was tougher for her to have the baby than to get rid of it.

Ducale continued as though reading Horton's mind, 'She told William she would keep the baby. He explained what that would mean, that she would have no claim on him and that he could no longer act as her boss or her lover. She was relieved. She didn't love him, and she couldn't see how she could end the affair. She was glad he had done that for her. The organisation took care of her.'

'Meaning you.'

'And my sister, as much as we could. Remember we were junior members of the organisation then. And I was posted around Britain and then abroad. Jennifer stayed in London with Eileen for a few years after you were born, then she moved to Portsmouth and recruited to work for us again, but obviously not with William.'

'Dormand was right then when he said she had provided intelligence on the IRA?'

'Yes. Jennifer was moved into a larger flat on a higher floor in Jenson House and got a job as a croupier in the casino where she was able to gather lots of intelligence. It was a well-known meeting place for those sympathetic to the IRA.'

'Then one day in November 1978, Gordon Eames walked in to the casino, a man she thought was dead.'

'Yes.'

And Gordon had told him the rest. But had he? 'Gordon told me he'd returned for his mother's funeral and to reveal the truth behind his family but got cold feet. He was going to get Jennifer out of the country and said he knew nothing about my existence. Was that true?'

'I doubt it very much. I think William took great pleasure in telling his son exactly what Jennifer had done and whose child you were because, according to our records, Gordon flew back to Australia two days after meeting Jennifer.'

'He didn't take a cargo ship then,' Horton said quietly.

'No. He did what he's always been good at. He ducked out. Richard also knew the truth.'

'More lies and cover ups. Gordon also said that William gave Jennifer the Portsmouth Blue brooch.'

'He did, and he thought she would have it on her when she came to meet Gordon, but she didn't because she didn't know that was the day Gordon had planned for them to leave.'

As Gordon had told Horton. That much was true at least. Horton said, 'She fully expected she could go back to the flat for her belongings?'

'Yes. William met her on his boat. He told her he was taking it out and that they would pick up Gordon on the way, either at Gosport or possibly, he said, the Isle of Wight. It was only after killing her that he realized the brooch wasn't on her. It was too late to go back.'

Horton took a breath. He'd already heard how William Eames had no scruples over killing, even his own son, Gordon, so why not his former lover?

'He ditched her body in the sea and then returned to his house on the island. He couldn't go to your flat and search it. And when William Eames managed to get someone into your flat and remove anything incriminating – you must have been at school – PC Adrian Stanley had already been ahead of them and helped himself. William assumed Gordon had met with Jennifer after he had seen her and before she had met him on his boat and taken the Portsmouth Blue.'

Horton ran a hand through his hair and assimilated this. His mind sped back to the awful days longing for his mother to come home, to rescue him from hell until finally he gave up and decided to hate her instead. The Eames family had done that to him, but he tried to hold on to the thought that hating them would achieve nothing. They would never know and, even if Richard and Gordon were still alive, his hatred would mean nothing to them. He would be the only person hurting from it. The hatred would curl up inside him and gnaw away at him, germinating bitterness and resentment, and possibly fuelling revenge and even murder. He'd put his hatred of Jennifer aside some time after Bernard and Eileen had shown him how to.

With exasperation he said, 'You haven't answered my question on why you planted the photograph. Why not tell me all this straight out instead of this cloak and dagger stuff and leaving me to discover who those men were and the significance of the photograph?'

'Would you have believed a word of it if I'd simply told you?'

'Yes. No. I don't know.'

'You're a police officer. You're trained not to trust easily, to disbelieve and to question, and you're also a good detective. When I discovered Jennifer had disappeared, I asked questions but, as you can imagine, I was rapidly discouraged from doing so. I was told that handing you over to my sister was all the concession that would be made, and I was posted abroad. Eileen, of course, was also sworn to secrecy. William was still one of the top people in the organisation then. He had enormous influence. But the powers that be had already begun to suspect him of having extreme right-wing leanings, which were getting worse. He was becoming more paranoid and obsessed, especially during the Labour administrations. He was a liability. Mortimer had already seen this and, after framing Michael Paignton for the murder of Roger Salcombe, which he committed, the last deed he did for William, he cleared out in 1970, receiving a generous payment from William. He changed his name, acquired a new passport through his dubious contacts because he wouldn't have trusted William to give him one – that would have enabled William to have him tracked and taken out whenever he wanted. Mortimer went abroad. In his new guise he became exceedingly wealthy, perhaps some of that wealth gained illegally, some legitimately. He was always a shrewd investor, brought up to appreciate fine wine and art, and he invested well, as you discovered. He was also incredibly adept at extracting secrets from people.'

'A blackmailer.'

'Yes. You remember Tom Brundell?'

Horton could hardly forget the charred remains of that man whom he and Cantelli had found on the boat in Horsea Marina the December before last. It had been the incident which had kick-started his curiosity into Jennifer's past with the vicar's press cuttings about him.

Ducale said, 'Brundell, a former fisherman, became a wealthy investor. He returned to his home town of Portsmouth from Guernsey, when he discovered he was dying of cancer, to confess to a crime he and his fellow fishermen had committed years ago, as you investigated, that they had killed a man. In Guernsey he had met Cedric Halliwell, who extracted that secret from him. Halliwell got a great deal of money from Brundell, and he also got the story about Jennifer Horton, a name he recognized from the past. He learned from Brundell that Jennifer had worked in the Portsmouth casino in 1978 and that she had a son, called Andrew, who was a police officer.'

'Did Mortimer know who my father was?'

'Yes.'

'And he bought Beachwood House on the Isle of Wight knowing that Richard Eames owned a property there. Mortimer thought it might be useful living so close to him. So it wasn't Paignton's idea, as Gordon told me.'

'Maybe it was a bit of both. But Mortimer was happy to go along with it because he knew, when he revealed to Richard what he'd discovered about his father and how you were William's son, he'd be in clover. And that maybe he should tell you.'

'Is Antony Dormand alive?'

'His body hasn't been found but we're certain he's dead.'

There was a small silence. Horton caught the faint sound of a halyard against the mast which meant the wind was rising. With it the fog would lift.

Ducale broke the silence. 'You know what happened to William Eames?'

'I read in the newspaper that he had an accident on his yacht in 1979 while sailing off the coast of France.'

'Officially, yes. When Jennifer disappeared, her background was checked. Had someone discovered she was passing on intelligence? Were the IRA involved? Nothing came back on that. There was a risk with her being loose. Could she be coerced into giving away intelligence? Had she defected or was it simply a case of running off with another man, which was the version that was circulated?'

'And which I believed until the Tom Brundell murder on the boat in Horsea Marina.'

'Her past file was examined and eventually it led to the Radical Six. The deaths of Timothy Wilson and James Royston were probed. Then there was Michael Paignton's prison sentence, the death of Zachary Benham as everyone believed in that fire, and the disappearance of Gordon Eames. And, as I said, the powers that be were getting worried about William's increasingly extreme opinions. Slowly Williams Eames and Rory Mortimer's secrets were unearthed. Mortimer had vanished. William was confronted. He knew that no one would reveal the truth, there was too much at stake for that, but equally he knew that one day he'd have a mysterious accident. He took off on his yacht, which was found abandoned just south of the

Portsmouth to Cherbourg ferry route on a heading for Barfleur, France. The file was closed. It came into my possession when I took over as head of the section ten years ago, but it wasn't until the alert sounded on your enquiry to social services in January and after that your access to the missing person's file on Jennifer, that I was notified. I retrieved the file.'

'Did Richard also know this?'

'Yes. But he knew nothing about the photograph. Not until you showed it to him, which must have worried him. The photograph I left on your boat was the only one that I had in my possession. The others, Jennifer had given direct to William who had destroyed them. I'm not sure why Jennifer gave me that picture, or why I kept it, maybe some sixth sense you develop, just as police officers do about a situation or a person. I put it away with my personal papers in a safe deposit box. If you hadn't started asking questions, that is where it would have stayed. I instigated a search for Mortimer without Richard knowing. He had to be kept out of it. I had my suspicions about him. I found the trigger for your enquiries had come after Brundell's death and we linked that with a man called Halliwell who had been an associate of Brundell's in Guernsey, as I mentioned, and who had bought a house on the Isle of Wight. Halliwell also had a secretary, who we were certain was Michael Paignton.'

'So you had them watched and followed and discovered that Paignton was friendly with Ben, a wood carver. And that Jethro Dinx, a talented artist, was Gordon Eames.'

'Then Dormand was discovered to be at Northwood Abbey. Richard Eames could have recognized him. He was, after all, a generous benefactor and visited the abbey regularly. Or he was told. Not by me but someone else in the organisation. But I don't think he was.'

Horton relayed his theory of how Richard had come across Paignton.

'It sounds highly likely,' Ducale concurred. 'It was only as I looked more deeply into the situation that I realized how much Richard knew about his father's past and how deeply he must have been involved in those deaths, even possibly in covering up Jennifer's disappearance.'

Horton took up the tale. 'But what Dormand didn't know, until Gordon told him, was the lies he'd been told by William Eames and

228

Rory Mortimer – that Royston and Wilson were spies. They weren't. They died along with all those men in the Goldsmith Psychiatric Hospital because William was afraid that his secret of being a fascist and a traitor during the war would be exposed.'

'Yes. Whichever way, and whoever got Mortimer first, Dormand or Paignton, or even Richard, that would be the end to it, and you would never know the truth. I thought you deserved a chance at it if you wanted it. You could have thrown away that photograph. You could have consigned it to a safe deposit box. It was down to you.'

'How far was Professor Thurstan Madeley involved?' Horton recalled the man in his late-fifties who he'd met in the Castle Hill Yacht Club on the Isle of Wight in August and who had compiled the archive file on the London School of Economics 1960s protests.

'Madeley was tasked by Richard under the guise of instructions from MI5 to make sure that there was no reference to the Radical Six in the London School of Economics archives and no photographs, also to ensure that the Eames family didn't feature anywhere in the files. A mission he achieved long before you visited and delved into the university's archives. He was surprised when you showed him the photograph. He wondered who had given it to you and the only person he came up with was Amos. He gave you his name, possibly to see what you would do, or because he felt it better to give you something than nothing, which might make you even more curious and suspicious. Besides, he believed that Amos's memory would probably be failing by then.'

'And Madeley told Richard Eames after I had left him at the yacht club what he'd done. Amos knew his days too might be numbered after I went to see him. He told me who five of the men were, but not the sixth, Gordon.'

'He probably didn't know him. Gordon wasn't a student there.'

'After I'd gone, Amos thought he'd leave a message for me with his solicitor, but it was just a set of numbers on the back of an envelope. By accident, while I was visiting Haslar Marina Gosport, in August, I discovered that, with a bit of manipulation, the numbers could be the marina's grid location. It hadn't been a marina in 1978 but it was in close proximity to MI5's communications and training centre and the hospital where Bernard had been a patient after being shot in Northern Ireland, so I thought Jennifer could have gone to meet someone there and been abducted.'

'You were on the right lines but the wrong location.'

Horton could see that now. If he took the numbers Amos had given him, 01.07.05 and 5.11.09 as degrees, minutes and seconds and made the five 50, then the numbers he got were 50deg 11min 9sec North, one deg. 7min 5sec West and in degrees this became 50.18583 deg. North and 1.11805 deg. West. Horton could pinpoint it on a map, but he didn't need to because he was convinced he knew what he would find; the place mentioned in that article he'd read in Walter's newspaper and which Ducale had told him was where William's yacht had been found abandoned. 'They're co-ordinates just south of the Portsmouth to Cherbourg ferry en route to Barfleur, France.'

'Yes.'

'Where he disposed of my mother?'

'I should imagine so.'

Horton drank from the water bottle. 'How would Amos know this?'

Ducale shrugged.

'You told him?' Ducale remained silent. Horton said, 'Did William Eames kill himself or was he killed?'

Again, Ducale shrugged.

'And releasing Ben's fingerprints from the intelligence files after his body had been discovered was down to you?'

'Yes. I thought that it might force Richard or Gordon's hand. Or both, which it did.'

'How did you know that Lomas or rather Gordon had given me that card?'

'Mike Danby is not the only one who has security and surveillance monitors at Richard's properties.'

'Which of them is dead? I heard a gun being fired.'

'Perhaps they both are. Whichever one of them is piloting the boat has disabled the automatic tracking system, but we'll pick it up somewhere. Whether there will be anyone on board…'

Horton exhaled and ran a hand over his face. He felt incredibly tired.

After a moment, Ducale said, 'Does knowing what happened make a difference?'

'I don't know,' Horton replied with weary exasperation.

'It doesn't change the person you are. And it doesn't change the person your mother was.'

'She *was* killed.'

'Yes, and you can't bring her murderer to justice. He's dead.'

'He should have been charged, tried and convicted.'

'You think that would have happened? There was no evidence and no witnesses.'

'Both Gordon and Richard knew their father had killed Jennifer. They should have come forward.'

'Seeing as Gordon was supposed to be dead, he didn't. It would have stirred up so much dirt that the authorities would have sat on it.'

'One law for the rich and one for the poor,' sneered Horton.

'There is no one to try for the murder of Rory Mortimer. And no one to bring to justice for the deaths of Timothy Wilson and James Royston, or of Roger Salcombe, all of whom were killed by Mortimer, not Dormand, and he too is dead. It's up to you to decide if you want anyone to know about your parents.'

And Horton knew that Ducale already had the answer to that. Even if Richard Eames was still alive, Horton would never be able to bring him to justice. And anything he said would mean exposing his mother's past. He shuddered at the horror of that. And Emma? What would she think of it? Would Catherine use it to somehow prevent him ever seeing Emma again?

'What will Gordon do now, *if* he's still alive? Will you pick him up off that boat?'

'I shouldn't think so. Gordon will do the same as he's always done. Disappear. He no longer has any responsibility for Zachary Benham or Michael Paignton.'

'But if Gordon is dead and Richard is still alive, he won't disappear. And I'll be around to remind him of his family's dirty secret. What's to stop him having me killed?'

'He won't.'

'You're so sure?'

'Yes.'

Horton understood. Ducale didn't need to spell it out. And perhaps Richard had already taken the same way out as his father. 'He'll always be there reminding me of how he left me to rot in those children's homes.'

'Then don't let him. You can't change the past, Andy.'

'Christ, don't I know that.'

'And Jennifer? What would she want?'

'Don't try that emotional crap on me.' Horton rounded on him, but the anger subsided as Ducale gave him a steady look.

'You discovered the truth, Andy, and it was never going to be a fairy tale ending. You of all people should know that rarely happens. The baddies don't always get banged up, the evil bastards live on to a ripe old age and get away with it, the good die young. There are no neat pink ribbons to tie up at the end. Life is often messy and shit and, at other times, it's OK. Getting revenge is not the way you're made, even if you think it is. You'll have a job finding Gordon or getting anything on Richard. And you'll never get a warrant to get that vault opened and the body of the man found on the Australian beach exhumed and examined.'

'Don't the man's relatives deserve something?'

'He has none.'

'How do you know?'

'We checked.'

'And the brooch, the Portsmouth Blue?'

'Oliver Vernon will be persuaded into thinking you were enquiring because it was stolen in the Trehams robbery.'

'Do the Eames family have it?'

'Why? Do you want it? William gave it to Jennifer.'

'I want nothing from them.'

Ducale rose. He stretched out his hand. Horton took the firm grip in his. He had a great deal to be thankful to this man for.

He watched Ducale leave. He knew he wouldn't sleep that night, even though he was tired beyond belief. His head was too full of the revelations of the last few hours. The mist was lifting, there was a light wind blowing, and it wouldn't be long before the sun rose to reveal a bright April day. He made the boat ready and set a course for France. There was one final journey he had to make.

For more information on Pauline Rowson and her books visit
www.rowmark.co.uk

Printed in Poland
by Amazon Fulfillment
Poland Sp. z o.o., Wrocław

58134977R00141